TOO YOUNG
to fall in love

USA TODAY BESTSELLING AUTHOR
LACEY BLACK

Lacey Black

Too Young to Fall in Love
Burgers and Brew Crüe, book 7

Copyright © 2023 Lacey Black

Cover Design by Melissa Gill Designs
Photographer Wander Aguiar
Model Chase Roback

Editing by Kara Hildebrand

Proofreading by Sandra Shipman, Joanne Thompson, and Karen Hrdlicka

Format by Brenda Wright, Formatting Done Wright

ISBN-13: 978-1-951829-36-0

Lacey Black

One

Kellen

Usually, a Saturday night brings a packed house, but not tonight. Tonight, our doors are closed to the general public, as we celebrate one of our own. Kallie and Leo were married this afternoon at his parents' house, and now we're hosting their reception.

Everyone is present, whether working or as a guest. Walker, Numbers, Jasper, and Jameson, the four owners of Burgers and Brew, are here, along with their wives. The employees not working are enjoying food prepared by Jasper, desserts handcrafted by his wife, Lyndee, and music by our own Jameson. A few servers take care of the food service, and I'm one of the two guys behind the bar, where I always am.

Where I belong.

I've worked at Burgers and Brew for nine years, starting at the ripe old age of twenty-one. It was a time in my life where everything around me was chaos, and finding my place here brought me solace and stability. It's unfortunate how a dysfunctional homelife can fuel the decisions you make impacting the rest of your life.

But I don't regret any of them.

Not a single one.

The best thing to come out of that time was a closer relationship with my sister, Kinsley. She was eighteen and a senior in high school when our parents' marriage imploded spectacularly, threatening to take us all down as the gossip mill did its thing and made sure the dirt on the McGregor family was spread from one end of Stewart Grove to the other.

The other positive was finding this place. Working beside Walker and the rest of the Crüe has been a dream. I get paid to pour drinks, listen, offer sage—and sometimes sketchy—advice, and flirt.

Yes, ladies, I get paid to flirt, and fuck, am I good at it.

They say it's the smile.

The Panty-Melter, and I'm not talking about the burger listed on the menu.

My smile could charm even the most prudish of women, my friends. It helped me get grades far better than I deserved in high school. It's gotten me out of traffic tickets—and on one particular occasion, helped secure a date later that night when the pretty lady cop got off work. I helped her *get off* twice afterward. It's gotten me free food and discounts at various places around town when I didn't ask for them. And it's netted me more tips than I could possibly imagine over the last nine years from female patrons. Apparently, when you give them a wicked little grin and a wink while handing over their drink, they'll give you a bigger tip.

And their phone number.

And their panties.

Oh, that's definitely happened.

More than my mom would care to hear about.

Fortunately, I don't have to worry about that kinda crowd in here tonight. Everyone is here for a different reason, and while I don't believe in all the hearts and flowers and love bullshit surrounding it, I can appreciate a good party, and that's what we have here tonight.

"Jack and Coke, please?"

"Comin' right up, darlin'," I reply with a wink, drying my hands off on the towel behind the bar.

"Quit flirting with my wife," Garreth practically growls at me, making me grin from ear to ear.

Leaning forward, I give Reagan my full attention. "He always like this? You know, if his caveman routine is too much for you—"

I don't get to finish my statement, because I'm hit in the face with a coaster. "Knock it off, or I'll fire you," Garreth demands, but even I can't feel the heat behind his words. He knows I'm joking, I'd never actually cross the line with Reagan or any of the wives. Hell, with any of the employees. The last thing I need is to make the work environment uncomfortable because I had to dip my pen in the company ink, if you know what I mean.

"You wouldn't fire me because I'm the best bartender you've got," I state confidently.

"Bullshit!" Kallie bellows as she catches the tail end of the conversation. "You're second best," she counters. "I can't believe you'd spread lies like that."

I can't stop the loud laugh that spills from my lips. Man, I enjoy working with Kallie. She's one of the best bartenders I've ever known. We've worked side by side for almost the entire nine years I've been here, her starting just a few short months after me. Sure, there was some attraction on my part early on—I mean, she's fucking gorgeous—but it quickly transformed into mad respect and friendship. Now I consider her more of a sister than anything else, which is why I'm incredibly happy for her today.

Even if the thought of marriage gives me the heebie-jeebies.

"Aren't you supposed to be dancing with your new husband?" I ask the bride, while making Reagan's Jack and Coke.

"We're getting ready to leave, and I was coming over to say goodbye. I'm glad I did, so I could refute your lies," she sasses, her playful eyes narrowing as she watches me from across the bar.

7

I flash a grin as I place Reagan's drink in front of her. "She's delirious from all the I do's. Something like that is bound to make a person loopy and confused."

"Jeez, here we go," Kallie replies, rolling her eyes. "Someday, someone is going to knock you on your ass, and I can't wait to watch. We'll all have front-row seats of Mr. Kellen McGregor, bachelor extraordinaire, falling in love."

A shudder sweeps through my body. "Bite your tongue, woman. That'd be a cold day in hell."

She just smiles back at me. "If you say so," she says in this happy little singsong voice.

"I say so. There's way too much—"

"Don't you dare say it, Kellen McGregor!" Reagan bellows, her mouth hanging open.

Holding up both hands in defeat, I insist, "I wasn't going to say *that*."

Lies. I was totally going to say pussy.

Reagan narrows her eyes at me. "Then what were you going to say?"

Reaching for a plastic cup, I fill it with ice water and take a sip. "I was going to say there's way too much *variety* in this world to settle with one woman for the rest of my life."

Both women roll their eyes and Garreth chuckles, trying to quickly cover it with a cough when his wife turns and glares at him. "Sure, you were," Kallie mutters.

"Are you ladies done harassing me?" I ask, tossing the hand towel over my shoulder and spotting Cameron carefully walking to the end of the bar, her tray loaded down with dirty glasses. "I have work to do."

"I was coming over to say goodbye," Kallie announces, walking away from me and around the end of the bar, her pretty dress swaying as she goes. First, she stops and gives Cameron a hug, thanking her for working tonight. Cameron returns the gesture and laughs at something Kallie whispers in her ear.

That sound gives me pause.

I've heard a lot of women laugh over the years, especially that fake flirty giggle women think all men want to hear as an invitation to dinner at the pussy buffet, but there's something about this particular laugh that makes my balls a little heavier and my chest feel a bit tighter. I'm sure it has something to do with the fact Cameron doesn't laugh nearly as often as she should. She's quiet, more reserved, but when she smiles, the room just seems a little brighter than before.

That's why I go out of my way to see that grin on her face as often as I can, the only way I know how. I flirt. Shamelessly. I don't get to do it as much as I'd like, considering we usually work different shifts and she's leaving when I'm coming in, but tonight, every time I see her, I'm laying it on extra thick.

Because it makes her smile.

"Ladies," I start, throwing my arms around both of their shoulders, "good news. I have two arms available, one for each of you."

Kallie barks out a laugh before elbowing me in the gut playfully. It doesn't hurt, much like my invitation didn't really mean anything, but I don't miss the adorable blush I spot on Cameron's face moments before I bend forward and drop my arms. Giving one good Oscar-worthy fake cough, I sputter, "You wound me, Kal."

"That little elbow was the least of your worries, *Kel.*"

I can't help but laugh as I turn to face Kallie's new husband, Leo Martinez. "Hey, Leo. Fancy meeting you here."

His eyebrows arch upward as he stares at me. "Yeah, weird I'd be here tonight, huh? You know, being the *groom* and all."

I step away from his wife because even though I'm joking around, my face is too pretty to be dented by his fist. My arm brushes against Cameron's, and I ignore the jolt of electricity that zaps my skin. Besides, it's probably just static anyway.

With a chuckle, I extend my hand toward him. "Congrats, man."

He offers me a rare smile as he takes my hand, his eyes instantly going to his new wife. "Thanks."

I want to tease him about that dreamy, lovesick look in his eyes, but I opt not to. Leo and Kallie's road to today hasn't been easy. It was paved with potholes and speedbumps the entire way. She's shared just a little bit about their relationship over the last few months, keeping the personal stuff private, but she has mentioned Leo's mother Valerie's health.

It's not good.

The fact she's still here is a godsend, because I don't think it was guaranteed she'd make it this long. The cancer is winning, slowly taking her strength and her life, but not her smile and her love for her family. That's one of the main reasons Kallie and Leo married as quickly as they did, so his mom could be part of their celebration.

"You guys can't leave yet. It's still early," I insist, glancing at my watch and noting it's before ten o'clock. Valerie and Bruno, Leo's dad, left shortly after the dinner to go home, taking Kallie's dad with them for the night.

"We've done all the traditional reception shit. Now I'm taking my gorgeous wife to the bed-and-breakfast my parents gifted us for our wedding night and doing all the dirty things I've been imagining since the moment I saw her in this dress," Leo states quietly, a naughty glint in his smile.

Kallie's face blushes three shades of pink.

"You don't have to brag, dude," I state, tossing my arm over Cameron's shoulder and sighing. "I suppose that just means I'll be left behind to entertain all the other lovely ladies in attendance this evening."

"Not this lady," Cameron chimes in, tossing my arm off her shoulder.

Dramatically, I hold my hands up to my heart. "Ouch, Cam."

She just laughs that glorious sound and shakes her head. "I'm sure you'll be just fine. That ego of yours will be sufficient padding for the fall."

"What fall?" I ask, stepping back and gazing down at Cameron.

"The one from that pedestal you've put yourself on."

"Oh!" Kallie hollers, holding up her hand for a high five.

"You wound me, love."

That makes her laugh harder as she turns her attention back to the tray on the counter. I jump right in, helping her remove the dirty glasses and load them in the small dishwasher we use behind the bar.

"All right, you two, we're taking off. I'll see you Monday," Kallie announces, giving me a quick hug before taking her husband's hand and heading off to make their rounds to say goodbye to the rest of the guests. The newlyweds aren't taking a honeymoon right now, because of Leo's mom's declining health. They don't want to be gone if something happens to Valerie.

"See you Monday," I holler before she goes to find our boss, Walker, and his wife, Mallory.

"Thanks for collecting these," I say once the washer is doing its thing.

Cameron shrugs, soft waves of auburn hair flowing around delicate shoulders. I was surprised to see her with it down tonight. Usually, like most of the servers, she pulls it back and out of her face. I suppose since her duties tonight are scaled back, she doesn't have to worry about it hanging in her face and obstructing her view as she writes. "It's the job," she quips.

"Hey, Kellen, I need a Seven and Seven, two Night Crüe drafts, and a sex on the beach."

My smile is wide as I glance up at Angie, the other server working this evening. "I'm your man, Ang," I insist, waggling my eyebrows at her.

She just rolls her eyes as she chuckles. "You're incorrigible."

"That wasn't a no," I tease, flashing her the same grin I give all my friends. It's similar to the one I use when I'm looking to get laid but doesn't actually hold any of the meaning behind it. I'm not trying to take one of my coworkers home for bedroom sexcapades. That was one of the suggestions I heard from Walker way back when I started and actually held on to all these years. I don't get naked with coworkers. Too much drama and entanglement, and I'm all about fun.

No drama allowed.

"You couldn't handle me, Kellen," she sasses with a sugary sweet grin.

I make the Seven and Seven and pour two drafts, placing them on her tray to deliver. "You're probably right, Ang."

"Now, Cameron, on the other hand," she says, the teasing evident in her voice.

I glance to my left to where Cameron is standing and find her eyes…downward.

On my ass.

Angie clearly notices too, because she perks right up and asks, "Something you care to share with the rest of the class, Cam?"

"What?" she whispers, her eyes looking up as realization sets in. Her face turns bright red, that light dusting of freckles on her cheeks more pronounced in her mortification. "Duty calls," she adds quickly, turning and practically running away. She bumps into the corner of the bar with her arm as she goes, dropping her tray with a clatter. "Shitballs." Ignoring everyone who turns their attention her way, she grabs the tray and scurries away to probably hide in a dark corner.

After a few moments of silence, Angie finally says, "She's a good kid," taking the final drink I mix and placing it beside the others.

"Everyone seems to like working with her," I note, leaning against the bar.

"They do. She's quiet and gets her job done. The customers love her too," she notes as she picks her tray up and turns around, ready to deliver them. Before she goes, she glances at me and adds, "Don't even entertain a thought in that pretty little head of yours."

My mouth gapes open. "What? I'd never," I insist, even though now that she's mentioned it, my mind most definitely goes there. Her. Me. Naked. Together.

Angie laughs. "Right," she chastises. "I've seen that look before. Right before you left with that questionably legal set of sisters from out of town."

I bark out a laugh. Oh, I remember that night about five years ago quite well. Two sisters in town for a work thing and definitely looking for some hotel room whirlpool fun. A good time was had by all.

Twice.

"You think I'm pretty?" I ask, batting my eyelashes.

"Of course that's what you'd take away from what I said," she replies with a chuckle.

Grabbing the towel, I toss it from left to right just to give my hands something to do. "They were celebrating their twenty-first birthday, so definitely legal. And no worries, Ang. You know I don't *entertain* coworkers."

"Keep it that way, cowboy. We all like her and don't want to see her get hurt." With that, she leaves to deliver the drinks on her tray, and I'm left with only my thoughts about her comment.

She's not totally off base, even though there are plenty of reasons why I wouldn't actually make a play for Cameron besides the fact we work together. One, there's quite a bit of an age difference. Seven years, to be exact. While gorgeous, Cameron is more reserved and quiet. I usually go for...easier, for lack of a better word. Someone looking for a good time and who knows the score at the end of the night. Or the morning. I don't do commitments and long-term anything. Don't expect to meet my parents.

I know that makes me sound shallow, and you're probably right, but there's no way I want anything to do with the heartache and mind fuckery that accompanies commitment and marriage. I've seen too much shit firsthand in my life to understand monogamy and forever don't go hand in hand, and when infidelity finally comes to light, it leads to heartache, tears, and a shit ton of anger.

Fuck that.

I want nothing to do with it.

I'm happy being single and will enjoy myself as long as I can. Then, someday, I'll find a quiet little cabin in the woods someplace, where no one can bother me. It's the perfect scenario. But until then, I'm going to live my life and have fun every step of the way.

The rest of the night goes quickly, and before I know it, the only guests left are the owners and employees who are working. It takes no time to get the place cleaned up and ready to reopen tomorrow.

"Take off, Kellen. I got the rest of it," Walker announces, closing down the computer system.

"I don't mind finishing. You're the one with a wife at home."

He flashes me a grin. "She's already sleeping, trust me. If there were a chance she'd be waiting up for me, I would have been gone thirty minutes ago, but she's already super exhausted with the pregnancy."

"Only a few months to go," Jasper says, slapping his friend on the shoulder and giving it a gentle squeeze in support.

I've heard about Mallory's difficult pregnancies with both boys, so everyone's hoping the fourth time around would be a little easier on her. In fact, she's not the only one pregnant right now. Numbers' wife, BJ, is expecting their second boy around the same time as Mallory is due. Two babies before Christmas.

It's still mindboggling how these four guys went from single to married and having a ton of kids within a handful of years, and I do admit, they make it look easy. Their marriages seem nothing like the shitshow one I grew up watching. Of course, I also know all too well, appearances can be deceiving, but I don't get that vibe from them. If I was looking for a future, I might even use one of their marriages as a model example.

Too bad I'm not searching for it.

"All right, I'm out," I announce.

"Here, take this with you," Jasper hollers, handing over an envelope. I already know what's in it. My cut of tonight's tips.

"Thanks."

Everyone hollers a goodbye as I head out the back exit and toward my truck. When I spot it, Cameron's one spot over, trying to start her old Cavalier. It's not turning over, however.

Bypassing my own vehicle, I approach her door. "Need some help?"

She startles, turning wide green eyes my way. "Shitballs, you scared the crap out of me."

"Sorry," I mumble. "Can I help?"

"No," she replies, climbing out of the driver's seat. "I'll deal with it tomorrow."

"Come on," I insist. "I'll give you a ride home," I add, turning behind me and facing my truck.

"It's okay. I'll walk."

"Not happenin', pretty lady." Pulling open the passenger door, I step back and announce, "Your chariot awaits."

With a deep sigh, she takes two steps and climbs inside my cab. "This is probably out of your way. I don't mind walking."

I blow out a deep breath. "This is Stewart Grove. Nowhere is out of the way." I have no idea where she lives, but it can't be too far of a drive.

Moving around to the driver's side, I get behind the wheel, instantly noticing a new scent. Not that my truck smells bad, but this new scent is definitely different than the pine tree air freshener hanging from the rearview mirror.

Vanilla.

And lavender.

I don't know what it is about that combination, but it goes straight to my dick.

At ease, soldier. There's no need to stand at attention.

Before I even have time to adjust my tight pants, she sighs the most seductive sound I've ever heard. It's all breathy and reminds me of sex, and it's right in this exact moment I realize I might very well be in trouble where she's concerned. Giving Cameron an innocent ride home is definitely not putting innocent thoughts in my brain.

The quicker I get her home and out of my truck, the better.

Cameron

Fidgeting with my hands, I search for something to say that doesn't make me sound as lame as I am. "Sorry to put you out like this."

Yeah, that's the best I could come up with.

"You're not," he insists, backing out of his parking spot. "Which way?"

"Oh, uh, left. I'm on Jefferson Street."

I don't know what it is about Kellen, but I've always felt super flustered when he's around. I've managed to perfect my outward reaction to him and remain completely aloof to his charms, like they don't cause my panties to become soaked and useless, but inside, I'm all fawny and awkward. It's a combination of his flirty personality and the devilish grin that makes you want to drop your drawers and offer up yourself on a platter.

I've known him since I first started at Burgers and Brew over a year ago, and he's one of the most charismatic guys I've ever known. However, even though he's always got some comment, I've never felt uncomfortable or threatened by him. It's just his personality. None of us take him seriously, even if he has the good looks to go along with the miles of charm.

"I used to live on Jefferson Street," he says, pulling me back to the conversation.

"Yeah?"

See? Lame.

"Yep. Right next to the Methodist church." He takes a turn off Main Street and proceeds toward the street I live on.

"I'm two doors down from the Methodist church. Six fourteen."

"No shit?" He glances my way quickly before returning his eyes to the road. "I lived at six twelve. When I was growing up, an old man named Haggerty lived in that house."

I nod, even though he's not looking at me. "I rent it from his daughter."

"Jane?"

"Yes."

"Huh, what a small world," he notes, almost absently, as he drives toward the place I live.

As we approach the area, I take in my surroundings with new eyes. The houses are mostly tidy ranch-style homes with small backyards and comfortable porches. The streetlights are bright, and you can almost feel the welcoming sense of kids-at-play all around you.

The house I call home almost seems out of place amongst the family residences. My rental is a tiny one-bedroom house with aging green shutters and a small wooden porch with a family of raccoons living beneath it. Inside, the hardwood floors are marred from years of use, the linoleum is cracked and faded, and the hot water heater never seems to last long enough for my liking, but it's perfect for me.

And it's all mine.

Well, thanks to Garreth and Reagan. Reagan found this place for me at a time when I needed, not only a friend, but the help and was no longer too proud to accept what she was offering. Her boss at the clothing boutique, Jane Honeywell, was dealing with her father's house after his death, and I was desperately needing to move out of the house I was in. The rent on this place was half of what I was paying, leaving me with a little extra money each month to pay debts.

To finally get out from under the mountain of trouble I was in.

"Here ya go."

I blink, realizing he's already parked in my driveway. "Thank you for the ride. Can I pay you for the gas?" I ask, pulling my envelope containing tonight's tips from my purse.

"I'd be offended if you did."

Nodding, I release my seat belt and open the door. I hesitate, not really knowing if I should just get out or if I should say something else. I opt to slide out of the seat, since there's no way I can just casually step out of this big thing, and turn to face him. I have to look up to keep eye contact. "Thanks, again," I state lamely, throwing in a wave.

"You're welcome. If you need help getting your car to Otto's let me know."

I cringe, worried how much that will cost me. Just when I start to think I'm getting ahead with my finances, my ancient POS car takes a crap. "I'm sure I'll manage, but I appreciate the offer."

He nods and just watches me. When neither of us speak, I realize he's waiting on me to go inside. Or shut the door. Something other than just stand here like an idiot and stare at him.

"Okay, bye," I practically yell, shutting the door with a little extra force and walking quickly around to the back door.

There's a slight tremble to my hands as I slip my key into the lock and turn the knob. What the hell is wrong with me? Why am I so awkward?

The moment I'm inside, I pause, noting I haven't heard his truck leave yet. Dropping my bag on the floor beside the door, I take off running into the front room, leaving the lights off. When I reach the mini blinds covering the window facing the front of the house and driveway, I carefully lift one of the closed pieces and peek through it. My breathing hitches when I spot Kellen's truck still sitting there, but more so because he's staring at my house. Not like a creeper, mind you, but in this confused way, like he's not sure why he's still parked.

I watch with wide eyes, pretty sure I'm not breathing, as he finally shakes his head, throws the truck in reverse, and backs out of the driveway. It isn't until he's completely out of sight that I finally release the breath I was holding and close my eyes. Dropping the blinds, I turn and sag against the wall.

Danger, danger.

Kellen McGregor is *exactly* what I *don't* need in my life right now. He reminds me too much of a wild and carefree time I've worked very hard to overcome and forget about. The last thing I need is someone as charismatic and charming as Kellen causing me to entertain ideas of a relationship. Not that this is what he was offering, but all it takes is one little seed to be planted, and the next thing you know ideas bloom.

I'm better off sticking to myself.

I have this house, a great job, and a few friends.

What more do I need?

"Order up!"

I spin around and head for the kitchen, anxious to serve my last table of the day their food. It's approaching four, and the evening servers have arrived to prep for their shift. I place the two plates on my tray and carefully make my way to the dining room where the sweetest couple waits.

They sit together on the same side of the booth, which makes me smile as I approach. Mr. and Mrs. Saunders have been married for sixty years and are what a lot of people call "relationship goals." They've been together since their early twenties and still act like they're in the honeymoon phase. It's the sweetest thing to witness, and I'm so grateful they're always seated in my section.

"A regular cheeseburger, hold the bun, with fries for you, Mrs. Saunders," I announce, gently placing her plate in front of her. "And a Paradise by The Dashboard Lights for Mr. Saunders."

He grins widely as I set his food in front of him. I'm pretty sure he orders this burger just because of the name. "Thank you, Cameron," he replies, reaching for the wrapped silverware I placed on the table.

"Can I top off your waters?" I ask, already reaching for their glasses.

"Please," Mrs. Saunders answers politely.

"I'll be right back," I state, taking their glasses back to the servers' station.

"I love those two," Meg says, glancing over the partition and watching the older couple. "Seriously, they are the sweetest."

Topping off the two glasses of water, I reply, "They really are."

"Someday, I'm going to find someone who looks at me exactly like Edwin looks at Silvia." Meg has this far-off look in her eyes, one I've seen often. She's a dreamer, the believer in all things love and forever. If you ask her, soul mates are real and until you find yours, you're just wandering aimlessly through life, searching for your other half.

I don't have the heart to tell her it's all bullshit.

I've been friends with Meg since she started here almost six months ago, and one thing I love about her is her extremely positive outlook. She clearly hasn't been hurt in the past or had life deal her a terrible hand. Not like me. She's also not one to judge a book by its cover, so to speak. In fact, she's one of the few people who doesn't seem to care much about the rumors flying about me.

Instead, she just waves them off, arguing everyone has a past, and who is she to judge?

She really is one of the best things to happen to me since my life imploded last year.

Like me, she's not a lifelong Stewart Grove resident. She moved here a few years back with her mom, who is a physician at the hospital. Meg didn't want to follow in her mom's footsteps, however. She chose to take photography classes at the local community college and supplements her income with shifts at Burgers and Brew. She's flexible and floats between the day shift and the evening one, which helps Garreth, the manager, who makes the schedule.

I became a Stewart Grove resident myself in high school, seven years ago. My dad's company transferred him to this small Ohio town the summer between my sophomore and junior year, and even though I didn't want to leave my hometown in rural Pennsylvania, I had no other choice.

The move wasn't as bad as I thought, and I quickly made friends that first summer in my new town. In fact, I became quite popular. Everyone was curious about the new girl, including Seth Garrison, the basketball and football star a year ahead of me. We dated the rest of my time at Stewart Grove High, until he went off to college on an academic and basketball scholarship.

After graduation, I stayed behind and worked full time, even when my father's job relocated him again. This time, I was a recent high school graduate and ready to take on the world. I also wasn't interested in moving a second time, so I stayed here, rented a small apartment with a friend, and started working at the diner in town.

That's where I met Cage Bronson.

My, how life has changed in the last five years since that day.

Shaking off those thoughts, I glance back over at the couple at the table. "They are super cute," I reply as I gather up their freshly filled glasses and returning to where they sit. "Here you go. How's the food?"

"Delicious, as always, my dear," Silvia replies, stabbing a small piece of the cheeseburger her husband helped her cut.

The Saunders have enjoyed an early dinner every Wednesday since I started working here fourteen months ago. They always come in at three thirty, on their way to a church group gathering, and always request to sit at the same table. That table just so happens to be in my section, and slowly, week after week, I've gotten to know the sweet older couple. They've become the highlight of my midweek workday.

"Did I ever tell you about the time Silvia's mother caught us necking in the back seat of my dad's automobile?" Mr. Saunders asks, his hazel eyes sparkling with delight.

He has, in fact, told me this story several times, but as I do most weeks, I shake my head and smile, the anticipation great.

"Well, it was nineteen sixty-one and JFK was just elected as our thirty-fifth president. We were parked behind the abandoned barn by the Wilmon bridge, and I had just gone in for my first kiss. That's when we saw the headlights," he states with a chuckle.

"It was past my curfew," Mrs. Saunders adds, her eyes only on her husband.

"It was, and her parents weren't too happy about it."

"They made me go straight home with my mother, but my father stayed behind."

"He wanted to have a little *chat* with me," Mr. Saunders states with a knowing grin. "That was the night I knew I would marry my Silvia. Told her father that too."

Silvia smiles over at her husband. "We were married six months later."

"And then I was shipped off to Berlin right afterward. Took a bullet to the thigh and was honorably discharged home to spend the rest of my life with the woman I love." He leans over and kisses her lips softly, and even though I've heard this story, and many like it, what feels like a thousand times, my heart still does this weird little skipping beat, and my eyes turn misty.

I blink away the moisture before it has time to gather and fall and give them my best smile. "I love that story. Why don't I leave you two to enjoy your meal. I'll be back to check on you shortly."

When I approach the servers' station, I find the day shift girls and the evening ones finishing up the switchover. I'll hang around though, waiting until the Saunderses are finished with their meal. Usually, the server who has my area after me will take over, but I always stay for them.

"Did you hear how good he looked Saturday night at the reception?" Angie asks Meg as I join them.

"Who?" I ask, straightening the bin with wrapped silverware.

"Kellen. Angie said his ass was amazing in a pair of dark jeans at the wedding reception," Meg announces, causing me to blush. "I'm sad I had that anniversary party to photograph and couldn't go."

"Oh, she's aware," Angie smarts off, a knowing smirk on her face. She clearly hasn't forgotten about my embarrassment Saturday night. While no one said anything after I was busted ogling Kellen's ass, my luck is just too crappy for someone not to bring it up at some point.

Meg turns wide eyes my way. "What'd you do? Did you smack it? Grab two hands full? Rub on it like it were a lamp and you were calling the genie?"

"Oh my God!" I break out in a fit of laughter. "Of course I didn't do that! What is wrong with you?"

"Absolutely nothing is wrong with me. I'm just saying, if I had a chance to smack dat ass, I'd totally do it."

"Whose ass are we smackin'?"

I gasp and spin around, stumbling backward when I realize how close Kellen is standing to me, his face practically against my cheek. He reaches out and catches me, keeping me from falling flat on my backside. "No one's!" I bellow, my heart trying to climb out of my chest.

"Hmm," he hums, the innocent sound causing my internal muscles to clench like a Kegel. "Too bad."

Meg and Angie both giggle, making me roll my eyes.

Before I can comment about having work to do, Kellen asks, "So, if you're not the ass smacker, does that make you the ass smackee?"

Cue red cheeks.

Angie laughs. "Leave her alone, Kel. We have work to do."

He pulls a surprised face. "Are you insinuating I don't have work to do? I'll have you know there's a ladies' book club coming in this evening, which means I will be working my cute little ass off to keep the ladies happy. Because I'm all about exceptional service," he boasts, placing a hand on his chest and smiling innocently.

"You're incorrigible," I insist, shaking my head as I glance over to see how the Saunderses are doing. "If you'll excuse me, I need to get back to my table."

As I start to walk away, I hear Meg gasp and whisper-yell, "Stop staring at her butt!"

It's followed immediately by Kellen, who says, "No! She stared at mine first. It's only fair."

I close my eyes for the briefest of seconds, mostly because I don't trust myself not to run into a chair if I'm not watching where I'm going, and casually make my way to where Mr. and Mrs. Saunders finish up their meal. Of course I can't stop thinking about the fact Kellen was just watching my ass. It's probably a good thing my back is turned to them all so they can't see the color of my face right now.

Not that I'm reading too much into the fact the flirty bartender was looking at my butt, because I'm sure he looks at all of them, but after the last year or so, I can't help the little bubble of pride that fills my chest. *Someone* actually checked me out. Yes, it was Kellen, but still. I'll take it. The ego boost does feel pretty good, especially after the crap-tastic year I've had.

Now, to put all thoughts of Kellen and his flirting out of my head, finish my shift, and head home to watch *The Office* on DVD. I'm up to season four where Toby is leaving Dunder Mifflin, and there's definitely something going on between Michael and Jan.

Just a typical Wednesday night in the life of Cameron Wright. Old hand-me-down DVDs and some leftover spaghetti in the fridge. But do you know what? It's *my* life, and I wouldn't change it for the world.

Kellen

I keep an eye on the pub tables across the bar, monitoring the levels of liquid in their glasses. I've been trying to give the group of nine ladies their space to discuss whatever book they have, but I'm not sure how much talk is actually about the book. Every time I stop to check on them, they're discussing the latest fashion trend they saw on social media or debating on who is sleeping with who around town. Looks more like a gossip night disguised as a book club than anything else.

But who am I to judge?

My second biggest duty at the bar, followed closely behind pouring drinks, is to listen but not judge. I've served my fair share of cheaters and other creeps over the years, and for the most part, I stay silent. There are a few instances where I don't—can't—like when you put your hands on someone else, or if you can't comprehend no means no. Unfortunately, there are some people— yes, I've seen it from the ladies too—who don't understand what the word no means. Nothing pushes my buttons faster than an individual who can't respect boundaries.

I'm a master at watching. I people watch nonstop, constantly taking in their demeanor, stance, mood, and how they react to others. I'm a touchy, feely person, which is why I make sure I'm in tune to those around me. I don't touch someone who seems guarded or not receptive to my overfriendliness. Like my coworkers. I may flirt and throw an arm over their shoulder in the name of fun, but I've already assessed I'm not overstepping by doing so.

Except Cameron.

She was someone I knew not to touch. Not in the beginning, anyway. She was guarded in a way I respected, so I kept my hands to myself when we were near each other. Oh, I still throw in the occasional comment and wink, just to get a rise out of her, but I'd never cross the line with her, if I could help it.

With anyone, really.

Recently, however, I've noticed the slight shift in her. There's humor dancing in her beautiful green eyes when I tease her. She was actually the first person to initiate physical contact between us. One rare night we worked together; she gently grabbed my arm when she was moving in beside me. The touch felt…good. Unexpected, yet right. I held completely still, not reacting in any way, just in case it was unintentional. But then the next time we were beside each other, she swatted at my arm when I made a joke about one of the burger names. She laughed in this carefree, happy way, her head thrown back as the sweetest sound spilled from her lips, and it was from that moment, I knew I'd spend every minute of my time here trying to hear it again.

Even after those two contacts, I was still hesitant to touch her. Someone as guarded as her, I didn't want to cause her any discomfort or see that light dim in those eyes. So, when she touched me a third time, I reciprocated and wrapped my arm around her shoulder as I spouted off a joke, making sure to keep it loose so she could pull away if she desired. I was pleasantly surprised when she turned toward me in her laughter and pressed her nose into my arm.

Internal alarm bells sounded.

Danger, danger!

Woman you can't touch too close.
Smells too good.
Soft and warm.
Abort, abort!

Since that night, there have been a few touches here or there, but always within the predetermined boundaries I placed on any physical contact we may have. Her comfort means more to me than getting a rise out of her, so I make sure to keep it light whenever she's near.

That doesn't mean I didn't want to lean in and sniff her neck when I was standing beside her earlier. Yes, you heard me. She smells fucking amazing, even after working around greasy food all day. The vanilla and lavender are almost overwhelming, which is weird because they're two common scents. Smells I inhale often in my line of work, but for some reason, I never feel a reaction deep in my balls like when it's emanating from her skin.

"Hey, there, handsome. I need two Night Crüe drafts and two lime margaritas with salt, please."

I glance up and smile at Meg. "Coming right up, darlin'."

As I pour two beers, a loud group of cackles fills the bar, making me internally roll my eyes. "Sorority meeting?" Meg asks, humor lacing her question.

"Supposedly, book club," I reply, risking a quick glance over to the tables. "But I haven't seen them open any books yet."

She snorts a laugh. "They're too busy taking bets on which one gets to take you home tonight."

That catches my attention, and as I gaze in that direction, I notice the entire table looking my way. Oh, I'm well versed on the looks on their faces. The flirty smiles. The glint of desire in their eyes. The way two of them lick their red lips seductively. I know immediately, if I wanted one of them—hell, probably a couple of them—they'd be game.

But an orgy isn't on my to-do list for tonight.

My cock respectfully disagrees.

"You want me to go over and get their refill orders?" Meg offers, taking the two margaritas I complete and setting them on her tray.

"No, I've got it," I reply, washing the lime and salt off my hands.

She chuckles. "I'm sure you do," she retorts before returning to the restaurant.

I slide a refill across the bar to one of the regulars who's here watching the game on TV before pasting on a big smile and heading in the direction of the lookie-loos. Their heads are all leaning in once more as they chat. Again, not one book is open.

"I heard she robbed them after they closed one night," one of the women, Chloe, states.

"And she still works here?" another one, Jackie, asks.

That makes me pause.

"Clearly, she's sleeping with one of the owners. I mean, who robs a place and still keeps her job?" Ali asks in disgust.

"Ladies," I interrupt with forced bravado. "How's the book club doing tonight? Are we ready for another round?"

"Definitely," Chloe coos, batting her overly blackened eyelashes my way. Since I'm standing directly beside her, she reaches her hand out and places it on my forearm, giving it a gentle squeeze. "Can we ask you something?"

"Of course," I reply, even though I'm not really sure I want to know.

She leans in toward me, the heavy scent of expensive perfume tackling my senses. "Is it true about that girl? Cameron? Did she really rob this place one night after work?" she asks, her brown eyes sparkling with the prospect of juicy gossip.

"I heard she used her key code to get in and out. How stupid are you to use your own key code to commit a crime?" This absurd question from one of the other ladies at the table, Dahlia.

I school my features, refusing to let my annoyance show. "Robbed us?" I ask with a lighthearted chuckle. "Ladies, come on.

You know that's just a rumor. We've never been robbed before. Not by a current employee or otherwise," I state, grabbing the empty glasses off the table.

"Yeah, but what if someone covered it up? Like when the mayor was sleeping with the chief of police last year, and everyone knew it. I mean, she was calling extra meetings on nights her husband was away for work," Ali adds, causing everyone to nod in agreement. "*Private* meetings."

"Late at night," Chloe tosses out there with a knowing glint in her eyes.

I can't help but smile, because even though I'm pretty certain the married mayor was very much screwing the equally married chief of police, I'm not going to comment on someone's marriage with a group of town gossips.

"I just can't believe she's still working here, after what she did," one of the others, who remained quiet up to this point, states.

I shrug, refusing to be baited into this particular conversation. "How about more margaritas?" I ask a second time. Once they nod in agreement, I turn and head back to the bar with their empty glasses.

By the time I reach the small dishwasher behind the counter, my blood pressure is elevated, and I'm more irritated than normal. Why? I've heard all the rumors about Cameron and the money, but unless I hear what really happened from her mouth, I won't believe any of it. I just *can't* believe it.

The story goes she stole money back when she first started last summer. The amount taken has varied from mouth to mouth and the reason for it is unknown, hence the speculation. And boy have there been rumors. Not just from patrons, but staff too. Some just love to gossip like the rest of the town, while others don't seem to buy the tales we've heard over the last year or so.

Me? I don't believe it.

At least not the shit I've heard shoveled my way. No way would the guys allow her to keep her job if it was as bad as rumored to be, nor are any of them sleeping with her. I've seen each of them with their respective wives too much to buy that load of crap. The owners and Garreth, the manager, are great husbands and employers to work for, but they're not going to let you take advantage of them without just cause. I just don't know what that cause is, and until I hear it from the source, I won't let it affect the job I do or how I treat those I work with.

"Hey, everything okay?"

I glance up and find Garreth standing across from me. "Oh, yeah. Right as rain," I reply, pasting on a big smile.

He snorts. "I can only imagine after dealing with the gossip vultures across the way," he says without looking over at the pub tables where the book club sits. "You looked tense when you walked away."

I shrug my shoulders and start making six fresh margaritas. He comes around to my side of the bar and helps, salting the rims of the glasses as I blend the fruity concoction. "Was it about your sister?" Garreth finally asks.

I pause, my gaze seeking his out. There's worry and compassion in his eyes as he waits for my reply. "No, actually, it wasn't this time."

My sister is a regular source of gossip and question, but when she's a famous country star, that's bound to happen. People are always trying to get the dirt on her life and usually go searching for it in the form of tabloids and internet fodder. Or me. They think they can get to her through me.

It feels like he's waiting me out, so I give him what he's after. "They were asking about Cameron."

I knew that would get a reaction out of him. Whatever happened with Cam involved Garreth, and he's incredibly protective of her. Like a big brother guards his little sister. The way I've always protected my sister, Kinsley.

"Fuck that. Doesn't anyone have anything else to gossip about anymore?" he practically growls his question.

"I hear ya," I reason gently, hoping to defuse his irritation.

"Tell them to mind their own business," he grumbles, turning frustrated eyes over to the table of women.

"Easier said than done in this town," I retort, placing the last of the drinks on the tray. When I reach where they sit, I'm greeted by more giggling. "Ladies, here're your drinks." One by one, I place them around the table, noting the way a few of them move to brush against me. I've had more tits pressed against my arm in the last ten seconds than I did at the Pearl Jam concert when I was twenty.

"May I ask you a very important question?" Chloe coos, leaning forward and invading my personal space, while setting her fake tits on my arm as if it were a shelf.

"Of course," I reply, bending forward just the slightest to make it appear I'm enthralled with anticipation.

She moves her mouth toward my ear and whispers, "Have you ever had your cock sucked in the back room?"

I cough, choking on the air I try to breathe. "Well, I can't say I have," I reply quietly, as if we're sharing a dirty little secret and keeping my work persona mask firmly in place. "Management frowns upon blowies while on the clock," I quip with a tsk.

"Who said they have to know? I'm quite good at it. Give me three minutes and you'll be coming so hard; you'll be begging me to come back tomorrow night."

I don't bother telling her I'm not on the clock tomorrow night.

With my smile firmly on my face, I reply, "That's quite the offer." That's also when I glance down and notice the large diamond ring on a certain finger.

"Don't mind that," she replies, taking notice of my line of sight. "He knows I like to *play*. As long as I come home to him at the end of the night, he won't say a word."

As tempting as it might be to take what she's offering, my gut tells me to bail. While she's offering exactly what I'm looking for, she doesn't scream hit it and quit it. The way her eyes darken, something tells me she's a clinger and getting rid of her might be harder than getting rid of the clap. Not that I'd know, mind you, but Chloe Reynolds screams good time with a side of crazy.

And that's not my jam.

Plus, she's married, and that's something I avoid like an STD.

"Aww, I appreciate the offer," I start, glancing over my shoulder and finding Garreth behind the bar and watching us.

"He can come too and watch," she states, her eyes zeroing in on my boss as she licks her red lips. "Or he can join. I have more than one hole, and I'm very bendy."

"Okay," I say loudly, pushing back from the table and dislodging her very perky double D's from my arm. "You ladies enjoy these drinks and your book."

As I walk away, I can't help but snicker. It takes a lot to get my feathers ruffled, and this isn't the first time I've been offered sex while on the clock, but it *is* the first time said invitation has included a coworker. Twenty-two-year-old me would have jumped at the opportunity, but I've learned over the years, not all fun comes without the strings.

Chloe doesn't just scream strings, but ropes.

And chains.

And probably those fucking bungee cords that stretch, but then those little plastic balls on the end whack you in the family jewels when you're least expecting it.

"Problems?" Garreth asks, drying the washed glasses and placing them back on the shelf.

"Nope, not at all. Oh, if you're looking for something—or someone—to do in a bit, Chloe Reynolds has several holes, and we can flip for who gets which one first."

Garreth's eyes bug out of his head, and he almost drops the glass in his hand. "For fuck's sake, are you serious?"

"As a heart attack, my friend," I state with a laugh.

He shakes his head in disbelief. "You hear just about anything on this job," he says with a snort. "I'll leave Chloe and her wild advances to you. I prefer to go home to my wife," he adds, filling a glass with ice and water.

"Yeah, I think I'm gonna pass on that invite. The husband at home is a hard limit for me."

He grins over at me. "Oh, *now* it's an issue."

I throw the first thing I can find at him, which happens to be a towel. "Shut up, fucker. I didn't know she was married until the asshole came looking for me the next day."

"You wore that black eye well, my friend."

I salute him with my middle finger and turn back to the customers at the bar, the sound of his laughter accompanying me as I get back to work.

Four

Cameron

The ringing of my cell phone interrupts my very busy Saturday afternoon of eating Chex Mix and putting together a complicated one-thousand-piece puzzle.

"Hello?" I answer, noticing my mom's name on the screen.

"Hello, darling. How are you?"

"I'm good, Mom."

"I haven't interrupted anything, have I?"

"Of course not. I always have time for you," I insist, setting down the puzzle piece in my hand and popping a pretzel in my mouth.

"Well, I won't take much of your time. I know you probably have plans tonight, being Saturday and all."

I cringe, wanting to tell her she's way off base, but opt to not make myself sound like a complete loser with that confession. "What's up?"

"Your father and I are going on vacation next month. He has a week's worth of paid time off available, so we're renting an RV and traveling out to Mount Rushmore and the Black Hills."

"That'll be fun," I state, even though traveling cross country in an RV doesn't exactly sound like a fun trip. My dad tends to get all road-ragey when in heavy traffic.

"We thought so. Everyone's doing that nowadays, and there are several rental companies down here. Anyway, we're going to travel up to Ohio first to see you, and we have an extra sleeping space if you wanted to go with us. The dining room seating area turns into a bed."

My eyebrows pull together in question as I try to picture how that would work and if it would be comfortable at all. Not only does that *not* sound like my idea of a good time, but the prospect of missing a week's work and tips sends me into a panic attack. Especially with my car still out of commission.

"Well, you know I welcome a visit from you and Dad anytime, but I don't think I'll be able to get the time off right now," I reason, choosing to let her down easily.

"Why not? Are they working you too much? When was your last day off?"

"I was actually off today, and no, they're not working me too much. There are just staff members getting married and having babies, so any extended period of time off can be difficult over the next few months," I counter, even though I don't really know how true that is. I've never asked.

"Oh, well, okay. That makes sense. As long as they're not taking advantage of you. I suppose we'll just stop by for a short visit then, and maybe you can go with us on a future trip."

"I'm sure we can discuss it when the time's right," I reply.

After a beat, she turns the subject to the topic I expect. "So? Anyone special in your life?"

I roll my eyes, mostly because I knew this question was coming. Mom and Dad were high school sweethearts, married by the time they were twenty. Even though I didn't come along for several more years later, thanks to Mom's endometriosis making it difficult to conceive, she's still a big advocate for finding your forever love.

That's why I never really told her the whole story about what happened with Cage.

She knew we dated, and even lived together, but thinks it was an amicable split between two people who wanted different things. I didn't tell her what really happened. *I couldn't.* I was mortified. Embarrassed by the decisions I made and drowning in the weight of the guilt I carry.

Clearing my throat, I return my focus back to the conversation. "No, no one special right now."

"Well, that's okay. Your someone is out there. You'll find him soon."

I don't have the heart to tell her I have no interest in finding him. I'm doing just fine on my own right now. The last thing I want, or need, is another man to complicate my life. Been there, done that. Don't even want the T-shirt.

My phone vibrates with a text, and when I glance at my screen, I see a message from Meg. "Hey, Mom, one of my coworkers is texting me. Can I call you back later this week?"

"Of course, love. Talk to you soon."

"Love you," I reply, her repeating the sentiment before I disconnect. Then, I switch to the messaging app and click on Meg's name.

Meg: Any chance you can work for me tonight?
I'm not feeling so hot.

I glance at the time, noting her shift is just starting. If I hurry, I'll make it in before the dinner rush hits, and even though I usually work the day shift now, I know the evenings usually net more tips, and that'll help me tremendously when it comes to paying to fix my car. That was an added expense I wasn't anticipating.

Me: Of course! Need me to bring you anything?

Meg: No, I'm good. Jasper is sending me home
with chicken noodle soup.

Me: Okay. On my way.

The moment I tap send, I jump up and run to my bedroom to get ready. Fortunately, I did laundry earlier today and have a pair of black jeans and a work shirt clean, so I quickly throw them on. I stuff my feet into my favorite pair of comfortable shoes and make a beeline to the bathroom to add a touch of eyeliner and mascara. I don't usually wear a lot of makeup, so it only takes me a minute to freshen up before I grab my hairbrush. Running it through my long auburn locks, I toss the brush on the counter, braid my hair over my shoulder, and quickly brush my teeth. I'm out the door a few minutes later.

Unfortunately, with my car out of commission right now, I'll have to walk to the restaurant, and today's September temperature is significantly warmer than yesterday. My brow is already drawing sweat by the time I reach the end of my block, which doesn't bode well for my appearance by the time I get to work. But since I can't turn down the money, nor would I back out on my agreement to work for Meg, I have no choice but to deal with the heat and humidity. Maybe tonight's tips will be good enough I can get my car looked at.

It's been sitting at Otto's since Monday morning. He was able to pick it up on his way to work, only charging me a forty-five-dollar fee to grab it. That was the easy part, sadly. He's pretty sure my alternator is bad, which might not be so bad by itself, but the power steering pump is shot too. That would explain why it has been turning harder the days before it broke down. Add in the fact my tires are so bad, he doesn't feel comfortable letting me drive on them anymore. Suddenly, my old car is in need of major repair, and I just don't have the money to fix it right now.

Every spare penny I have goes to repaying my debt to Garreth, so until that's finished, I'll just walk to and from work. The weather hasn't been too bad. Well, until today. The sun is trying to bake me, and I'm kicking myself for not putting sunscreen on my face. I'm going to have red cheeks the rest of the night, I'm sure of it.

By the time I approach Burgers and Brew, I'm panting. Apparently, I could use a little more daily exercise on top of it, but I don't have time to think about that. Right now, I need to get inside, cool off, and get to work.

Entering my code at the back entrance, I slip inside and am wrapped in glorious air-conditioning. I lean against the wall, closing my eyes and letting the coolness wrap around me.

"Hey, you okay?"

I look up and find Isaac, or Numbers as everyone calls him, coming down the stairs from his second-floor office. "Of course," I reply, pasting a bright smile on my face. "It's warm out there." He's studying me a little too closely for my liking, so I push off the wall and start walking to the employee break room. "I'm covering for Meg. Gotta go!" I holler, swiftly rounding the corner and entering the room.

There's no one in here, so I have the space all to myself. I slip my small bag in the locker I use and secure it behind me. I head inside the small bathroom and groan, recognizing my appearance is as rough as I expected it to be, but there's nothing I can do about that now. Grabbing a paper towel, I wet it quickly and run it over my face, hoping it helps draw out the redness from my skin quicker, but I don't notice any change. With a sigh, I toss the paper towel in the trash and head out to get to work.

"Oh, hey, glad you can come and help," Garreth says, flashing me a grateful smile. "I sent Meg home already."

"No problem. Just tell me what section I'm taking tonight," I reply, grabbing a waist apron and tying it behind me.

"Actually, we're changing things up," he starts, sighing and running his hand through his long hair. When he meets my gaze, I know. I can feel his sadness before he even says a word. "Kallie got the call a bit ago. Valerie is unresponsive."

My heart hurts for my coworker and her new husband. "Oh no."

He nods. "They've been expecting it. It's only a matter of time now, so she'll be taking some time off. Walker will be in later after the kids go to bed. He took tonight off for his mom's birthday dinner, and I wasn't letting him miss that. Until then, I'll help Kellen behind the bar, and I'll have you cover the tables. Have you ever worked that side?" he asks, referring to the booths and tables in the bar.

"Nope, but it won't be a problem," I assure him.

"I know it won't. Use the computer behind the bar for your orders so it doesn't get too congested at the servers' station. Holler if you need help," he insists, leading me in that direction.

Even though it's barely five o'clock, the room is half-full with patrons. I survey the room, taking note of who has menus and who doesn't, and jump right in. After dropping off menus and promising to come right back for drink orders, I move to the bar and start filling water glasses.

"Hey."

I look over to Kellen and instantly notice his demeanor. His usual bright smile is sadder this evening and his ocean blue eyes don't hold the same sparkle. "Hi," I reply.

"You heard?" he asks, reaching around me to grab a glass.

"Yeah. Sorry to hear about Valerie," I confirm.

He nods. "Me too. Kal left in a hurry and was a mess."

"I'm sure. I couldn't imagine," I say, filling the last glass and placing it on my tray. "I'm going to deliver these and start taking orders."

"Sounds good. The two booths over by the door already have drinks, but that's it. I'll cover the bar."

"And I've got the tables," I insist, carefully lifting the tray and heading out to take care of the customers.

I'm surprised by how fun it is to work on this side of the business. The tables are spread out more and the crowd seems a little more laid-back, more content to just have a few drinks and a good time.

On one of my many trips behind the bar to place an order with the kitchen, I spin around to grab a glass off the back shelf, since the ones beneath the bar are gone, and run smack into a hard chest. It's warm and smells amazing, and my immediate instinct is to curl into it, not push it away.

"Whoa there, love. You're gonna hurt yourself," Kellen says softly, his hands wrapping around my upper body to keep me from falling flat on my ass.

"Shitballs, I'm sorry. I wasn't paying attention," I quickly reply, gazing up…and up and up…into those hypnotic blue eyes.

He flashes me a devilish grin as he winks. "Women are practically falling at my feet nonstop, love. It's a curse, really," he states with a shrug.

A very unladylike snort slips from my mouth, as I shake my head. "You're something else."

Again, he grins proudly. "Thank you."

Rolling my eyes, I tell him, "That wasn't exactly a compliment." That's also when I realize he's still holding me against his body. I can feel the warmth of his skin through his work tee and the slow and steady tickle of his breath against my forehead.

Things are also *happening* south of his belt, if you know what I mean.

I can definitely feel that, and I'm not sure which is worse. The way my throat goes Sahara-dry in embarrassment or the fact my panties are very damp suddenly with excitement.

Kellen must know it's happening. I mean, what man wouldn't realize he's getting hard when he's pressed against a woman, which means he clearly knows his body is reacting to me. What I don't understand is why.

I'm nothing to write home about.

Nothing special, as Cage used to remind me.

Often.

I find myself licking my lips as I gaze up at him. Not because I'm thinking about kissing him—okay, maybe I'm thinking about it...or maybe wishing—but because it's suddenly hot in here. Hot and dry and my brain isn't quite working properly. The respectable thing to do would be to politely back away, apologize again for running into him, and then carry on with my night.

However, that's not where my brain goes. It lodges firmly in a no-fly zone of dirty images starring none other than Kellen McGregor. Naked images, thanks to a certain hard appendage wanting to come out and play. Seriously, is that thing a third leg?

Oh my God, stop thinking about it!

A loud crash causes me to jump, and even though his hands tighten for a fraction of a second, they loosen just as quickly. I step back, allowing oxygen to infiltrate my brain again. Clearly, his cologne is some voodoo drug that makes women horny and reckless, like that pheromone patch they used with Matt Damon in *Ocean's Thirteen*. If I hadn't moved back at that exact moment, I was liable to lick his neck and likely strip myself naked before I even realized I was doing it.

"You okay?" he whispers, his voice deep and husky.

"Yep, fine, great!" I insist loudly and unnaturally. "I'm going to take a quick restroom break." Then, I spin back around and power walk toward the hallway. I really just need a minute or two to clear my head. You know, work shit out and all.

I don't waste as much time as I'd like trying to calm my racing heart, because this isn't my allotted break time. I'm needed on the floor, waiting tables. That's what I get paid to do, and every tip helps chip away at the pile of debt I accrued, thanks to falling in love with the wrong man.

Never going to let that happen again.

With one final once-over in the small bathroom mirror, I release a deep, calming breath and return to the main hallway. The moment I step out of the break room, I find Garreth standing there.

"You okay?" he asks, his eyes full of concern.

"Oh, sure," I insist, plastering on a big smile.

The problem is, if anyone knows how to read me, it's Garreth. Well, him and his wife, Reagan. They both became the friends I so desperately needed last year, and even though they're both older than me, Reagan about ten years, and Garreth right around sixteen, they don't treat me like I'm a dumb kid who can't make her own adult decisions.

Though, history has recently proven those decisions to be questionable.

The truth is, they helped me get on the right track, and I will forever be grateful and in debt to them.

"Do you need to switch with someone? I can have Angie or Cece take the bar side," he offers.

"No, I'm good. Promise. I like working the bar side."

He stares at me for a few long seconds before nodding. For a moment, I thought he was going to call me out on my weird reaction to being so close to Kellen, but fortunately, he doesn't. The situation is embarrassing enough without Garreth noticing me getting all hot and bothered around a coworker. "All right," he finally concedes. "Holler if you need help or another breather."

I nod in reply and quickly move around him, heading back to the bar. It's a busy Saturday night, and I have a job to do, money to make.

Sexy man behind the bar with a panty-melting smile be damned.

Kellen

I keep my eye on Cam for the rest of the evening and tell myself it's because she's new to this side of the business. But my dick keeps calling my bluff. He remembers exactly what it felt like to have her pressed against me. She molded to me like a second skin, her much smaller body fitting perfectly to mine like a puzzle piece. Soft, full tits pressed to my chest and lithe fingers gripping my arms. That's exactly why my little soldier is doing his best to stand at complete attention once more, ready to be called up to active duty.

Only, there will be no saluting the golden pussy tonight, my friend.

And definitely not Cameron's.

Unfortunately, he doesn't heed the commands from my brain, and for the last hour, I've done everything I can to conceal a half-mast dick, especially when she's near, and because she's working my side, that's pretty much nonstop. I'm not sure how to take this reaction to her. Yes, I'm a guy, so I have this particular reaction from time to time when around a gorgeous woman, but it doesn't happen at work with coworkers.

"I need two Night Crües, two American Crües, and a Bud Light, all drafts, please," Cam announces when she approaches the bar, placing the order slip in front of me.

My eyes, the traitorous bastards they are, automatically go to where they shouldn't. Namely, her tits. Even for the briefest second, they catch a glimpse of the way the work polo hugs those luscious mounds, and I know it'll take bleach to my corneas and a significant brain injury to forget just how amazing she looks in a work shirt.

"You got it, darlin'," I reply, starting to pour the frosted mugs of brew. As I place the first one down on the bar, our fingers brush against each other as she grabs it. Jolts of electricity course through my veins with startling potency, something that's never happened before when I touch another person.

What the hell?

Keeping my features schooled, I finish her order and place the slip back on her tray, anxious to send her on her way. Not because I don't enjoy working with her, but because she's fucking with my mind. She doesn't even realize she's doing it, which is the frustrating part of it all. At least when I encounter women who are flirting back and trying to ride me like a roller coaster, I'm prepared. I'm comfortable. In my element. I know exactly how to respond, because that's exactly how they expect me to.

However, with Cameron, she doesn't even realize how sexy she is and how everyone in the bar seems to track her movements with their eyes. She's gorgeous, with those auburn locks and big green eyes. Not to mention the light dusting of freckles across the bridge of her nose and cheeks. Fuck, I didn't even realize I was a sucker for freckles until now. She's like the girl next door you watch through the fence, secretly jacking off every time she's doing something as simple as reading in a lounge chair.

But the best part about Cam is she doesn't even realize how the guys check her out. She's oblivious to their watchful and appreciative eyes, going about her business as if she's not the object of every male fantasy in the room. Hell, even I didn't truly see her for the beauty she is until recently. Very recently, actually.

Ever since the wedding last Saturday night, I can't stop stealing glances and picturing her in ways I've never entertained before.

Dirty ways.

"Earth to Kellen." Garreth waves his hand in front of my face. "You all right? You were spacing out. I don't think you heard anything I said."

"Shit, sorry, man. I was off in my own world there for a minute," I reply with a grin. "What can I getcha?"

"Nothing. I was just telling ya the grill was shutting down for the night. Walker texted he's on his way, so when he gets here, I'll send Cam home. Most of the tables in here are done eating anyway."

I nod, surprisingly saddened to know she's leaving soon.

The realization I've developed a little crush on Cameron is startling. Thirty-year-old men don't get crushes.

They get laid.

Clearly, that's what I need. One quick glance around the room confirms I could easily pick one of the eager women currently giving me the fuck-me eyes and take her home. It would probably do me good to release a little *stress*. It's been...

Holy shit!

Okay, a little math lets me know it's been a little longer than anticipated since I got laid. I remember bendy Sherry, the yoga instructor who works at the same gym I frequent, and that was almost six months ago. I recall the exact weekend because it was St. Patrick's Day and she was wearing an *Irish You Were Naked* tank top, her fake tits practically spilling out of the fitted top.

Her wish was my command, because we barely made it back to her place before I was naked.

Yeah, I definitely need to get laid.

But as I hear Cameron laugh at the end of the bar, her long, smooth neck on full display and begging to be bitten, I know that's not happening. Not tonight. The thought of going home with some random woman leaves a guilty feeling in the pit of my gut, and that's just stupid. Stupid and fucked up, considering we're nothing more than friendly coworkers. Why should I feel bad about getting a little dick action?

But I do.

All the more reason I need to get over this sudden and crazy crush I seem to find myself with.

"All right, I'm out of here. Hope I didn't mess up too bad tonight."

I spin around and find Cameron leaning against the bar, a tired but happy smile on her face. "You did fine," I reassure her, propping my hip against the cooler and fighting myself between wanting to step closer and knowing I need to keep my distance.

Jameson is on the stage, playing his guitar like he does every Friday and Saturday night. It's one of the big draws to this place, his acoustic performances while you have a few drinks. It won't be until after he performs that the energy turns up, the atmosphere shifting. First, with the playing of a Mötley Crüe song at the stroke of eleven, followed by upbeat rock music until last call.

She rolls her eyes playfully before yawning. "Sorry." She chuckles as she covers her mouth. Of course, my stupid dick sees her smiling like a donut and suddenly he's entertaining ideas of exactly what to slip between those plump lips. "I forgot how exhausting it is to work the dinner shift."

"Been a while, huh?"

With elbows resting on the bar top, she smiles casually and rocks herself forward on her toes. The motion pushes her chest toward me, but I resist the urge to look.

"Yeah. I've been working the lunch shift since Christmas. It's not always quite this busy, but you still make decent tips."

"Well, we'll have your cut from the bar put away for you next time you work. Numbers will have it."

She seems surprised. "What?"

I shrug my shoulders and cross my arms over my chest. There's no missing the way her eyes drop to my arms for a brief second before returning to my face. "Well, everyone who works behind the bar splits all the tips at the end of the night. You'll get a cut."

Her mouth falls open.

Fantasies, fantasies...

"But...I didn't work behind the bar. I covered all the tables," she insists quickly, seeming a little flustered.

I grab a cloth and wash down the bar in front of where she stands just to give my hands something to do. "You think I didn't notice you refilling those two drinks while you were putting in an order?"

She seems flabbergasted. "Those were just Cokes."

"Doesn't matter," I reply casually, tossing the cloth in the warm, soapy water.

"No...but...that's not right. I only helped one or two times. That doesn't warrant me getting part of the tips. I have plenty from the tables I served."

I give her a big smile. "Cam. You think I didn't notice you jumping in almost every time you saw someone who needed something? You might not have poured beers or mixed drinks, but you took care of people sitting at the bar all night long."

Her face blushes a beautiful shade of pink. "That was nothing," she all but whispers, her words so soft I almost miss them.

"It was everything. You deserve a part of these tips too."

She's already shaking her head. "I won't accept them. It's not right."

"What's not right?" Garreth asks, coming around the bar and standing beside me.

"Kellen says I'm getting part of his tips behind the bar because I helped pour a few waters and sodas."

"You did more than that, and you know it," I state, giving her a pointed look.

"That's the rules, Cam. You were a huge help over here, especially when I got pulled over to the restaurant," Garreth insists. "You'll have an envelope with Numbers for tonight."

She sighs and closes her eyes for a few seconds. "I'm not going to win this argument, am I?" she concedes, though her question really doesn't sound like a question at all.

"Nope," both Garreth and I state at the same time.

"All right then, I'll leave you both to it," she says, looking over her shoulder and watching Jameson play for a few beats. When she's unable to hide another yawn, she stands up and offers a wave. "I'm headed home, unless you guys need anything else?"

Before I can open my mouth to probably reply something dirty, Garreth steps in. "Nope, we got it. Walker's here. Clock out. Or stay and enjoy the music for a bit."

"I should definitely go," she replies just as Walker approaches. She moves behind the bar, her scent tickling my nose as she passes, and taps on the tablet.

"Hey, Cameron. Thanks for helping out tonight," Walker greets with a grateful smile.

"Of course. Anytime," she insists, finishing using the device. "You guys have a good evening." Then, she heads away from us, her ass hypnotizing me with every step she takes.

I've always been an ass man.

"I'll walk you out," Garreth states, following Cameron to the door to make sure she doesn't have any problems, but just before they reach the back entrance, someone stops him. He says something to Cameron, who pushes through the door, as he walks toward the kitchen to deal with whatever issue has suddenly arisen.

I jump back into work, trying to put all thoughts of Cameron and this pesky little crush I seem to have developed as of late. However, about ten minutes later, I look over and find Cameron walking toward us and taking a seat at the end of the bar. There's something on her face I can't exactly read, and whatever it is has me moving in her direction, forgetting all about the order I was working on.

"Hey, everything okay?" I ask when I reach where she sits.

She gives me a smile, but it doesn't quite reach her eyes. "Yeah, of course. I got outside and thought I might stay for a bit. You know, watch the magic happen behind the bar and listen to Tank play," she says, using the nickname many have for Jameson.

I nod, not quite buying her story, but not really knowing her well enough to call her on it. "Can I get you a drink?" I ask, already reaching down for a glass.

She seems hesitant, but eventually replies, "Just a water, please."

Nodding, I fill the glass with ice and water before sliding it her way. "Anything else, love?"

Her eyes seem to relax a bit as the faintest smile plays on her lips. "No, thank you."

I tap the bar before returning to my post and finishing the order I was originally working on. The woman seems a bit annoyed with me, but I don't care. Making sure Cameron was all right was top priority.

"Sorry 'bout that," I say, placing her and her friend's drink on the bar. "Seven fifty, please."

The woman leans forward, pressing her tits up and out of the top of her skimpy tank top. "I don't get a free drink for my birthday?" she coos, batting her eyelashes.

Funny, I'm pretty sure she asked Walker about a free birthday drink not twenty minutes ago. We don't do that, especially for women who think it'll lead to sex, which clearly this one does. "Sorry, darlin', no free drinks. Maybe you could find someone to help you celebrate and buy you one later." I throw in a wink and my flirty smile, falling easily into my work persona.

She leans forward even more. "Or..." she starts, reaching her finger out and running a red nail along my forearm, "*you* could help me celebrate later."

"Aww, you know, I'd love to, darlin', but I'm busy tonight." I flash her a grin, even though I'm flat-out turning down her offer.

And why am I turning her down, again?

Without any prompt from my brain, I glance over to the end of the bar to where Cameron is sitting.

The woman makes a tsk noise and a pout. "Well, if your other friend isn't interested, give me a call," she states, slipping her credit card and one of our bar napkins across the hardwood top. There's a number written across the paper with the name Alexis above it.

I take both, running the card through the machine and slip the number into my pocket. I'm sure she thinks I'm keeping it as a backup for later tonight, but she'd be wrong. I don't make a habit of throwing the given numbers away in front of the women. That's when you get your tires slashed or a dead raccoon thrown in the bed of your truck.

Has happened.

Not to me, but I know a guy.

The bartending world is surprisingly small.

Finishing up her tab, I place a pen and the slip of paper in front of her and grab the next guy's order. Once the lady up front finishes paying, I collect her slip, which also now has her number written on it, and put together the beer order for the next customer. And that's how it goes until last call.

Jameson walks a few ladies out, while Walker, Garreth, and I tackle the shutdown behind the bar. A chuckle to my left has me in search of the owner, and I find both Jasper and Numbers standing over by Cameron. She throws her head back and laughs again, and my heartbeat does this weird tap dance number. It's unsettling, really, and starting to piss me off.

When the last stool is placed on the bar, everything cleaned up, and the coolers are restocked, I clock out on the tablet and grab the envelope Garreth holds out for me. He takes another one to the end of the bar and places it in front of Cameron. She shakes her head, pulling her hands back as if it were a snake about to bite her.

"Don't be difficult," Garreth counters as I approach. "Just take the money."

Cameron sighs deeply and reluctantly takes the envelope off the counter. "Thank you," she mumbles, even though I can tell she's not a fan of taking this additional portion of tips. "I'll be sure not to help next time."

I can't help but laugh as Numbers takes the cash register drawer and walks toward the hallway. I've seen this process happen enough to know one of the owners will stay behind with Numbers while he locks the money in the safe and makes sure the building is secure to leave.

"Let's go," Garreth announces.

Cameron hops off the stool and seems a bit fidgety as she slowly walks toward the back exit with the small group. Jasper is there, as well as Jameson, who are talking about Elliott's latest antics at school.

I get to the door first and push it open, the warm September night air hitting me in the face with a slap. Damn, it's warm out here, not completely uncommon for September in Ohio, even at night.

First thing I do is look around the lot, checking to see if anyone lingers or what vehicles remain. It's happened before where we come across patrons making out in the open, having not made it to a car yet, or witness naked asses pressed against a car window.

The next thing I notice is the way Cam seems to be searching the area. It's more than just a casual glance or two around the parking lot. It's as if she's uncomfortable, keeping her eyes moving and observing her surroundings.

"Night," Jameson states, walking over to his Harley.

I'm heading to my own truck, when it hits me Cam's car isn't in the lot. I pause, taking in another quick surveillance of the area, but don't see it. Before I can ask about it, Garreth stops and face her. "Where's your car?"

She looks down, hesitant to answer, but eventually does. "It was such a great night, I walked."

"You walked?" Garreth asks, his eyebrows drawn together. You can tell he wants to ask more but opts to just point at his SUV. "Come on. I'll drop you off on my way home."

"You don't live that way. It's fine. I can walk," she insists, turning and heading in the direction of the front of the building.

"Cam. Get in." Garreth uses that older brother tone, leaving no room for argument. It's comical to watch.

She huffs, her shoulders dropping as she realizes she's not going to get out of this. "Fine," she grumbles, turning and walking toward Garreth's SUV.

A bubble of something foreign festers and tickles my gut. Is that...*jealousy?* Am I really jealous Garreth is jumping in and helping her? *They've always been close*, I tell myself, but the truth is, I wanted to be the one to offer. The one she went to when she needed help. Not that she was asking for assistance. The stubborn woman would have no doubt walked home at one thirty in the morning.

"See you, Kellen." Her soft voice pulls me out of my own thoughts.

"Night, Cam," I reply, lifting my hand to wave.

She's in his vehicle and they're pulling out before I can offer to take her myself. Not that it's any closer to my own place, but I still felt like it needed to be me who offered.

All the more reason why I should get in my truck and as far away from Cam as I can. She's stirring up way too many weird feelings in the pit of my stomach I'm not prepared to deal with. Crushes are weird and hard, especially when you don't want them.

It's not going to be easy avoiding her, especially if we work together, but it's necessary. Until this pesky little infatuation I suddenly have is gone, I just need to steer clear of the sexy Miss Cameron Wright.

Shouldn't be an issue.

Cameron

I startle awake, my breathing labored as I stare wide-eyed up at the ceiling.

Was that a noise outside?

Listening intently, the only sound I hear is a car starting nearby. I let out the breath I didn't realize I was holding and glance at the clock. It's almost eight, which means I've gotten less than four hours of sleep.

When Garreth brought me home early this morning, I struggled to calm down enough to fall asleep. He knew something was up with me, but never pushed the matter. When I got inside, I must have checked the doors and windows a dozen times before finally convincing myself I was safe enough to go to bed. Relaxing enough to actually fall asleep took forever and even then, it wasn't good sleep. I was plagued with dreams of a time I'd rather forget all about.

Finding Cage Bronson in the parking lot behind Burgers and Brew last night when I got off work was shocking to say the least. I had intended to slip out the back as if my car was there and walk home before anyone became the wiser, but then I found him waiting for me. It's been well over a year since I saw my boyfriend—or, *ex-boyfriend*. Almost a year and a half ago, our relationship imploded my life, blanketing me in humiliations and bad decisions. I did things I'm not proud of, things I can't take back, despite wanting desperately to.

All I can do is move forward and right the wrongs I committed.

But now what?

Just when I think my life is almost back to normal, the man who turned it upside down declares he's back and grateful I took care of paying his debt. What the hell is that? He gets himself into trouble, leaves me to take the fall and deal with the consequences of his actions, and then thinks he can breeze back into town? As if I'd be waiting for him? Pining away for the man I thought I knew, when in reality, I only saw the façade he wanted me to see?

How did I go so wrong with him?

Was I so blinded by the prospect of love and forever I couldn't see the man he truly was?

I mean, it's not like my friends didn't try to tell me. They warned me about his reputation. Hell, I'd heard all about it, and I'd like to say I fought my attraction to him in the beginning, but I'm not sure if that is true. From the start, I was smitten with the sexy bad boy with the tattoos and the naughty glint in his dark eyes, and slowly over the course of our time together, he alienated me from my friends, making sure I depended on him for everything and anything.

Freeing myself from Cage, despite the reason why, was the best thing that ever happened to me, followed very closely by finding friends like Garreth and Reagan. Now, he's back, and in his words, anxious to just pick up where we left off.

Well, that's not going to happen.

Not now.

Not ever.

I get up and rub my tired eyes, knowing instantly I won't be finding any more sleep this morning. The worry plaguing my exhausted brain has me glancing around the room, taking stock in everything nearby. For what? I'm not physically afraid of Cage. He never hurt me, at least not with his hands. He was a master manipulator, so it was always his words he wielded like a weapon.

Besides, he doesn't know where I live, which is a blessing.

The place we shared last year is long gone, his items inside left for the landlord to deal with. I took my own belongings, not that there were many. Cage already had that house when we got together, so by the time I had to vacate the premises, I only had some clothes and a few random personal effects to deal with.

I yawn dramatically and slip into the hallway bathroom. A shower would do wonders for my weary bones, as would a big cup of sweetened coffee. Unfortunately, coffee is a luxury I don't have, despite missing it desperately. I have no coffee pot, nor do I make stops at Lyndee's bakery for a fresh—and slightly expensive—cup of Joe. That five dollars could be used in other ways, like making sure I have my utilities paid and a roof over my head.

After a long, hot shower, I feel slightly better. I slip on a pair of cutoff shorts and a tank top, comb out my wet hair, brush my teeth, and add a touch of mascara. Donning my favorite pair of flip-flops, I grab my keys and wristlet and head out the door.

It's early enough in the day that it doesn't feel like the sun is trying to cook you, so at least the walk to the grocery store won't be completely miserable. Plus, without having my car, it'll ensure I don't spend too much money on food, since I'll have to carry everything I buy home with me. There's also the fact I have to be at work at ten thirty, so this trip needs to be quick and only getting the necessities.

The walk doesn't take too long, but I'm definitely grateful for the air-conditioning the moment I step inside. I retrieve one of the smaller carts and make my way past the soda and bottled water aisle to reach the produce section. There, I place a few bananas in my cart, as well as a bag of fresh peaches that are on sale, and even though I'd love to stock up on some vegetables too, I don't want to have to carry them back home right now.

Once my car is fixed, I'll come back and fill my fridge.

Famous last words.

I reach the very back of the store where the frozen foods are kept, and even though I know I shouldn't even entertain the idea of getting ice cream—no way will I make it home before it melts—I stop and stare at the flavors longingly. Chocolate cherry chip? Peach cobbler? Oh my God, my mouth is watering just reading them.

"You always had a sweet tooth."

The hairs on the back of my neck stand straight up and goosebumps pepper my skin, and it has nothing to do with the temperature in this aisle. I turn to face Cage, standing up straight and moving my cart between us like a shield. "What are you doing here?" I ask, my tone clipped.

He grins at me, and I shudder. His smile was always nice. Not Kellen nice, but nice nonetheless. Of course, now that I know what lurks behind that grin, I don't feel any reaction to it the way I used to. "Well, it's a grocery store, Cameron," he states, as if he's speaking to someone who's unable to comprehend.

"I know that," I counter, taking a step back and moving my cart with me.

"Then you can probably figure out what I'm doing here," he replies breezily.

I don't miss the fact he doesn't have a basket, cart, nor is he carrying any food. Swallowing over the lump in my throat, I shift my cart and try to walk around him. "If you'll excuse me, I need to finish my shopping."

Cage steps to the left, blocking my retreat. Even though my brain is screaming *Danger!* I steel my spine and meet his gaze, refusing to let him see me react. "Where ya going, Cameron? I thought maybe we could hang out later," he says quietly, reaching his hand out as if to cup my cheek.

I take another step back and move my cart, hitting him in the foot with the wheel. He grunts, annoyance filling his features as he stares down at me. I take one more retreating step and startle when my legs hit the cool glass of the frozen food case behind me. My mouth opens to decline his suggestion when I hear a familiar voice behind me.

"Hey, Cam."

Cage and I both turn as Kellen walks up to stand beside me. Unlike Cage, Kellen is holding a green grocery basket with a few items placed inside.

"Oh, hi," I squeak out, my voice surprisingly pitchy.

He offers me a friendly smile, his eyes searching my face. I wonder if he can see the stress lines around my tired eyes or see the uneasiness I feel coursing through my body. If he does, he doesn't say anything, choosing to turn his attention to the other man standing near. "Hey. Kellen McGregor," he states with a confident smile, extending his hand toward Cage.

My ex looks like he wants to sneer at Kellen and perhaps refuse to shake his hand. However, after a few uncomfortably long seconds, he finally reaches forward and shakes. "Cage Bronson."

"Nice to meet you, Cage." Then, he turns those sapphire blue eyes back to me and asks, "Ready to go?"

I'm about to ask him what in the world he's talking about, but realization sets in and hits me hard in the chest. He's offering me an out. He knows I'm uncomfortable around Cage and is throwing me a lifeline without causing a scene. I could kiss him, really. Actually, that idea has some merit, but I won't be kissing Kellen now or anytime soon, so I might as well just get over that fantasy.

Clearing my throat, I reply, "Yep. Ready."

Then without a glance back at Cage, I spin my cart around and walk beside Kellen toward the checkout lines. My heart is doing its best to try to pound out of my chest and my legs feel a bit wobbly, but somehow, I manage to get from point A to point B without embarrassing myself.

He waves his hand for me to go first in the checkout, and as I'm placing items on the conveyor belt, I notice the tremble in my hands. Giving them a quick shake, I pick up the pace in emptying my cart, desperate to get out of the store before Kellen and Cage can follow.

Just as I'm swiping my card to pay, I see Cage exit the building and stop just outside the door. I close my eyes for a brief moment, realizing my narrow window for escape has slammed shut.

Now what?

As if sensing my turmoil, Kellen reaches out and lightly cups my elbow. "Wait for me, please."

I take my receipt and step forward, deciding if I'm going to go outside and face Cage or wait inside for Kellen. Without having my car, I won't be able to get away as easily, meaning my ex might be able to follow me home, and that's the last thing I want. So, placing my cart back with the others, I pick up my few grocery bags and wait for Kellen to complete his purchase.

"All right," Kellen says, taking his two bags in his left hand and placing his right one against my lower back. The warmth and protection it offers sends shivers of awareness up my spine, and suddenly, I'm picturing that very hand touching other parts of my body.

The moment we walk outside, Cage moves toward a newer Cadillac Escalade. Of course my dirtbag ex would be driving an SUV like that, while I was barely scraping by, no thanks to him. He walks over to his driver's door and gets inside his vehicle. I keep my gaze in front of me, but I know he turns it over and is waiting. I can hear the engine sitting idle.

Kellen places his bags in the back seat of his truck before taking mine to do the same. Once he shuts the door, he turns and stares behind me, his blue eyes narrowing a bit as he watches. I already know what—or *who*—he's looking at.

"Listen," I start, but am cut off.

"Hang on." He opens the passenger door behind me and stands close.

Something in his voice gives me pause. It's not so much his firm directness as it is the concern behind it. He steps toward me, crowding my personal space even more, and places his hand on the door behind me. The stance cages me in, but I don't feel threatened or unsafe. No, the action does the complete opposite for my lady bits. They are suddenly standing at complete attention, taking notice of everything surrounding Kellen McGregor. The shape of his body, the hardness of his muscles, and the scent of his soap. It all tickles my senses and makes me want to lean into him.

I don't, however.

I hear a vehicle backing out of a parking spot nearby and stomp on the gas a little too hard as it drives away. Realization sets in and I sag against the door with relief. Even then, I still look over to where the Escalade was once parked to find it gone.

"He took off," Kellen confirms, his warm breath hotter than the summer air around me.

"Thank you."

He watches me intently, those sapphire eyes searching my face. After a beat, he drops his arm and moves back. "Hop in."

"Oh, that's not necessary. I can walk home."

With a sigh, he waves at the inside of his truck. "It's not a problem, Cam. Let me take you home." His eyes seem conflicted, as he waits for me to argue with him.

Realizing I have to be to work soon, I turn and climb into the passenger seat. He shuts the door behind me and walks around to the driver's side. Without saying a word, he starts the truck, backs out of his parking spot, and takes off in the direction of my house. I don't miss the way his eyes search his surroundings, and I can't help but wonder if he's looking for Cage's SUV.

I know I am.

After a few blocks, he finally speaks. "So, Cage Bronson..." he starts, leaving the door wide open for me to finish the statement.

I clear my throat. "Ex-boyfriend."

"Ex?" he asks, looking my way for a brief moment as he seeks confirmation.

"Yes, definitely ex. Apparently, he's back in town."

"I thought I heard he left for a while." He pauses, glancing to me again as he asks, "Is he bothering you?"

I consider lying to him, insisting he's not. The truth is, he's not really doing anything wrong except making his presence known. He might crowd my personal space a little, but he hasn't threatened me in any way or touched me. "I guess he's bothering me only because he's suddenly reappeared. He showed up in the back lot of the bar last night, and—"

"He what?"

Fidgeting with the fringe on my cutoffs, I mumble, "Umm, well, he was in the back parking lot when I got off work last night."

His jaw tightens, as does his grip on the steering wheel. "I knew something was up," he mutters, almost to himself.

"He didn't do anything."

Why am I defending Cage?

I rush on to add, "I walked out last night, and he was there. He told me he was back in town and insinuated we could pick things back up where we left off. I told him not a chance in hell and went back inside. That's it."

He doesn't reply for several blocks, and I don't know if that bothers me or if I'm grateful. When we turn onto my street, he finally asks, "No chance in hell?"

I shake my head. "None. That train has left the station."

Kellen relaxes a bit in his seat and moments later pulls into my driveway. When he puts it in Park, he turns his body toward me. "Would you tell me if he was causing you problems?"

Okay, that's not what I was expecting.

"Umm…"

He exhales loudly and holds my gaze. "Promise me if Bronson causes a problem for you, you'll let someone know. If not me, tell Garreth, okay? I know you're friends with him. Everyone just wants you safe, and if someone is threatening that or your comfort, we want to know."

I nod, my throat suddenly too thick to speak words.

Kellen relaxes even more with my confirmation and flashes me that familiar smile. It's friendly and calming in a way I wasn't expecting.

"Thank you for the lift," I state, releasing my seat belt and opening my door.

"Want some help taking your stuff in?"

"No, that's okay. It's not much." I close the passenger door and open the one right behind it. I wonder if he's going to argue with me, insisting he help me inside, but he doesn't, and for that, I'm thankful.

"See you at work, Cam," he says when I have all of my bags in my hands.

"Bye."

When I shut the door, I carefully make my way to my back door, praying he doesn't see me trip over the uneven concrete in the driveway. It's all good, though, and as I jiggle my keys in the handle, my mind goes right back to Kellen. To his offer to help, if I should ever need it.

Does he know about what happened last year? I know there are rumors and speculation about me. Does he believe any of them? I'm sure he's heard them all. Who hasn't?

My cheeks burn with mortification as I set my bags on the counter.

The thought of Kellen knowing the truth almost makes me physically ill, mostly because it will change the way he sees me. He may not be offering to help me after he hears what I did.

And that thought saddens me more than I could have possibly expected it to.

Kellen

There's something that doesn't sit right with me about my encounter with Cameron and Cage in the grocery store this morning, and the more I dwell on the rigidness of her posture and the apprehensive look on her face when he was standing directly in front of her, the more uneasy I get.

They clearly have history.

Yes, it can have everything to do with a bad breakup. Fuck knows if I ran into Gina Cooper right now, I'd probably look a little tense too. That woman ripped the ass seam out of every pair of gym shorts I owned, burned the word 'asshole' in my front lawn with a blowtorch, and poured soured milk into my athletic shoes. Didn't matter how many times I washed them, they still stunk like rotten ass afterward.

This is why you don't screw around with flight attendants.

They're slightly unhinged.

Thankfully, the vandalism charge and restraining order prompted her to relocate to another state, and I haven't seen her brand of crazy here in about four years. On the rare occasion I fly somewhere, I make sure to avoid Bliss Airlines like an STD, because running into Gina is the last thing I want.

I pull into the parking lot behind the bar and head inside. It's not as hot today as it was yesterday, thankfully, but it's still hotter than Satan's ass out here. We were definitely hit with a late summer. August was warm, but nothing compared to how September has gone so far.

I'm absolutely looking forward to cooler fall weather.

Inside, I head straight to Garreth's office, knowing he's on duty tonight and should already be here. His office is the one next to Walker's, in the main hallway across from the bathrooms, and when I approach the entrance, I find the door cracked open. "Knock, knock," I say, carefully pushing the door inward.

"Hey, Kellen. Come in." Garreth leans back in his chair and offers me a friendly smile.

"Sorry to interrupt," I say, stepping into the room and closing the door behind me. "I won't take much time."

He waves me off. "I'm just making adjustments to next week's schedule. Kallie's going to take two full weeks off, so I'm just filling in the holes."

"Well, you know I'll help anyway I can," I state, stepping up to his desk, but not taking a seat.

"I know, but you need a day off every now and again," he replies with a chuckle. "So, what can I do for you?"

"Actually, I wanted to talk to you a moment about Cameron."

His left eyebrow draws heavenward, but other than that, he doesn't respond beyond that.

"I ran into her at the grocery store this morning and there was a man crowding her. Cage Bronson."

That gets a response. Garreth sits up straight in his seat, his eyes drilling straight into me. "What happened?"

"Nothing, really. I noticed them and could see the tension in her posture. I walked over and introduced myself, even though I recognized him right away." Everyone knows Cage Bronson. Local asshole drug dealer who flew under the radar a long time. When the cops became aware of his business and started watching him closer, he managed to always slip away, keeping a low enough profile, they had a hard time pinning him down. Then, one day, he disappeared—gone—only to have half a dozen other dirt bags slip into his spot and take over his operation.

"He waited in his SUV for her to come out but left when he saw her getting into my truck."

Garreth's eyebrows pull together once more in question, so I continue to answer the question I know is coming. "She was going to walk home, and I insisted I give her a lift. She seemed fine, but the whole thing just struck me as odd, so I thought I'd mention it to you. I know you two are friends."

"I appreciate it," he responds, leaning forward and resting his elbows on his desk.

"Listen, I've heard all the rumors," I start, but he cuts me off.

"I'm not talking about it. It's not my story to tell."

Holding up my hands, I add, "I'm not expecting you to. I'm just telling you I know something happened, and the fact he was here last night and then appeared earlier this morning—"

"Wait, what?"

Shit. I forgot about that detail.

"Last night when she went to leave, he was outside, waiting. That's why she came back in."

"Jesus fucking Christ," Garreth grumbles, standing up fast. His chair moves back and hits the wall behind him.

"She said he insinuated they could get back together, but she told him no. Apparently, he hasn't tried anything, but he's shown up twice now in twelve hours. I could just feel the anxiety in her when I asked about him, so I made her promise she'd tell someone if it ever escalated to the point she was scared."

Garreth stares, perhaps trying to get a read on me. "I appreciate that. I'll talk to her."

I nod, taking that as my cue to leave.

Before I get to the door, he asks, "What's with your sudden interest in Cam?" There's a warning laced in his question.

I stop and turn to face one of my bosses. I've loved working for Garreth. From the moment they hired him to manage this place, I've always respected the hell out of him. He's fair, honest, and always has both the business and the employees' best interests at heart. "Just making sure she's all right," I reply, not liking this feeling spreading through my chest. I feel annoyed with Garreth for even asking, even though I understand it.

I'm not exactly the guy you bring home to meet your mom. I'm considered a player, have been a bit of a manwhore over the years, and will flirt with anything in a skirt, but most probably don't realize it's more of a front I put out there. Everyone knows the score up front, so no one loses, and both parties get to have fun while it lasts.

Easy, breezy.

Yet, I still don't like the tightness in my chest. He knows I'm not good enough for Cameron, and while I wholeheartedly agree, it doesn't make it any less painful to hear. Of course, if I wasn't nurturing a damn crush on the girl, none of this would matter. I wouldn't care he doesn't want me anywhere near his friend, and his unspoken warning wouldn't pack the punch it does.

Goddammit, how do people deal with these crushes?

"Thanks again for letting me know," Garreth says, his features relaxing a bit.

"No problem, boss. I'm gonna head out and get started."

Before I can turn the doorknob, he announces, "The visitation for Valerie is Wednesday. We were going to close down for an hour or two so we can all attend, but Kallie refused to let us do that. We'll discuss it during the owners' meeting tomorrow afternoon, but we'll probably figure out a rotation for anyone working who'd like to attend."

I nod, recalling I'm working that evening. "I'd like to attend, if possible."

"Done. We'll make sure it happens. I'll let you know what we come up with."

"Sounds good, boss. I'll leave you to it," I say before exiting his office and walking to the bar.

Max is there today, having taken Kallie's day shift behind the bar, but that's not where my eyes go. The traitorous bastards look to the restaurant, hoping to catch a peek of Cameron as she's finishing her shift. I know she's working today, because the creepy fucker I am checked the schedule to see if we were working together any other time this week. We're not, of course, but most of the days I'm here, she's on too, so I knew we'd cross paths for a very short time.

When I don't spot her right away, I greet my fellow bartender, who's typing away on his phone. There's only a handful of customers on the bar side, mostly Sunday regulars who stop by to have a drink, watch a game, and shoot the shit with the other regulars.

"Hey, man," he replies, slipping his phone into his back pocket. "We were busy at lunch but slow this afternoon. Hopefully it'll pick up for you for dinner."

"Here's to hoping," I reply, waving at Larry and Fred at the end of the bar. They're here most Sundays, bickering over anything and everything. If you listen to them for more than a minute, you'd assume they didn't like each other much, but, really, they're great friends.

Max goes through the process of closing down his register, while I start my own from the one Garreth brings out to me. Once Max clocks out and empties the tip jar, I dive right into refilling drinks and talking to the customers.

I spot Cameron at the servers' station in the restaurant and throw her a big smile when she looks my way. She gives me a small one, along with a wave, before looking down to complete whatever task she is finishing. When she's finally done, she hollers a quick goodbye to the evening servers and follows behind Angie as she heads this way.

"Well, hello there, handsome," Angie says as she reaches the bar.

"Ladies, how was the lunch rush?" I ask, leaning forward with my hands on the bar, giving them both my complete attention.

"Busy. Good tips. Right, Cameron?"

The auburn beauty blushes ten shades of red. "Stop."

I can tell there's a story there, so I move even closer, like I'm letting them in on a big secret. "Did something happen, Cam?" Even I can hear the flirtiness in my question, which is perfect. I need to remember she's a coworker and nothing more.

Before she can reply, Angie steps in. "Oh, it did! Cam got a huge tip and a phone number."

Even though my stomach clenches with the news, I keep my big smile plastered on my face. "Really?"

Cam rolls her eyes. "It was nothing. He was just trying to be funny."

"Girl, there was nothing but interest in that man's eyes."

Cameron huffs, "It was slightly insulting if you think about it."

"He left her a hundred-dollar tip."

I stand up straight. "A hundred bucks? Seriously?"

"*And* his phone number," Angie reiterates, making me grind my molars down to keep from reacting.

"Why so much?" I find myself asking.

"He told her the service was *exceptional*," Angie states, waggling her eyebrows suggestively.

"It wasn't any better service than I give everyone else," Cameron mumbles.

"Are you going to call him?" I find myself asking, even though speaking the question feels like I'm trying to gargle gravel.

She shrugs, averting her gaze. "Probably not."

Good.

"Oh, she'll call him. He was good-looking and clearly has a little extra cash to throw around. Anyway, I'm heading out. I've got a date with Ben and Jerry's and streaming that new Brad Pitt movie." Angie waves before heading down the back hallway toward the break room.

Cameron exhales loudly, her gaze somewhere behind me. I can't help but wonder if she's thinking about the fucker with money who tipped her so big today. And if she is, why does it bother me so much? I don't mess around with coworkers.

Period.

"Hey, Cam, mind if I talk to you a minute?"

We both turn toward Garreth's voice, and a small lump forms in my throat. I wonder if she'll look at my conversation with him as a betrayal. She shouldn't. I did ask her to promise to talk to him. I just gave him a heads-up the conversation is coming.

"See ya later," she says quietly, spinning and walking toward our boss, who's standing outside of his office.

I try not to stare, but my gaze keeps going to where they talk. Garreth reaches in his pocket before heading my way. "Hey, I'm going to run her home real quick. I'll be back in ten."

I nod, feeling better about the fact she won't be walking. Not with that asshole Cage back in town and always seeming to find her. "No problem. We're good here," I reassure him.

Twenty minutes later, he returns and goes back to his office. I want to barge in there and demand he tell me what they talked about, but I can't do that. Frankly, it's none of my business, even if I feel like it should be. She's not my problem to worry about.

Just after five, the back door opens, and Jameson's large frame fills the space. I'm making a few drinks for a table in the other room when he approaches the bar and takes a seat at the end. I didn't even realize someone else was with him until this moment, and I instantly smile when I see Tucker Dunn. "Hey, guys," I greet.

Jameson gives me a head nod, while the other man says, "Hi, Kellen."

As soon as I have the order finished, I turn my attention to them. "Whatcha drinking?"

"Ice water," Jameson states.

"Same," Tucker adds.

Filling two glasses, I ask, "You guys eating?"

They both nod, neither of them taking the menu I set in front of them. "Garreth's joining us in a minute," Jameson informs me, so I go ahead and fill a third glass of ice water, knowing he won't be having a drink while on the clock.

When the back door opens again, we all look that way and see Numbers entering the building. He's casually dressed in dark jeans and a short-sleeved button-down, something we rarely ever see from the straitlaced man of the group.

Numbers waves, points to his office, and takes off up the stairs. "I'll be right back," Jameson says as he slides off his barstool and heads toward the direction his friend and brother-in-law went.

"So, how's it going?" I ask the man remaining at the bar.

"Good. We finalized the recipe for the brew he's releasing this summer. It's pretty exciting," he informs me before taking a drink of his water.

Tucker works as the assistant brewer at Crüe Brewery next door. He started not that long ago and has been working with Jameson on adding a new brew to their line-up. I've also known Tucker most of my life. He lived down the street where I grew up, but not only that, he dated my sister for a while.

"Can't wait to try it," I say, grabbing a fresh beer for one of the guys just down the bar.

When I return, I ask, "How's Grayson doing?"

His smile is instantaneous and lights up his entire face. "He's awesome. Spending the day with my parents and talking nonstop about tractors and how he's going to be a farmer. He sweet talked my mom into a pair of boots and bib overalls a few weeks back," he says with a chuckle.

I can just picture the little guy now, and it brings a smile to my face. Grayson is four and has the biggest blue eyes I've ever seen. He's the spitting image of his dad, actually; dark hair and quick with a smile. He's probably the happiest little fella I've ever known and gives the best hugs, even to someone he just met. He also has Down syndrome, and I know that's presented its own set of challenges to both Tucker and Grayson.

I grin back at my old friend. "Tell him I said hello."

He nods. "I will." After a few long seconds, he finally asks the question I know is coming. "How's your sister?"

"She's good. They just started her tour. Last I heard, she was on the northern part of the East Coast," I reply, restocking clean mugs in the small freezer.

I don't miss the flash of excitement that crosses his eyes. Tucker was Kinsley's biggest supporter. They dated two years in high school, and he always knew she'd make it big someday. He was the one who encouraged her to go to Nashville, to really give professional singing a try. I know it broke his heart to see her go, but he's never said one ill word about how their relationship ended.

He was also a constant anchor for her when life at home got sucky. Our parents were constantly fighting, the divorce wreaking havoc on everyone, and she found solace in our friend down the road. I wasn't sure about them dating at first, but then I saw them together and realized Tucker was a goner for her. He worshipped the ground she walked on and treated her like a queen. There was no one better for my little sister than Tuck, and I'll always appreciate what he offered her during that tumultuous time.

Now, the douchebag she's currently married to?

Zander Houston is a big wanker, if you ask me. I didn't like him from day one, but it wasn't my place to cause a stink. He made her happy, and while it wasn't quite the same as when she was with Tucker, I'm grateful. I may not like the jackwagon, but I can be civil. Of course that would mean he'd have to come around every now and again, but that rarely happens. Anytime Kinsley comes home for a visit, she's always alone, saying how Zander is working on new music for her. Something has always bothered me about that guy.

Zander is my sister's bass player. They met when he auditioned for her band and hit it off. They've been married for three years, and I do admit, it brings me a little comfort, knowing he's out on the road with her, considering she's headlining her own small ten-city U.S. tour right now.

"I heard about that," he says with a small smile. "Proud of her."

I excuse myself to make the drink order for one of the servers, but I can't help but wonder what might have happened with those two if my sister wouldn't have gone to Nashville to pursue music after high school. Not that it matters, really. Their roads took them on two different courses, but I've always thought Tucker still carried a torch for his old flame. There's just something in his eyes every time he asks about her.

Like regret.

It's only a flash, but I swear it's there.

Too bad that ship has sailed.

Eight

Cameron

Another Saturday night, another shift covered for someone else. It rarely happens that someone no-shows, but it happened tonight when one of the regular servers didn't show up. I quickly volunteered to cover the extra hours, especially because of the night it is. Saturdays are one of the busiest of the week, which means the extra tips will be plenty.

And welcomed.

I'm so close to paying off my debt to Garreth and Reagan, and another extra night or two could mean the difference between making that final payment sooner than anticipated.

Walker, of course, didn't want me to do it. He insisted pulling a double would be too much for me, but I was adamant. He knows why I need this shift, so after only little grumblings, he finally relented, telling me to take an extra fifteen-minute break the moment I could to get off my feet. I'm certain he's already texted Garreth, who is off tonight, to let him know I was covering for Alyssa, a now former server who has no-showed twice this month. Twice without notice means termination.

There's a very short line of patrons awaiting tables, but I pay no attention to them. I focus on my tables, at making sure drinks are refilled and dinners delivered as quickly as possible. Numbers is down here, helping serve meals as they're ready, which is a rarity for me to witness. Even though he's the man in the office, out of sight most of the time, he's charismatic and pleasant with the customers and everyone seems to smile.

When the evening finally starts to slow down, my legs are throbbing, and a slight headache is forming. Being on your feet for almost ten hours isn't my idea of a good time, but it's a small price to pay for the extra cash I'll earn.

"Cameron, take a break," Numbers says as he approaches the servers' station.

"I'm okay," I quickly insist, hating to leave my tables to be covered by someone else.

"It's not a suggestion. The Department of Labor doesn't take too kindly to us not giving breaks. Do me a favor and save me the paperwork hassle, will ya?"

I can't help but smile. "Fine. I'll be back in fifteen."

"Thirty. There's a meal waiting for you in the kitchen," he states, leaving no room for argument. "I've got your section."

With a sigh, I tap on the computer monitor, indicating I'm taking my required break, and head for the kitchen. The moment I walk through the door into organized chaos, I'm hit with the delicious aroma of fresh grilled burgers and deep-fried goodness. My stomach growls, a reminder I haven't eaten in almost seven hours.

"What do you want on this?" Jasper hollers without even looking up from the grill.

Of all the guys, he's the one who makes me the most nervous to be around. Not because I'm afraid of him or anything, but because he's intense and can yell a lot. He's never yelled at me, but I've heard him get on the kitchen staff before. Though, I've been told, he's much better now than before he got together with his wife, Lyndee.

"Just plain," I quickly reply.

That earns me a look. His full attention is now on me as his eyes narrow. "It's against my religion to make a plain cheeseburger, Cam."

A giggle slips from my lips, and I quickly go to cover my mouth with my hand. He doesn't seem bothered by my laugh, however. In fact, it seems to be the exact reaction he was looking for because he smiles in return.

"I'll have to repent for days, Cam. Don't make me repent," he counters, clearly teasing me now.

"Yeah, don't make him do that. Lightning will probably strike if he gets religious on us," Patrick, the former dishwasher turned chef's assistant, hollers. Patrick started at the age of twenty when the business opened and is one of the best guys I know. He's also one of the only people to stick around and not seem fazed by Jasper's grumpy moods.

"Get back to work before I fire you," Jasper announces, barely able to cover his smile with the stern look he sends Patrick's way. You can clearly tell they have a good relationship, and he wasn't serious about firing him.

Patrick just laughs, loading a basket of piping-hot steak fries onto my plate. "You got it, boss."

When Jasper looks my way again, I finally concede. "Fine. I'll take the Cowboy burger."

He flashes me a big smile. "See? That wasn't so hard, was it?" Then, he makes quick work at adding barbecue sauce and fried onions to my burger.

"Thank you," I reply, taking the plate once it's handed to me.

"No, thank you. I heard you volunteered to stay and cover Alyssa's shift."

I shrug, as if it was no big deal. "I don't mind helping."

He studies my face for a few seconds before nodding. "Go take a load off." And then he's gone, disappearing into the chaos to keep preparing orders.

I leave the kitchen out of the hall entrance and slip into the break room. My legs sing in hallelujah the moment I sit, my mouth watering as the scent of my dinner punches me in the nose. I practically inhale my burger and fries, not even bothering to get a bottle of ketchup from the fridge. They're so good when they're fresh like this, you don't even need dipping sauce.

I spend the rest of my break resting my feet, and before I know it, my time is up. I deposit my dirty plate by the sink for the dishwasher, earning me a wink from Jasper as he continues to work, and return to the servers' station. Once I indicate I'm back from my break, I jump right in with my tables, as Numbers takes over another section so the server can take her break.

I'm so busy trying to get caught up with the new faces sitting in my area, I almost miss the familiar one in the farthest booth from me. It takes a moment for my brain to catch up, but when it does, I can't hide the shock I feel at seeing Cage sitting there. He's watching me, and I'm just standing here, staring back at him.

The bell dinging, signaling an order up, snaps me out of my trance, and I slowly make my way toward where he sits. "What are you doing here?" I ask numbly, not bothering to set a straw and wrapped silverware on the table.

"Having dinner," he states, that cocky smile spreading across his lips.

My brain tells me to run away, to get as far away from this man as possible, but I know that's not an option here. This isn't my business, and as much as I despise him, Cage Bronson is a customer.

Period.

"What can I get you to drink?" I ask, trying to sound strong and as if him being here is not affecting me at all.

"Jack and Coke, please. You remember my favorite, right?" he asks smugly, lifting the menu in front of him and giving it a look-over.

My jaw is tight as I turn and head for the bar, jotting down his drink order as I go. Fortunately, I don't run into anyone, and when I reach the bar, I only have to wait a minute to place the order.

"Hey, Cam," Kellen greets with that trademarked grin on his face.

"Hi. I need a Jack and Coke, please."

His eyebrows draw together as he searches my face. "Everything okay?"

"Yep, of course!" I insist, pulling out a smile to try to punctuate my statement. Unfortunately, I think it falls a little short of looking natural, so I shove my nose into my order pad and pretend to scan the receipts.

A minute later, he returns with the drink. "Here ya go, love."

His usual flirting doesn't make my heart jump like it seems to do lately. Maybe that's because my heart rate is already elevated. "Thanks." Placing the drink on my tray, I turn and make my way back to the restaurant, ignoring the way it feels like his eyes are on my backside.

"What's wrong?" Numbers asks the moment I cross the threshold.

"What? Nothing," I insist again.

Except Isaac's eyes aren't on me. They're on the room.

And he spots Cage sitting at the end of the restaurant. "Is that...What the fuck is he doing here?" he asks quietly so no one can overhear.

"Eating dinner," I mumble.

"No. Absolutely not. He needs to go. Garreth told us he was back in town, but he's not welcome here."

And then he's moving before I can say anything else.

I watch in part horror, part fascination, as he walks straight to Cage's booth, leans in, and has a word with my ex. There's no doubt in my mind the man knows who Cage Bronson is, as does most everyone in the room. A few patrons turn to look that way, speculating on what's happening. My face must be cherry red as my eyes are pinned to the scene. Cage's angry voice carries across the room, but I can't tell what he says. He's leaning toward Isaac, his angry eyes narrowed into slits.

Holding my breath, I watch as Cage slowly slides out of the booth, shoves his hands in his pockets, and casually strolls to the front entrance without so much as a backward glance. The moment he crosses the threshold, and the heavy door closes behind him, I exhale loudly.

"What the hell is going on?"

Kellen's sudden question barely registers as I work to slowly draw air in and out of my lungs. When he places his warm hand on my lower back, the comfort it provides seems to snap me out of it. I'm saved from having to provide an explanation when Isaac returns to where I stand, places a gentle hand on my elbow, and guides me toward the servers' station. Thankfully, it's empty right now.

"You okay?"

"Yes, of course. I'm so sor—"

"Don't apologize," Isaac insists, his eyes gentle and kind. "You did nothing wrong. He's not welcome here."

"Who?" Kellen asks beside me. I didn't even realize he followed us over here.

Isaac replies, "Cage Bronson."

"He was here?" he asks, wide eyes on me as he looks me over from head to toe, making sure I'm not injured or something.

"He was. Insisted he was just having dinner and wasn't bothering anyone, but I don't care. Anytime he's here, he's gone. Get one of us and we'll escort him off the property."

I numbly nod, realizing I'm still holding a tray with his drink. "I'll pay for this," I mutter.

"That his?" Kellen asks, lifting it off the tray. The moment I confirm, he draws the glass to his full, kissable lips, and chugs the contents.

My mouth falls open as I watch a bead of moisture slide down his chin. Isaac chuckles as Kellen brings the now-empty glass down to my tray and licks his lips. That trail of moisture is still on his chin, and I almost reach out and swipe it away with my own finger. Before I can embarrass myself by doing just that, he uses the back of his hand and wipes it away, making a satisfied sigh.

That sound.

My thighs clench and my core spasms in a mini orgasm.

"There. Now I'll be paying for the drink." He throws me a wink and turns to head back to the bar.

Isaac is still standing here, so I say, "We should get back out there." I don't add the fact customers are starting to look our way.

He searches my face with those same kind eyes before nodding. "As long as you're sure you're okay."

Taking a deep, cleansing breath, I insist, "I am. Promise. Seeing him sitting there caught me off guard, but he didn't say or do anything."

After a beat, the corner of his mouth turns upward. "Okay, then. Let's get back to work."

I hesitate at the back door, listening to Jameson play his guitar in the bar. A part of me wants to stay again, not only for the good music, but for the good company too. Sure, Kellen and Walker would be busy working, but they're always entertaining to watch.

And neither are bad on the eyes, if you know what I mean.

But my body is exhausted.

Actually, I think it's ten steps past exhausted. I'm so tired, I might sleep the entire day tomorrow.

Thank goodness I'm off until Monday.

Pushing out the back door, I pause and glance around. The other server left a few minutes before me, and even though we've worked for the same place for a while now, I didn't want to put her out and ask for a ride home. Oh, don't get me wrong. My aching feet and back wanted me to, but I just felt bad for asking.

Now, here I am, having to walk home.

Again.

Thank God it's not as hot out tonight. As we approach the end of September, the cooler fall days are definitely around the corner. The evenings aren't as damp and there's a touch of pollen in the air that makes my eyes itch.

Stupid ragweed allergy season.

I turn to my left to walk around the building to the street, but someone blocks my path. A gasp slips from my mouth as I take in the form, instantly recognizing it as my ex. "What the hell, Cage?" I ask, taking a step back.

He follows my retreating form and invades my personal space. I continue to move backward until I hit the brick wall of the building. "What was that, Cameron? You think you can have me thrown out of here?"

"I-I didn't do that. I was bringing you your drink," I insist, my heart starting to creep up into my throat, making it hard to breathe.

"You clearly said something to the assholes who own this place if that's how they react. You do *not* want to piss me off, Cameron." As he bites out my name, the agitation as clear as the liquor on his breath, he brings his face level with mine.

I've never been scared of Cage. I mean, not really. I did hear him get mad a few times on the phone and make threats to whoever he was speaking to, but that anger was never directed toward me, and at the time, he brushed it off as work drama.

Work drama.

Right.

Now that I know all about his specific line of *work*, it forces all those issues I brushed off at the time to the surface. Like a tidal wave of emotion, I'm overcome with grief over the decisions I made in the past. I shouldn't have dated him, shouldn't have moved in with him, and most definitely shouldn't have had to deal with the consequences of him up and leaving.

Yet, here we are.

"Listen, Cage, you need to leave."

The corner of his mouth tics, like he's trying not to smile. "That's not what you said last summer," he coos, leaning forward and running his palm against my cheek. "I heard you were looking for me, baby. You didn't want me to go then."

My mouth drops open as I shake off his touch. "Are you kidding me? You took off while I was at work without so much as a goodbye. I was looking for you because I didn't know where you were. I was worried!" I counter.

He leans against the wall beside me, his arm wrapping around my stomach to keep me close. "I would have taken you with me if I could have, baby," he croons gently, his finger gliding down my arm.

"Instead, you left me to deal with your mess," I argue, shaking off his touch. It has the exact opposite effect it used to have on me, as my body shivers in disgust.

"You took care of that though. You're such a good woman, babe."

The gasp pulls from somewhere deep inside me. "Are you kidding me? That man showed up on our doorstep and threatened to kill me, Cage. Kill. Me. If I didn't give him the money *you* stole from him."

Just then, the back door opens to my right. I turn toward the sound, expecting to see some of the kitchen staff leaving for the night, but am shocked when I find Kellen standing there, holding a bag of garbage. He takes a few steps in the direction of the large garbage dumpster at the back of the lot but pauses and looks to his left. That's when he spots me.

And Cage.

He suddenly pivots, heading our way. I'm able to sidestep Cage's touch, though I'm still pinned against the wall.

"Cam, I was wondering where you got off to. Whatcha doing outside, love?" he asks, his normally sparkly eyes zeroed in on my ex.

"Just stepped out for some air."

Kellen stops directly in front of Cage, as if daring him to try something. "Cage, I wasn't expecting you to be out here," he says with a fake smile.

"Just stopped by to see Cameron," he says, pulling himself to his full height and facing Kellen. Kellen has him by a few inches and maybe twenty pounds. He definitely has him in muscle mass too. Kellen's not bodybuilder big, but you can tell he spends time in a gym.

"Oh yeah?" Kellen asks, dropping the bag of trash at Cage's feet and throwing his arm around my shoulder. "Whatcha want with my girl?"

Cage jerks as if something shocked him. "Your girl?" His eyes bounce between Kellen and me before landing on the arm casually slung across my shoulder.

"Yep," Kellen boasts proudly. "Finally sweet-talked this gorgeous woman into going out with me."

My entire body is still, but not necessarily because he's touching me. Really, I have no clue what's happening right now. Why is Kellen acting like we're together? Did I hit my head or something? The only reason I can think he'd be telling Cage we're together is if I'm suffering from some sort of brain injury right now and my subconscious is playing tricks on me.

Cage clearly isn't buying it either. There's an incredulous smile on his face, and he shakes his head in disbelief. "Whatever," he says with a laugh.

As if the thought of Kellen and I being together is hilarious.

Or is it the thought of me being with someone else that makes this so funny?

Kellen turns to face me, a wicked gleam in his blue eyes. "I guess we're just going to have to prove it, love."

Warm hands cup my cheeks, the tips of his fingers sliding into my hair. He slowly lowers his mouth, pausing just for a fraction of a second. It's as if he's asking permission, and all I can think about is what it will be like to kiss him. My eyes close automatically and my ability to breathe ceases.

Just when I think he's not going to do it, I feel his lips against mine. Soft at first, then with a little more urgency. His tongue coaxes my mouth open and delves inside, tasting and consuming as if we've done this a million times before. Except this is a first kiss. *The* first kiss. One you write fairy tales about, and it's with Kellen.

Holy shit.

Kellen McGregor is kissing me.

And it's the best thing ever.

Kellen

I have no idea what possessed me to kiss Cameron, but I'm not sorry. Not in the least. She tastes like heaven and hell, all wrapped up in one adorable little package.

My tongue glides along hers and the softest little mewl squeaks from her throat. My left hand moves down her cheek, exploring the softness of her neck and feeling the erratic beat of her pulse beneath my finger. My cock throbs in my jeans, begging for just a little attention from the vixen with the magical mouth. Of course he has come up with his own plan for said mouth and is anxious to show her what he has in mind.

Dirty fucker.

I end the kiss before my brain can completely shut off and let my body take over. As I pull back, I open my eyes and gaze down at her freshly kissed lips. They're partly open, swollen, wet, and send the wrong message to my brain. All it wants to do now is jump into round two.

"Wow, I guess you *do* work fast, McGregor."

The statement catches Cameron's attention first before registering in my sex-fogged brain. Her wide eyes turn his way, followed quickly by mine. Pushing the lust from my head, I sling my arm over her shoulder once more and draw her into my side. "You gotta work fast when you see someone as amazing as Cameron in your sights. If you're too slow, someone might steal her out from under you." I give him a smug grin and pull her even closer.

The security lights in the lot help me see his features perfectly. Cage snarls at me, and I wonder if he's going to take a swing. I'd love it if he did. I've never been much of a fighter, but I'd lay this fucker out if he took a swing first.

He must think better of it because he spins on his heel and walks away. "I'll see you around, Cameron. You can bet on it."

I watch as he walks to the same Escalade he was in last Sunday, and don't move until he's pulling out of the lot. Only then do I feel some of the tension she's been carrying ebb from her body. "You okay?" I ask, giving her my full attention.

She nods, looking everywhere but at me.

"Come on, let's go dump this trash before they send a search party out for me," I tell her, taking the garbage back in my left hand and her soft one in my right.

She doesn't say a word as we walk to the back of the lot, and I toss the bag in the dumpster with a loud clank. When I turn around, her eyes are cast down at the ground, her foot kicking a small rock.

"I'm sorry," I blurt out.

She looks up, her embarrassment written all over her face. "It's okay," she says before bringing her fingers to her lips and touching them. "I know it didn't mean anything."

Ahh, hell.

Didn't mean anything? That was the single best kiss I've ever had. The feel of her molded against me, the taste of her lips, the naughty sounds she made and probably has no idea she made them. All boner-inducing. I'm pretty sure I'm gonna be jacking off to those images and sounds for a long damn time.

"No, not that. I'm sorry I was touching the garbage bag first and then had my hands all over you. That was pretty gross, and you'll probably want to shower as soon as you get home. But that kiss?" I start, shaking my head as the memories assault me again. "I don't regret that. Not one second of it."

Wide green eyes stare back at me, as she continues to touch her lips. Is she thinking about that kiss too? I'd like to think my kissing game is top-notch, but for the first time since I was fifteen and about to lay a big smacker on Natalia Chesmaki, the foreign exchange student, I'm a little worried it wasn't my best work.

"Oh," she replies, dropping her hand and clearing her throat. "It was nice." Again, she blushes. Even in the darkened lot, I can see the pink staining her cheeks.

"Nice? I can do better," I insist, taking a step forward.

Before I can lay it on her a second time and really knock her socks off, the back door opens and Numbers steps out. "Did you get lost? Walker's gonna lose his shit if you don't quit jerking off by the dumpster—Oh shit. Sorry, didn't realize you weren't alone," Numbers hollers from the back entrance.

"Come on," I say, taking her hand once more because I like it, not because it's necessary.

"I should head home," she insists, though I can hear the hint of worry in her voice.

"Let someone take you home. I'll do it, but if you don't want to stay to close, have Numbers or Jasper do it."

She seems hesitant, but reluctantly agrees.

Together, we walk in the back entrance, where Numbers is staring at our joined hands. "I'm going to use the restroom," she says, pulling her hand from my own and stepping inside the ladies' room.

I'm torn between wanting to wait for her to finish and getting back behind the bar where I'm needed, and I can already tell Numbers isn't going to let slide what he saw outside. So, while she's inside the bathroom, I pause and say quietly, "She went to leave, and Cage was waiting for her." Numbers stands up straight, his eyes widening. "I defused the situation and made him leave."

"Defused the situation how?" he asks, taking a quick glance toward the bar.

My gut twists as I consider how much to tell him, but ultimately know it'll have to come out. It'll also explain why I was holding her hand. Or at least they think it'll explain the main reason. I'll leave out the part about the stupid crush. "I can explain later but promise me you'll keep an eye on her. Her car is down, so she's been walking. I don't want her to walk home tonight."

"I'll make sure she gets home safely," he says. There's a finality in his tone, and I know he'll do just that.

"Thanks. She doesn't think Cage knows where she lives, so you gotta make sure you're not being followed. We don't need him showing up at her door."

Numbers nods in agreement. "Consider it done. If I get busy, I'll have Jameson do it once he's done playing."

"Okay." I take a deep breath, feeling as if I can actually let it out completely again without that crazy tightness in my chest making it difficult. "I better get back up there."

"He's gonna give you shit. He already looks pissed."

I snort and give him a grin. "No worries. I can handle Walker."

As I approach the bar, I can see my boss's narrowed eyes on me. I ignore him, however, and jump right into filling drink orders. After a few minutes, Walker makes his way toward me, grabbing a bottle of tequila off the shelf beside me and says, "Glad to see you decided to get back to work."

"Sorry. I'll explain later."

He snorts and shakes his head. "If your explanation has anything to do with the blonde who's been trying to eye-fuck you the last three hours, I don't want to hear it."

I give him a big, cheesy grin. "Don't want all the dirty details?" I tease, even though there are no details to give. The blonde most certainly wasn't outside—or anywhere—with me, but since I have a reputation to uphold here, I add, "She does this thing with her tongue and my—"

"Jesus Christmas, Kel, I said I don't want the details."

I'm already laughing, mixing vodka into the orange juice in the glass I'm working on. "Did you just say Jesus Christmas?"

He grumbles something about damn employees who should be fired before saying, "We have little ears, man, and apparently, I have a cursing problem."

My laughter turns into a snort as I shake my head. "What did Duncan say now?"

"Not Duncan, Waylon. Apparently, he told his teacher the truck in whatever book she was reading was killer because it had dope rims and sick pipes. When she picked her jaw up off the floor and asked him what sick meant, he replied badass."

I double over, unable to control my laughter. "That's great."

"Yeah, except the teacher called Mal first, so by the time I got home, she stewed for about two hours and was fit to be tied."

I spin around and set the mixed drink in front of a patron, flash her a big grin, and swipe her credit card. When the woman signs the slip and returns to her group, I take a few steps over to where Walker is. "There was an incident outside. That's why I wasn't back from taking out the trash. I'll explain later, but Cage was out there with Cameron."

Walker's eyes turn fierce. "Mothertrucker, I'm going to kill that bastard."

"Bastard's probably a no-no word," I remind him.

"Yeah, but nothing good can replace it but fucker, and that's at the top of the no-no list."

"True. Anyway, Cage left, and that's why Cameron is still here with Numbers hovering like an eagle." We both casually look over to the end of the bar and find Cameron sitting on the end stool, enjoying the music, Numbers and Jasper both standing beside her, whispering.

"Someone needs to make sure she gets home."

I'm about to volunteer my services, but don't have a chance. A large group walks through the front door and heads straight for the bar. We spend the next ten minutes getting their order together. By the time Jameson is wrapping up his playlist, the place is packed. I do everything I can to keep an eye on the gorgeous woman at the end of the bar. Each time I look that way, one of the guys is right there. I also watch the crowd for a now-familiar, not welcome face. I don't think he'd be dumb enough to come back tonight, but you never know.

Crazier things have happened.

At the stroke of eleven, Jameson exits the small stage as Walker heads to the jukebox to play a Crüe song. The room is silent as we await to hear his choice for the evening, which turns out to be "Live Wire," and I quickly look to my left. I always love this part of the evening, mostly because it's when things get a little crazy.

The bar erupts, hands fly in the air, holding drinks up in salute. I see Cameron smile, which brings a grin to my own face. It's a real one, and after finding her in the back lot with her no-dick ex, I was worried it might be a while before I see it again. Fortunately, she's all smiles when Walker holds his arm up and belts out the words to the song. He may no longer get up and sing and dance on the bar top, but he still has a damn good time when his favorite band is playing.

Hell, we all do.

The moment the song ends, it's chaos. The drinks are flowing, the tips piling up, and the patrons enjoying themselves. I barely have time to check on Cameron, but I know the guys are taking care of her. Jameson is there now, along with his sister, Numbers' wife, BJ. She's drinking water, since she's pregnant with their second child. Last I heard, she, along with Walker's wife, Mallory, is due around Christmas.

Just as Walker hollers last call, I grab a glass of ice water and down the contents. The drink I chugged hours ago has long worn off, but I made sure to flush it out of my system with water early on. We don't usually drink while working, so I made sure to tell Walker what happened to the Jack and Coke when I returned to the bar. I tried paying for it so Cam didn't have to, but he refused to take my money. Said he would have done the exact same thing, and there's no doubt in my mind he would have.

When the crowd starts to disperse and it's time to jump in and get the work done, Numbers comes over to where I stock bottles of beer. "Hey, I'm going to run Cameron home, and then take Beej home. The others are staying to help close down."

I nod, grateful he's ensuring Cam gets home safely, yet still a little irritated I'm not the one doing it. But as the night wore on, I could tell she was getting tired. She worked a double today, which means she's been here well over thirteen hours. I'm sure she's exhausted, and as much as I'd like to ask her to wait for me to take her home, that's a dick move. The sooner she gets home, the sooner she can crash.

"Sounds good, man. We got it here," I assure him, even though I know I don't need to. These guys have been shutting this place down well before I started working here.

He nods, throws a wave to Walker, and gathers his wife in his arms. Cameron looks like the third wheel as they head for the back exit, and at the last minute, she pauses and turns. My heart does this weird little giddy up in my chest as she gives me a small wave. There's also no missing the smile on her lips. The one that speaks of appreciation and exhaustion.

I lift my hand and offer my own wave, making sure she receives a grin too. Only this one is usually reserved for family and friends. It's not flirty or dripping with wicked intent. It's bathed in sincerity and alliance, two things she desperately needs right now.

Finishing up my job for the evening, I try not to think about her. *Try* being the keyword there, because lately, that's all I seem capable of. When I get the cue to clock out, I take a quick moment and pull up the employee cell phone list. I have my fellow bartenders in my phone for work purposes, but I've never had a reason to keep the servers or kitchen staff.

When I spot her name, I quickly add the number into my cell and slip it back into my pocket before someone notices. Not that they'd care, but I'm pretty damn sure they'd give me shit over it for a while.

Finally, it's time for me to head out. With a stack of cash in my pocket from tonight's tips, I say goodbye to the guys and make my way out the back. The night air is warm but doesn't hold the humidity it did in recent days. That doesn't stop me from cranking up the air-conditioning as soon as I get in my truck and have the key turned in the ignition.

Only then do I pull out my phone.

I try to consider my options here, but I just keep coming back to checking in with her. Granted, she left only fifteen minutes ago, so I'm sure she's fine, but for some reason, I want to hear it from her. Spotting Cage and Cameron out back tonight shook me up a bit too, especially because I could see the intent in his eyes. He wants her back, and that thought just burns my gut like an ulcer.

Me: This is Kellen. Just making sure you got home all right.

I click send and place my phone on the console before backing out of my parking space. I spot the rest of the guys exiting the building, so I throw them a wave as I drive by and pull from the lot. Just as I reach the stoplight, my phone rings. The moment I spot the name on the screen, I pick it up.

"Hello?"

There's no response, which has the hairs on the back of my neck standing on end.

"Cam? Are you there?"

"Kellen?" Her voice is so small, so soft, I almost can't hear her, but it's the sound of fear that has my blood pumping through my veins.

"I'm here, love. What's wrong?" I glance up, noting the light's still red.

"Someone was here. I'm so sorry to bother you. I was getting ready to call Garreth, but then your message came through," she starts, the sound of her tears my complete undoing.

With one quick look around to make sure no one is coming, I run the red light, whipping a U-turn in the middle of the intersection, and flooring it toward her house. "I'm on my way. Where are you?"

She exhales. "In the kitchen."

I press down a little harder on the gas pedal and hightail it to her neighborhood. "Do me a favor and stay on the line, okay? I'm on my way, Cam. Hang tight. I'll be right there."

I don't know who I'm trying to calm more.

Her or me.

Cameron

When I walked inside my house, I just stood there. I seriously thought in my overly exhausted state, I was hallucinating. But when the tossed kitchen didn't disappear, and realization started to seep into my brain, panic set in.

Someone has been in my house.

Not only that, this person trashed it.

I stood in the kitchen for several minutes, listening. Was the intruder still here? Was he lying in wait, hiding in the closet for that perfect opportunity to jump out and snatch me?

Man, I watched way too many crime shows back when I had satellite.

I'm sure it was just kids up to no good.

Except why did they have to be up to it in my house?

And why does the feeling of violation settle in my gut like a lead balloon?

I pull out my cell phone, knowing I need to call someone. I feel terrible for waking Garreth and Reagan, but I'm certain his reaction will be much worse if I don't call him. However, as my fingers hover over the screen, a text message pops up. I wasn't expecting an unknown number to appear, but a wave of relief washes over me when I see the first line of his message.

I read the rest of his words, and instead of replying in a text, I click on the number at the top. Do I want to call him?

Yes, yes, I do.

It only rings twice before his voice echoes in my ear. "Hello?"

I open my mouth, but nothing comes out.

"Cam? Are you there?" he asks softly, his voice soothing, yet firm.

"Kellen?"

"I'm here, love. What's wrong?"

"Someone was here. I'm so sorry to bother you. I was getting ready to call Garreth, but then your message came through," I start, my tears falling for the first time since I returned home to chaos.

"I'm on my way. Where are you?"

I tentatively look around. "In the kitchen."

"Do me a favor and stay on the line, okay? I'm on my way, Cam. Hang tight. I'll be right there."

"Okay," I mumble, sliding down the cabinet and sitting on the floor. I draw my knees into my chest and rest my cheek against my knee.

"What do you see? Can you hear anything?"

"Everything's a mess. My stuff is everywhere, but I don't hear anything. Do you think the person who did this is still inside?" I whisper, that same fear I felt minutes ago returning.

"I'm sure they're long gone, Cam. I want you to stay inside though, okay? I'll be there in less than a minute."

I nod, even though he can't see me. Just knowing he's on the other end of the phone line is comforting in a way I never expected. When Cage left and I was forced to face the lies I'd been unknowingly living, I told myself never again. Never would I let a man snowball me into believing one thing, when the truth was something completely different. Never will I stand by and let him make all my decisions for me.

97

"I'm pulling into your driveway now," he states softly. "I'm coming around to the back door. Do you have a weapon?"

"N-no," I insist. The thought of using something to hurt another person makes my stomach churn even more than it already has been.

"Good. I'd hate to walk in and get whacked with something, love. My face is too pretty to be dented with a frying pan."

And just like that, the tension filling the room and threatening to choke the life out of me slowly ebbs. A bubble of laughter spills from my lips. "You're safe," I reply.

Then, he's standing there, slowly pushing through the back door of my house and taking a look around. "I'm gonna have to call you back, okay?"

A small giggle slips out at his antics, and I disconnect the phone. When I place my hand on the old linoleum flooring beside me, he holds out his hand. "Wait right there, all right? I want to check the rest of the house."

He glances around the small kitchen before moving into the living room. I hear the crunch of broken glass, which pisses me off. There are only two things in that room that are glass, and that's the television and a framed family photo from my high school graduation. The thought of either one being ruined is depressing as hell. I'd rather not have to purchase a new TV right now, but the thought of that particular photo being destroyed makes my heart hurt.

I can hear him moving through my space because there's not much square footage to cover, and within a few minutes, he returns to the kitchen. He already has his phone out and is making a call.

"Hey, man," he says into his cell, offering me an unhappy little grin. "Yeah, sorry to call so late. Listen, I'm at Cam's place. Someone broke in." He listens for a moment before adding, "I'm calling them now, but—" He pauses before adding a final, "Perfect, see ya soon."

Kellen moves toward me now and crouches in front of me. "You okay?"

I nod, glancing over his shoulder. "Do I want to know?" I ask, referring to the state of the rest of my house. If the kitchen and broken glass in the living room is any indication, I'm going to assume the remaining rooms didn't fare well either.

He clicks his tongue, sympathy filling his sparkling eyes. "Probably not. The bedroom is trashed. Probably the worst room in the house."

I sigh, watching as he clicks away on his cell phone before bringing it to his ear, while remaining very close. "Walker's on his way over to help. I'm gonna call the non-emergency police number and get someone over here."

My heart drops. "Is that necessary?"

He meets my gaze head-on. "Yes," he answers before talking into the phone again. "Hello, I'd like to report a break-in," he says as he stands up, then continuing to fill dispatch in on the situation as he paces the small room. "Thank you."

Kellen places his phone on the counter behind me and drops back down in front of me. His blue eyes search my face, searching for what, I'm not sure. Maybe for signs I'm struggling or ready to crack. "There's a police officer on the way to file a report."

Just hearing those words, I sag against the cabinet door behind me. Closing my eyes for a moment, I whisper weakly, "It's probably just kids."

There's no missing the way his throat works as he swallows. "Could be, Cam, but with…everything that happened today, we can't be too careful."

And there it is.

The verification I didn't want to hear. "But he doesn't know where I live," I point out, referring to Cage.

He shrugs and brushes a strand of hair off my forehead. "We don't know that for sure. He could have followed you at any point over the last week," he gently reasons.

I concede with a sigh.

Everything from that point on happens fast.

Walker arrives at the same time as two uniformed officers. We step outside while they clear the scene, even though Kellen had already walked through my house, and when they determine it's safe for me to return inside, I do so readily. The night air feels cooler than normal. Perhaps that's because of the emotions coursing through my veins and worry I'm being watched.

"We didn't find any signs of forced entry. Does anyone have a key, or have you misplaced your key at any point?" the polite female police officer asks.

I shake my head. "No, never. I always have my keys on me, and the only other person with a copy would be my landlord, Jane Honeywell."

The woman nods, making notes on a pad of paper. "We'd like you to look around and see if anything was taken. Are you okay to do that?"

Now it's my turn to nod. Kellen and Walker are right beside me as I slowly make my way through the kitchen and into the living room. Tears fill my eyes as I take in the destruction. The glass I heard Kellen stepping on is from both my TV, which is now lying on the floor in pieces, and the framed photograph of my family. The thousand-piece puzzle I was working on is everywhere, as is what little furniture I have. The end table is on its side with a broken leg, and the coffee table where I worked on my puzzle is smashed to smithereens. My entire life looks like it was hit by a bomb, and I can't help but realize how reminiscent it all is of last summer.

Kellen places his warm, protective hand on my lower back and guides me into the only bedroom in the house. The tears burning my eyes start to fall as I take in the room. He was right. This room is way worse than the others. While the living room and kitchen are trashed, it seems like someone took out a lot of anger in my bedroom. My clothes are everywhere and slashed with either a knife or scissors. My mattress is cut, my curtains are torn from the walls, and my dresser is lying in three pieces. The window is broken, thanks to part of my nightstand being thrown through it.

But what really holds my attention is the words painted on the wall.

Die bitch.

In blood red.

A shiver sweeps through my body, leaving me cold and empty.

All I want to do is run away. My safe haven no longer feels safe.

Wrapping my arms around myself to ward off the chill, I spin around and run out of the room, desperate to get away from the wreckage that was once my peaceful life. I move past the broken glass and puzzle pieces, step over the measly kitchen utensils and broken dishes on the old linoleum, and straight out the back door, desperately sucking in greedy gulps of oxygen.

"Hey," Kellen says, wrapping his arms around me and pulling me into a hug. "It's going to be okay."

Ignoring the way my body craves the contact, I tell myself it's because of the situation, not the man.

Of course, even my own subconscious knows I'm full of crap.

It's very much the fact it's Kellen hugging me right now. I've never had this sort of racing heart and failure to breathe normally when I've been around any other man, and thanks to my line of work, I've seen plenty of good-looking guys in my short twenty-three years of life. I even flirted with them a little, back before Cage left me with an inability to trust my own instincts.

"This wasn't kids, Cam," he softly whispers into my hair, the warm tickle of his breath causing goosebumps to appear on my skin.

"I mean, it could have been," I mumble uselessly.

The truth is, I agree. Deep down, I know it was Cage who broke into my house and destroyed my stuff. I just don't know what to do about it.

"What the hell?"

I turn around at the sound of a new voice and find Garreth standing in my driveway at the back of my house. His eyes are wide and full of worry as he pauses long enough to take in the scene in the backyard and head in our direction.

Pulling myself from Kellen's embrace, I walk straight into my friend's arms. Garreth pulls me against his chest, providing the comfort only a friend can give. I try not to dwell on the fact I don't feel any of the same zings in my body like I did with Kellen and focus on the fact he's here. "What are you doing here?"

He pulls back and shoots me a look. "Walker called me." He glances over his shoulder at the house. "What the hell happened?"

Before I can reply, Kellen steps in. "Numbers dropped her off after work and she found her place ransacked."

Garreth pulls back and meets my gaze. "It was probably just kids," I mumble once more.

This time, it's Walker who speaks. "It wasn't."

Feeling the cold chill once more, I recount to Garreth about finding Cage in the restaurant, Numbers kicking him out, and then seeing him in the parking lot when I went to leave. I mention Kellen coming out and running him off but leave out the part about the pretend dating. And the kiss. That's the last thing I need Garreth and the rest of the guys hearing.

His jaw tics as the police officers step outside. "We've documented everything. This could be a random B&E, but something tells me you were targeted. Was anything you noticed missing?" she asks, the male officer walking the perimeter of my house with a flashlight.

I shake my head. "Not that I noticed." Not that I could really tell anyway. Everything I own is broken.

She jots something down. "We'll file the report for your insurance. You can stop in and pick up a copy Monday," she informs me, bringing on a plethora of additional stress.

I don't have renter's insurance.

It's an expense I couldn't afford, and never in a million years did I think I'd actually need it. Realization sets in that everything I have will have to be repurchased. Little things like shower products, makeup, and clothes. Money I don't have will need to be spent, some of it sooner rather than later.

"Any idea who might have done this?" The male officer asks when he rejoins our small group. "Having any issues with anyone?"

I sigh and close my eyes, but before I can answer, Garreth steps forward. "Her ex is back in town. Cage Bronson."

"What can you tell us about Mr. Bronson?" he asks, eyes on me.

I go through the brief encounters I've had with Cage over the last week, starting with his first appearance at Burgers and Brew and ending with what happened earlier tonight. I'm starting to feel a little numb, the shock of everything wearing off and the exhaustion I felt earlier back tenfold.

"Thank you," he states, sliding his own notepad into his pocket. "Do you have somewhere to stay tonight?"

"Yes."

I'm able to hide my surprise at the response to the officer's question, mostly because it comes from Kellen, not Garreth.

The officer nods. "If you want to file a restraining order, you're welcome to do that too."

My heartbeat kicks up at the thought.

"She'll be there Monday morning to do that." This time it is Garreth who replies.

Both officers say their goodbyes, and I'm left with Kellen, Walker, and Garreth. "Come on, kid. Let's see if there's anything we can pack. You can't stay here."

I fight through the yawn threatening to erupt from my soul. "I'm not staying with you, Garreth. You two have a baby. You don't need me underfoot."

"You can stay with me."

My entire body turns and faces the voice. "What?"

Kellen shrugs his shoulders. "I have plenty of space. There's a guest room already made up with a private bathroom. My sister uses it when she's in town."

My brain is spinning, as it tries to wrap around what he's saying. "I can't stay with you," I finally spit out.

"Sure you can. I have the room. I'm not a messy roommate, and I promise not to leave the toilet seat up."

Narrowing my eyes, I reply, "I thought you said I'd have my own bathroom."

He flashes me a wide grin. Even in the darkness of night, I can see perfectly white, straight teeth. "You do."

My legs start to throb from the sheer exhaustion of the day. "Wait, you said it's your sister's room," I start, but am cut off.

"And she's not planning to visit for a while. She started a tour, so it'll be a few months before she visits."

Okay, I'll come back to that one when my brain is working properly.

"Listen, there has to be another way. I don't want to put anyone out," I argue.

This time, it's Garreth who steps forward. "You're welcome to stay with us, but you'd be on the couch. It's yours, if you want it. Don't get me wrong. You can come stay with Reag and I, anytime, but this does seem like a logical solution, until we get your house back in order." He steps close, lowers his voice, and whispers, "Unless there's another reason you don't want to stay with Kellen."

I get what he's insinuating, but how can I tell him that's the furthest from the truth. The thought of being around Kellen, in his private space, should probably be filed in the bad idea category.

Not that I think he'd do something to me. More like I'm afraid of what I might do to him.

Climb him like a tree and replay that kiss from earlier, for starters.

"You're not putting me out, Cam, I promise," Kellen insists, never moving any closer to me than a few feet. "Plus, I'd feel better knowing you're there and safe until we can figure out what to do about Cage."

Walker nods his head. "I agree. I think staying with someone until the issue is resolved is your best scenario."

"And what issue is that?" I ask, rubbing my temple where a headache is starting.

"Until Cage understands you're not interested in him anymore and leaves you alone," Kellen states.

Garreth holds my gaze. "I agree, Cam. If not with Kellen, then somewhere. We can find you a place, but that message he left on your wall worries the hell out of me, okay?"

I don't ask how he knows about the painted message. I assume one of the other two told him about it.

With a deep exhale, I close my eyes and mutter, "Fine."

"Great. Let's go inside and see if we can salvage any of your stuff, and then we'll go to my place and get you settled," Kellen says, placing his hand on my lower back and guiding me to the house.

"I've got a piece of plywood. Garreth, help me get it and we'll get that broken window secure," Walker adds, heading toward the driveway.

All I can think about is the theme song from *The Fresh Prince of Bel Air* reruns I've watched late at night when I can't sleep.

This is how my life got flipped, turned upside down and how I became roommates with the sexy bartender from work.

This has bad idea written all over it.

Eleven

Kellen

She's fallen asleep.

By the time we found a few things that weren't completely destroyed and got the window boarded up, she was practically the walking dead. It's hard to comprehend the fact she worked a double before all this shit happened with her house. Now, it's almost three in the morning and the stress and exhaustion of the last sixteen hours or so has caught up with her.

Honestly, I'm just happy to see her sleep.

To me, that says she trusts me enough to let her guard down and nod off.

Or she's just too tired to fight it.

Stupid subconscious.

Pulling into my driveway, I press the button for my garage door, waiting while it slowly opens before proceeding inside. The moment I have my truck turned off, I angle my body to face her sleeping form. She's still wearing her work uniform, the small pile of personal effects we brought with us sitting in a paper sack on the floor in front of her. Her hair is a little wild, and there are bags beneath her eyes, evident in the shadowed moonlight reflecting through the garage window.

God, she's beautiful.

As much as I hate to wake her, I don't want her to sleep in my truck any longer than necessary. I push open the driver's door and hop out before walking around to her side. Slowly, I pull open her door so I don't startle her awake. When she doesn't stir, my hand moves in her direction, completely on its own. I brush hair off her forehead, something I never thought I'd find so alluring, yet do. A simple, intimate touch.

Her eyes slowly open, big, green, and unfocused. She looks at me and sighs before turning her head so she's able to place her cheek into my palm. Then, she exhales once more and closes her eyes, her sweet little tongue slipping between her lips for just a moment.

My cock is suddenly so hard, I could hammer concrete.

Clearing my throat, I whisper, "Cam, love, we're here."

Those amazing emerald eyes open once more, and as if someone flips a switch, she jumps up. In the process, she hits her elbow on the console. "Ouch, shitballs," she mutters, rubbing the place she smacked.

"Sorry 'bout that. I was hoping not to startle you."

She glances around the garage. "I can't believe I fell asleep so quickly."

I reach for the bag at her feet. "Well, you've had a pretty long and stressful twenty-four hours. What do you say we get you inside and comfortable?"

After releasing her seat belt, she climbs out of my truck and glances back inside. "I can take my bag."

I step back, giving her space to move, and when she's clear of the door, I close it. I also don't hand over the bag in my hand. There's not a lot in there, and it's not heavy. "Come on, love. Time for bed."

She straightens her spine at my comment but doesn't say anything. I mentally kick my own ass for how it must have sounded. No, I wasn't inviting her to my bed—even though I'd love to have her there.

When we reach the back door, I pull out my key and slide it in the lock. She steps inside the mudroom, and I've never been more grateful at the fact I cleaned the dirty dishes and swept the floors than I am right now.

I quickly press my security code into the keypad to shut off the alarm. "Make yourself at home," I state, shutting the door and locking it behind me. I'll worry about resetting the alarm in a bit.

Cameron walks into the kitchen and slowly looks around. The light is on over the sink, a habit I got into when I started bartending and would get home in the early hours of the morning, but I go ahead and flip on the main switch. She spins around, taking in the light, handcrafted cabinets, dark countertops, and rustic décor, and I try to see it through her eyes.

"My sister helped me. Kinsley has a great eye, and rather expensive taste," I quip with a chuckle.

Cam turns and faces me. "It's gorgeous."

"Thank you." I reach for her hand. "Come on, I'll give you the five second tour on the way to the guest room."

We walk through the living room with the office alcove—which I use to display my old record player, records, and drums—and head for the hallway. "There's a half-bath between the kitchen and mudroom," I tell her, realizing I forgot to show her that. "This room here is just storage and crap," I add, indicating the first closed door on the right. Moving farther down the hallway, I pause in front of the only open door.

My bedroom.

"This is mine," I state, pointing to the room and pushing through the door.

Cameron brushes past me and steps inside. Her eyes automatically go to the large king-size bed and matching dresser. There's also a comfortable chair in there, again, thanks to my sister's love for decorating and shopping. She has no problems spending my money when she comes for a visit.

I point to the two doors, both of them open. "Bathroom and closet."

Cameron nods and turns to face me. Every part of me wants to take her in my arms, kiss those soft, full lips, and carry her to my bed. Her scent wraps around me, tantalizing me, begging me to run my nose up the slender column of her neck.

But that's not why she's here, so I clear my throat and take a step back.

"And the guest room," I finally add, walking across the hall and throwing open the door.

I wait for her to enter first, watching her eyes as she takes in the room. Kinsley did everything in this room too. Though it's not quite as big as my own room, it's still a decent sized bedroom. The walls are painted a soft green color, which matches the floral bedding. There are warm, plush rugs and extra cozy throws, because she is always cold, and a small reading nook.

"There's a small closet you can use, and the bathroom is in there. The door goes into the other guest room, but I'll make sure it's locked from that side," I state, placing the paper sack on top of the bed.

"This room is gorgeous," she whispers, slowly taking a second look around.

"You can use anything in here. There might be some clothes in the closet and dresser, and I know she'd be fine with you using them. You're probably her size." My sister is the most generous, kindest person I've ever known, and if she knew Cam was here and the situation surrounding it, she'd insist giving her whatever she left here over the last few years.

"I couldn't, but thank you for the offer." She turns stunning, tired eyes my way, and I have to ignore the fact she's standing in front of another bed. Otherwise, I'm liable to throw her on it and ravish her from head to toe.

"I'll let you get settled. There are towels and some toiletries in the bathroom. Use whatever you need, Cam, really. You're not putting me out."

She gives me a look like she doesn't believe me, and that's okay. I'd probably feel the same way if I were in her shoes. "Thank you, Kellen. Truly."

I nod, turning to the doorway and walking through it before I'm unable to. "I'm right across the hall if you need me."

Cameron nods, her throat swallowing hard as she gazes at me. With that, I close the door behind me before the temptation is too much and I do something I shouldn't.

If only I could lock it from the outside.

I make a quick sweep through the house, checking all the doors and windows, even though I know they're secure. With Cameron staying here for the foreseeable future, I'd rather be safe than sorry. Once I'm satisfied everything is as it should be, I reset the alarm, reminding myself I need to show Cameron how to use it, grab a bottle of water, and head for my bedroom. Pausing outside her door, I almost knock, but then I picture her trying to fall back asleep, and I don't want to be that asshole. So, I force one foot in front of the other and slip inside my own bedroom, leaving the door cracked open a few inches.

First thing I do is jump in the shower. I hadn't made it home yet from work when I got her call, and I can smell the beer and liquor clinging to my skin. After stripping out of my work clothes and tossing them in the hamper, I turn the water on a little colder than normal. I'm hoping the water will help cool my overheated body, but the way my cock stands up and begs for some attention, I don't think it's working as planned.

As I lather up my body, I try to ignore the way desire races through me, but it's futile. I'm too tired to fight it, which is why I take my cock in my hand and give it a hard squeeze at the root. A groan spills from my mouth, thankfully drowned out by the water, as I slowly glide my hand to the head of my cock. Pleasure courses through me and I pick up the pace.

My balls are already tight, my spine tingling in anticipation. This might be the quickest I've jacked off since I was fifteen, but now isn't the time to dissect that thought. Not when my orgasm is barreling at me, my muscles taut and my blood pumping. There's no stopping this freight train of desire.

I close my eyes and picture her. She's on her knees in front of me, her hands replacing mine and her mouth open eagerly. That sexy little tongue of hers snakes out and licks the droplets of cum from the head of my cock before she takes it inside her warm mouth. Her tongue swirls around the tip moments before she sucks it deep in her mouth, swallowing my entire length in one fluid motion.

"Fuck," I groan, coming so hard I see spots.

I ignore the pain in my balls, just keep stroking myself off until I have nothing left to give. Leaning forward, I sag against the shower wall and try to catch my breath. Guilt nags at the edges of my mind, but I push it away as best I can. Even though I probably shouldn't have pictured Cameron in that way, there was no stopping my subconscious from conjuring up those dirty images.

Grabbing the shower gel once more, I re-lather my body and rinse it off. Then, I nudge the temperature dial a little toward the right side and force myself to stand under the cold water.

Fucking hell, I hate cold showers.

When I start to shiver, I turn off the water and grab a towel. Once it's wrapped around my waist, I make a pit stop at the sink to brush my teeth and then flip off the light. My room is dark, but I don't need light to see. I toss my towel over the closet door to dry and grab a pair of shorts from the dresser. I much prefer to sleep naked—especially during the hotter months—but with a houseguest, I don't want to be caught without pants on if something happens.

Finally, I throw back the covers and climb in.

And toss and turn.

Toss and turn.

There's no comfortable position. Not one. My shorts are riding up and the sheets feel clingier than normal. I keep listening, my brain trying to pick up any sound it can, both inside and outside, but it comes up with nothing. Everyone, and everything, around me is sleeping.

I don't know how long I lie there, but eventually, exhaustion wins. My mind tries to fight it, but I'm just too fucking tired to stay awake another second.

I hope Cam was able to get to sleep easily.

I pray she's comfortable in my guest room.

And what's more concerning, I wish she were here, in bed, with me.

That's my last thought before finally drifting off.

The creaking sound has me opening my eyes. I hold completely still, my ears listening for any noise so I can spring into action. I'm able to control my breathing, but my heartbeat is another story. It's trying to pound out of my chest, and I can't help but wonder if the person in my house will hear it.

I don't hear footsteps but catch the slight movement of my bedroom door. I'm about to jump up when I see auburn hair and hesitant green eyes peek through the doorway. "Kellen?" she whispers, causing my heart rate to spike. This time for a completely different reason.

"Is everything okay?" I ask, sitting up in bed. I have no idea what time it is, but considering it's still dark out, I'd say we haven't been asleep long.

"Umm, yeah." She fidgets, stepping inside the room farther. "Actually, no. I, uhh, had this dream, and it scared me," she whispers.

Before I can even consider potential consequences of my actions, I flip open the blanket in invitation, and while my dick could clearly get on board with this plan, that's not what I'm offering.

Cameron doesn't hesitate. She pads over to my bed and climbs in. My dick gets very excited, completely ignoring the cues from my brain telling him to calm down. I throw the covers over her, trying to keep a respectable distance, even though my body craves hers. In the soft moonlight seeping through the shades, I notice she's on her back, her arms at her sides, and stiff as a board. I almost reach out but stop myself. Me getting all up in her business when she's had a bad dream is the last thing she needs.

Then I hear a sniffle, and I'm unable to keep from touching her. I scoot toward her, carefully wrap my arm around her waist, and pull her against my body, careful to keep my groin back so she can't feel how much she affects me. I've never been a snuggler, but I find myself easily slipping into the role of the big spoon, her petite body molding so perfectly within mine. My left arm is beneath her neck, my right thrown over her waist, and all I can do is hold her while she cries.

"Why is this happening?" she asks with a sniffle.

"I don't know, love."

After a few moments, she whispers, "You think it's Cage, don't you." It's not a question.

"Yeah, I do." There's no reason to sugarcoat it. Watching people is a big part of my job, and I didn't like any of the vibes I got from her ex.

"What are we going to do about it?" she murmurs softly.

"We're going to go to sleep, Cam. There's nothing we can do right now. You're safe here, so we're going to try to catch a little shut-eye and deal with this in the morning."

"It is morning," she mumbles, a hint of humor in her voice.

"True," I agree with a chuckle. "I suppose we'll just talk later."

She yawns before snuggling deeper into my embrace. I hold her against me, doing my damnedest to ignore the feel of her basic cotton tee and shorts that do so little at concealing her curves. It's all fruitless, however, because there's no way in hell I'll ever forget what she feels like in my arms.

And that is a huge problem.

Eventually, she drifts off to sleep. The soft sounds of her light snores fill my room, and even though it's still dark outside, the room feels lighter. Freer than ever before. It's no longer just a place to catch some sleep or bring the occasional woman home. It feels different now that she's been here, and that's the biggest problem of all, because even though it feels good—right, even—I know it's not real. It's a façade. A mindfuck. I've seen what happens to lives when the love runs out and the gloves come off, and it's bound to happen.

No one stays happy post-honeymoon phase.

It's all undermined decisions and hateful comments.

So why bother?

Have fun and move on. That's my motto.

Best for me to remember that, especially now, when I'm unable to focus on anything other than Cam being in my bed. That good feeling wears off eventually.

But that doesn't stop me from adjusting my position against her back and shoving my nose into her hair like some creeper. It doesn't take long before my eyelids grow heavy, and I feel myself starting to doze back off. I'm sure it's the fatigue setting back in and has nothing to do with the way Cameron feels in my arms.

Nothing to do with the way she fits so perfectly against me.

Nothing to do with this overwhelming sense of contentment at having her here.

Nothing at all.

Too Young to Fall in Love

Yeah. Keep telling yourself that.

Cameron

I move my arms, stretching them high above my head, and smile.

Then last night and early this morning hits me, and that smile falls from my face.

My eyes pop open, and it only takes a moment to recall I'm not in my bed. I'm in Kellen's. It's big, comfortable, and very tempting. A part of me wants to curl up with his pillow and drift back to sleep, but the fact it's after noon tells me that's probably not the best option.

It's a damn good thing I didn't have to work today, or I'd be in a world of trouble for being late.

Slowly climbing from the bed, I scan the bedroom, even though I know he's not in here. I'd feel his presence, or at the very least, hear him. Since I'm blanketed in silence, I decide to slip out of his room, desperate for another shower. I took one earlier this morning when we arrived here, but it was mostly because I felt so dirty, so contaminated, after walking through the debris of my house.

I pause in the hallway, grateful to hear movement in the kitchen. At least I wasn't left alone. Before, that thought never frightened me, but now, it sends a cold shiver down my spine. Moving quickly across the hall, I stop in my tracks when I see the bags sitting on the guest bed. Creeping forward, I spot the small stock of work shirts first, all folded in a neat pile. There's a piece of paper on top of them, and my eyes are already tearing up when I see Reagan's familiar penmanship.

Cam – Just a few things to tide you over until we can go shopping. If there's anything you need, please let me know. We love you! – Reagan

I peek into the first bag and burst into tears. Dumping the contents onto the comforter, I find two packages of new underwear, some basic cotton bras, a bundle of socks, and a few pairs of cotton pajamas. The second bag holds a couple of T-shirts, two pairs of jeans in my size, and three pairs of black work pants. The third and final bag is stocked with bath and beauty products, most of it better brands than the basic stuff I used before.

"You okay?"

I startle, spinning around to face Kellen. He's leaning against the doorjamb, a worried look on his handsome face. "Yes, sorry," I insist, swiping at the wetness on my cheeks. "I wasn't expecting all of this."

"She said it was just some necessities," he says, slowly taking a step into the room, then another.

I nod in agreement. I don't tell him, when you start with practically nothing, everything is a necessity. "I'll never be able to repay her," I whisper, realizing I'm going to have to add the cost of this stuff to the total I already owe her and her husband.

"I don't think that's necessary," he states, coming to a stop beside me.

"It is." And the cost to replace the rest of my clothes is a daunting number.

"This is what friends are for, Cam. They're here to help when you need it."

"But this probably set her back a couple hundred bucks," I mumble, taking in the piles of clothing once more. "I wouldn't feel right not paying her back for it."

His arm brushes against mine as he reaches for the pair of blue and white striped pajama top and shorts. I notice the packages of panties right beside it, and I suppose I should be grateful he's not picking those up. The last thing I need is him checking out the basic cotton panties I'll be wearing. I mean, in my dreams, that wasn't exactly how I pictured his hands on them.

He drops the pajamas back onto the bed and takes a step back. "I'll let you get ready. Let me know if there's anything you need." He turns to walk out of the room. "Oh, and there's lunch on the stove."

I swallow over the sudden lump in my throat. "Thank you."

Then, he's gone, gently closing the door behind him and leaving me alone once more.

I take a few minutes to remove the tags from the new clothes and get them ready to wash. Unfortunately, I need to leave some of it out to wear today, but I'll make sure to wash those tomorrow. I have a few pieces of clothing in my bag from the house, but I didn't tell anyone the stuff I found that wasn't cut up were things I found buried deep in the hamper in the bathroom. And there wasn't much there either.

Once I get the bath products put away, I slip off my pajamas and stand beneath the hot shower spray. I remain rooted in place for several minutes, letting the water wash away the tear remnants. Unfortunately, with it goes the scent of Kellen that clung to my skin from sleeping in his bed. I try not to dwell on the disappointment I feel at no longer smelling him or the way my body felt both alive and safe while I was wrapped in his arms.

Stupid girly hormones.

I have no business recalling how amazing his arms felt.

Or the erection he tried to hide.

Oh, I definitely felt it. Despite him doing his best to keep his groin from contacting my body, I knew it was there. It brushed against my backside when he curled his bigger body around mine. I keep telling myself he was only offering comfort in my time of distress, and any man would get a hard-on while a woman lay in bed with him, but the niggle in the back of my brain telling me there was more to it can't be ignored. Especially after feeling how that kiss we shared behind Burgers and Brew affected him too. I mean, I'm not an expert on male erections, but the fact he's gotten one twice in the last twenty-four hours when he was either kissing or holding me is telling, isn't it?

Unless he usually sports them when he's around the opposite sex.

I've seen how flirty he gets with the ladies.

Perhaps his hard-on wasn't that uncommon after all.

I finish up my shower and slip on my new clothes. Grabbing the brush Reagan included, I take a few minutes to run it through my hair before pulling it onto the top of my head in a messy bun. I'll deal with the tangles later. Deciding to forego makeup, I use the new toothbrush she sent and hang my towel on the bar to dry. Finally, I pick up the pile of new clothes, throw them in the bags, and carry them out of the guest room.

Even if I wasn't going toward the kitchen, my nose would carry me in that direction. Whatever is on the stove smells amazing. It's a rich mixture of garlic and marinara sauce, and I'm suddenly starving. My stomach growls angrily, and I'm incredibly grateful Kellen wasn't in front of me to hear it.

Stepping into the kitchen, I find Kellen sitting at the table, eyes down on his phone. He must hear me or sense my nearness, because he quickly looks up and places his phone down in front of him. "Hey."

"Hi. I was hoping to wash some clothes," I start, hating the feeling of hesitancy at asking for help.

"Whatever you need, Cam. You don't have to ask permission," he replies instantly, standing up and leading me into the small, attached room.

He shows me how to use the machine, and moments later, my first load is running. My stomach chooses that moment to growl once more, ensuring my face is warm from embarrassment. With a chuckle, he adds, "Come on, Cam. Lunch is ready."

When we return to the kitchen, he points to the chair he vacated. Reluctantly, I take a seat and watch as he goes to the counter, retrieves one of the two plates, and fills it with food. I do mean *fills* it. A mountain of spaghetti noodles, sauce with big fat meatballs, two slices of garlic bread, and some green beans with bacon pieces is placed in front of me, and all I can do is stare at it. "Is someone else coming over to help me eat this?"

Kellen snorts. "Nope, that's all for you."

My wide eyes find his humor-filled ones. "I can't eat all of this."

He shrugs, turning around and filling another plate with an obscene amount of food. "Cold spaghetti makes the best leftovers," he insists, taking a seat opposite me.

Picking apart a piece of the garlic bread, I take a small bite. "I disagree. Cold pizza is far superior."

He twists a small mound of pasta around his fork and shoves it in his mouth. As he chews, he points his fork at me and mumbles, "I concur. As long as the pizza has ham and pineapple on it."

The fork I'm moving toward my mouth stops suddenly. "Seriously? You like Hawaiian pizza?"

He wipes the marinara sauce off his kissable lips. "Does admitting that kill my street cred?"

A smile spreads easily across my lips. "Nope. It makes you cooler. Only the cool kids eat pineapple on their pizza."

His laughter stirs something in my chest, and I try not to focus on the way his full lips curl up in the sexy way women fawn over daily. "Well, just don't tell Jasper. He thinks adding fruit to pizza is a cardinal sin."

We eat in comfortable silence, and I can't help but glance around the tidy kitchen. I saw it early this morning but seeing it now in the light of day is something entirely different. It's gorgeous, with its farmhouse feel. The living room has big comfortable pieces of furniture, but what sets the room off isn't the big screen TV on the wall. It's the fact there are coordinating portraits on the wall and decorative throw pillows. It doesn't scream bachelor pad. Not by a long shot.

"Your house is beautiful."

"Thanks," he replies between bites. "Like I mentioned when we got here this morning, I wish I could take credit for it, but really, my sister did it all for me."

I've heard him reference his sister on a few occasions but have never been brave enough to ask about her. I mean, it's not every day you meet someone related to an up-and-coming country music star. Kinsley McGregor is a household name in this neck of the woods, and even though she's three or four years older than me and was already out of high school by the time I moved to town, I've heard all about her.

Plus, I'm a big fan of her music.

"You can ask."

I glance up, a little off-kilter that he can easily read my thoughts. "I don't want to be rude."

Again, he points his fork at me. "And *that* is why you can ask me anything. Most people, that's the first question to come out of their mouths. Everyone wants to know about her, and that's okay, but the fact you don't want to ask because you think it's rude tells me a lot about you, Cam."

I twirl a little pasta around my fork and take a much smaller bite than Kellen did. "Why don't you tell me what you want me to know," I suggest, wanting to respect both of their privacy. I can't imagine what it's like to be related to someone who's famous, and the last thing I want to do is appear to only be interested in him because of her, or worse, be thought of as some big fangirl where she's concerned.

"She's fucking awesome, and I'm not just saying that because she can sing. She's genuinely the coolest person I know, and now that you see how great I am, that's saying something," he quips with a teasing grin and a wink.

My thighs clench.

"She's always been crazy-talented. She can play a few different instruments, but singing was always her passion. She's actually the one who taught me to play the drums. Never took any lessons. She just picked up a set of sticks one day at the grade school and started pounding out a solid beat. She's married to some douche I pretend to like; her bass player—"

"Zander Houston," I state, blushing instantly at the interruption.

Kellen just smiles though. "Yeah. Him."

"I don't know him, but he seems all right." My knowledge of her husband is pretty limited. I've seen the guy in photos and in her music videos, but that's it.

"He's not. He's a self-absorbed, controlling wanker, who's too good to come back to her piddly little Podunk hometown with her. They've been married three years, and he's only been here once. Always has some excuse as to why he can't come relax and hang out with his wife's family."

Clearly, Kellen isn't a big fan of Zander Houston's, and I can't help but feel bad for his sister, Kinsley. I know what it's like to have someone you love not get along with other important people in your life. My friends all hated Cage, which is why I no longer have friends. They slowly pulled back until I was completely isolated from everyone I knew and loved. I'm certain that was his goal anyway.

"She just started a small tour on the eastern side of the US. It's not huge by any means, but it's her first time headlining, so that's pretty fucking sweet. Ten cities in seven weeks, and there's talk about extending it if it goes well. I'm trying to figure out if I can get to the Philly show coming up in three weeks. It's the closest to Stewart Grove, but with Kallie off, I didn't want to add stress to the load at work by asking for it off."

"She should be back by then, though, right? I mean, how amazing would it be to surprise her at that show?" I'm suddenly sitting up straight and leaning forward, as if the concept of him going to a concert—a *Kinsley McGregor* concert at that—is the most exciting thing in the world.

Of course, Kellen doesn't know I've never been to a concert at all, so he probably doesn't get my excitement. For him, it's probably a regular occurrence, but for me, it would be once in a lifetime.

"Yeah, you're probably right. I'll talk to Garreth about it." He takes another bite, his sexy blue eyes trained on me. It takes everything I have not to wiggle under his scrutiny.

We finish our meal in more comfortable silence, and when I say finish my meal, I'm not referring to cleaning my plate. It'd take me two days to eat this amount of food. I slide from my seat and head to the counter, prepared to look for some foil to wrap up my leftovers, when Kellen meets me there. Without a word, he reaches into a drawer and pulls out a roll of ClingWrap, carefully sealing my plate for a later reheat.

We work in tandem, even though I don't do much, to finish placing the leftover food into bowls and in the refrigerator. When I reach for the washcloth to clean the counter, he finally speaks again. "There's something I wanted to talk to you about."

I set the wet cloth down in front of me and slowly turn to face him. Is he about to kick me out? I mean, I did crash his bed early this morning, and not in the way I'm sure he's used to.

Fumbling with my fingers, I whisper a hoarse, "Okay."

Kellen holds my gaze as he says, "I think you should stay here, and not just because your house was trashed and right now is uninhabitable. I think you should stay here and be my girlfriend."

Excuse me while I pick my jaw up off the ground.

"I'm sorry, what?" My voice doesn't even sound like my own.

He grins, knowing he's completely shocked me. "*Pretend* girlfriend, just like we told Cage."

"We?" I ask, my brain spinning, trying to wrap around what he's saying.

"Okay, technically, *I* told Cage we were dating, yes, but there's a reason I did that. To get him off your back."

All I can do is stare at him in disbelief. "But you think he trashed my house because of what you said."

"True, but men are fickle creatures. We don't like to be continually shot down. Hurts our ego. He did it out of anger, Cam. Once he realizes you've moved on, he will too," he states matter-of-factly, like he didn't just suggest we pretend to date for the foreseeable future.

"For how long?" I whisper, my head trying to wrap around the fact we'd be dating.

Pretending.

He shrugs his muscular shoulders. "For however long it takes."

The spinning in my brain just continues to twirl. "This seems so..."

"Extreme?" he asks with a chuckle. "Yeah, I'm an extreme man, Cam." He sobers as he holds my gaze and adds, "You're going to be staying here for a bit, so it's not a stretch to pretend to be dating, right?"

Except it is a stretch. No way would this man actually date me. Not when he has gorgeous women flocking to him daily. Women who know how to flirt in return and aren't afraid to take what he's suggesting, even for just one night. I've seen how they respond to one flash of his devilish smile. It's like Kryptonite for ladies everywhere.

Myself included.

"I don't know," I whisper, more for myself than for him.

"Listen," he starts, reaching over and taking my hand. He doesn't hold it too tightly, allowing me the opportunity to pull back if I want. I don't, of course. "If you don't want to do this, we don't have to. I was just thinking it would be an easy way to get Cage out of your life for good. He can slink back to whatever hole he crawled out of. Plus, you get to date me for a few weeks. I promise to be on my best behavior and be the best pretend boyfriend you've ever had." He punctuates his declaration with the waggling of his eyebrows.

A slow smile spreads across my lips.

Yes, I could pass on his offer and try to deal with Cage myself, but to be honest, having a friend beside me, prepared to help me eradicate my ex from my life, once and for all, doesn't sound so bad either.

With a sigh, I meet his intense gaze and nod. "Okay, let's do it."

I'm rewarded with a huge grin. One that makes my heart jump and my nipples to pebble. "Great," he agrees, pulling me into a light hug. I catch a whiff of his soap, deodorant, and whatever cologne he's wearing. The mixture is like a bomb dropped on my ovaries.

When he releases me, he finishes cleaning up the kitchen and I practically run off to the guest bedroom for a little space. Really, I just needed a few moments away from the hormones because his scent is definitely wreaking havoc on me.

I lean against the closed door and inhale deeply.

I'm sure being his pretend girlfriend will be easy, right?

I just have to remember it's not real. At the end of the day, he's not my boyfriend, and when Cage is gone, I'll be all alone again.

Just the way I want it.

Keep telling yourself that.

Thirteen

Kellen

This has bad idea written all over it.

In Sharpie.

Why I proposed having a fake relationship is beyond me, other than the fact I want to do this for her. I mean, I did already lay the groundwork where Cage is concerned. I did already tell him we're dating, and I even kissed her in front of him. I wasn't kidding when I told her guys don't like to be turned down repeatedly. A few times of him seeing her with me, and he'll get the hint she's not interested. I know I would. No guy wants to be rejected over and over again, especially when she's not playing hard to get.

Having her stay here with me is an added bonus. Not only do I seem to enjoy being around her, but I can keep an eye on her too. Until this guy gets it through his thick skull she's over him and not interested, I know she won't be too far away. Plus, having her in my space is surprisingly calming, and it has nothing to do with waking this morning with my arms wrapped around her. There was definitely nothing *calm* about what was happening with my dick. He was very excited to be pressed against her ass, nestled in tightly and eager to take the snuggle to the next level.

And that won't happen.

As much as I'd like to, Cameron is off-limits.

Yes, I realize there'll probably be some touching and hopefully, some kissing, but it's all for the sake of acting. A means to an end, if you will. Any kisses we share will be for the sole purpose of showing someone we're dating, and when Cage is out of the picture, the relationship ends.

Period.

No way do I want to entertain the thought of actually having something with Cameron. Relationships lead to hurt, and that's the very last thing I want to inflict on her or myself. That's why I always find the humor, the fun in any situation. Life is too short to spend it upset or hating someone else. Might as well enjoy it while you can, and if that comes in the form of a mutual agreement for a fake relationship with Cam, then I'm game.

My phone rings, and I'm not surprised to see Garreth's name on the screen.

"Hello?" I answer.

"Hey, how's she doing?"

Propping my backside against the counter, I pin the phone between my shoulder and ear and cross my arms. "Seems to be doing okay. She was appreciative of the bags of stuff you guys dropped off earlier."

He sighs. "It probably stressed her out though."

I don't confirm. She was very stressed when she opened the bags, fretting about how she'll repay for the stuff Reagan bought.

"She's probably trying to figure out how she's going to pay us back. If I know Cameron, she'll insist on it. She's very firm when it comes to repaying debts and there's no doubt she'll see those clothes as that," he continues absently, and I can practically hear him rubbing his forehead.

"Listen, there's something else I want to talk to you about," I start, realizing I should probably rip off the Band-Aid and tell Garreth the plan.

"Shoot."

"Well, Cam and I were talking, and we're going to pretend we're in a relationship until Cage gets a clue and fucks off."

I'm met with silence on the other line.

Then, suddenly, the call disconnects.

I pull the phone away from my ear and glance at the screen, confirming what I suspected. He hung up. Before I can set my phone down, it rings again. Only this time, it's a video chat.

The moment I accept the call, his angry face fills the screen. "Say that again? I want to see your ugly mug as you say those words."

My mouth falls open. "I'm not ugly! My mom says I'm the most handsome little guy in the world."

My joke falls on deaf ears, and if anything, only seems to annoy him more.

"Sorry," I mumble, clearing my throat. "Bad joke. Anyway, what's a better way of getting rid of your ex than with a new beau?"

Garreth's eyes narrow. "No."

"No?" I ask, now my own annoyance amped up. "What do you mean no?"

"You're not messing around with Cameron."

"What? Of course I'm not."

His eyes narrow. "Listen, don't take this the wrong way, Kellen, but I know how you are."

Okay. Totally taking that the wrong way.

"What does that mean?"

I know exactly what it means, but I'm making him say it.

"You're a player, man. And that's fine. You do you, but that doesn't mean you can fuck around with Cameron."

My ears are burning red, I know it. "I'm not fucking around with her," I reply calmly, even though my ire is starting to simmer.

"Then what are you doing?"

"Helping her," I insist to the phone screen. "We already sort of told Cage we were dating, so now we're just taking it to the next level."

"Whoa, stop. When did this happen?" he asks, rubbing his forehead as I imagined him doing earlier.

"Yesterday when I found them outside, I might have told Cage we were dating to get him to back off."

Garreth's jaw tics. "And you didn't mention this to me because..."

"Listen, man, I know you've got some big bro thing going with her, but I promise I'm not fucking around with her," I counter, completely ignoring his question. I also gloss right over the fact I kissed her. No need to cause the man to stroke out.

"Then what is this?" he asks calmly, even though I can tell he's teetering the line between control and out of control.

"I just want to help. I consider her a friend, G, and she needs help. Not only a place to stay, but someone to help Cage get a clue."

"Well, Jameson did offer to just beat it out of him," Garreth mutters, making me smile.

"The last thing he needs is an assault charge. And even though she's planning to get the restraining order, we both know it's just a piece of paper. I don't know Cage well enough to know how far he'll take this. I don't think he's an idiot, which is why I'm thinking a few flashes of me and her together in front of him will help him get the message, but also it keeps me close, in case he tries something else."

He closes his eyes and shakes his head. "I don't like it, but I don't like her alone either."

"The only time she'll be alone is when I'm at work."

Garreth stares at me for a few long seconds. "I might be able to help with that," he says, referring to his management position and the fact he can easily move one of us to the other shift.

"Let's hold off on that until we need to make a change."

He nods in agreement. "Who are you telling your relationship is fake?"

"No one. You and Reagan, but I'd like to keep it to must-know so there's less potential of Cage finding out we're not really dating."

"I'll have to tell the owners."

"That's fine but let them know to keep it to themselves."

"They will. Especially if it's for the safety of an employee." He pauses before asking, "And you're sure she's on board with this plan? The last thing I want is for her to feel railroaded or uncomfortable."

"She said she was okay with it, but you have to know, if she ever is uncomfortable, she has an out. I don't want to cause her more problems, G. She's dealing with enough after finding her house ransacked and discovering her ex is back in town. I don't want to add to it."

He watches me closely for several seconds before nodding. "Okay. Just keep your dick in your pants, my friend," he adds. "I'd hate to have to kill you."

"You know she's an adult, right?"

His eyes narrow into little slits, and it's in that moment I realize I said the wrong thing. "That may be true, but she's too good for you."

I snort, because his statement is completely accurate.

He knows it.

I know it.

"Listen, I get where you're coming from, but you have nothing to worry about, okay?"

I'm not really sure he believes me, but after a few very long, very tense seconds, he finally nods. "Okay. Just know I will let Jameson kill you if you fuck with her. I don't care how pretty your mom thinks your face is. I'll let him fuck it up."

I chuckle, even though I'm certain he's not joking. The mood seems somewhat lighter as he leans back in his chair and closes his eyes.

"Keep me updated on any developments, yeah?" he asks once more.

"Of course, but only as long as she's okay with me sharing details. I don't want her to feel like she's being railroaded, as you said. She needs to feel in control, and I won't go around her like a tattletale because you think you're entitled to information."

Again, his jaw flexes in irritation, but I know I'm right here. If he doesn't respect her as a woman and her ability to make her own decisions, then that's not my problem. "I understand, but know she comes to me or Reagan with everything anyway, so remember we'll find out eventually."

I sigh, feeling dizzy and wanting off this merry-go-round. "Everything will be fine," I counter, hating this big brother routine he's pulling, yet completely understanding and appreciating the fact she has him and Reagan in her corner. "Have faith."

He exhales loudly. "I'll see you soon, right? You're on tonight?"

"Yep. I'll be in shortly."

"All right. Later." Then, he's gone, and I'm left staring at a blank screen.

I drop my phone on the counter a little harder than I mean to and run my hands through my hair. I understand his concerns, really, I do, but he shouldn't need to worry. I'm not going to steal her virtue and send her out the door with a pat on the ass and a thanks for the good time.

"Hey."

Looking up, I find Cameron leaning against the doorjamb, offering me a small grin. "Hey."

She fidgets with the hem of her shirt, looking a bit hesitant. "You work tonight, right?"

"I do," I confirm, reaching for a glass and filling it with tap water so I don't walk over, take her in my arms, and kiss the hell out of her.

"Umm, I can go to Garreth and Reagan's house while you're gone, if you want."

"That's not necessary, Cam. You're staying here, which means you can be here without me. I trust you."

She seems surprised by my declaration. "You do? But you don't know me."

"Not well, no, but I've observed you at work for over a year, and I'm a pretty good judge of character. Besides, Reagan and Garreth are two of the best people I know, and if they have faith in you, then I do too."

I don't really know what I said to cause her reaction, but tears fill her eyes.

I hate tears. Seen too many of them growing up. My mom was always crying, my dad getting madder because of it. He always said she'd whip them out to get her way, but I saw the pain she tried to hide. She cried because she was sad and hurting, not because of ulterior motives.

"They are good people," she confirms softly.

"And so are you, Cameron Wright. I trust you here. Have at it. Snoop wherever you want."

A sexy smile spreads across her lips, instantly making my dick twitch eagerly. "Really? Even in your nightstand drawer?"

I give my own wicked grin. "Anywhere, love. Who knows? You might actually like what you find in there," I tease with a wink.

She blushes the cutest shade of pink and for a flash, her eyes drop to my groin. It takes every ounce of self-control I possess to not throw her over my shoulder and cart her off to my bed.

"My point is, you have free rein of my house while you're staying here."

"I'll pay," she insists, again with the fidgeting.

Not wanting to insult her, I go with a simple, "We'll discuss it later."

She doesn't seem to buy it, but she doesn't say anything either. "All right."

Moving her way, I reach out my hand, noting only slight hesitancy as she reaches and takes it. "Come on, Cam. I'll show you how to use the alarm system."

I've never been a big fan of sitting at home and doing nothing, but for the first time in my life, I'd rather be there than here.

The bar isn't very busy, which is typical of a Sunday evening without a big sporting event on TV. Right now, the regulars are engrossed in an auto race, debating whether the guy leading will actually win. I tune them out, mostly because I've never gotten into the whole racing thing. I mean, they just turn left the whole time. What's exciting about that?

"How's it going over here?" Garreth asks, appearing from the kitchen, where he's spent a good chunk of his night, thanks to the dishwasher going home with a stomach bug.

"Good. Nothing I can't handle," I insist, placing clean glasses on the shelf.

"I figured you'd be fine, but if it gets bad, let me know. I can call Max and see if he can come help ya."

I wave off his concern. "I'm good. How's the kitchen? Got dishpan hands yet?"

He rolls his eyes. "I don't mind washing a few dishes. It's dealing with Jasper when he's acting like a prima donna that has me ready to chuck a plate against the wall."

"I heard that," Jasper states, walking up behind him.

"I wasn't whispering. Besides, I knew you were walking up behind me."

"Came to find out where my dish boy went. It's not your break time," he quips, the hint of a smile playing on his lips.

"I was just making sure everything was all right out here. You'll be back to barking orders at me in a few minutes."

"Excellent. I love bossing you around."

"Do I need to leave you two alone for a few minutes? You have this weird bromance thing going on. I don't want to interrupt," I joke, getting the expected rise out of Jasper.

"Fuck off."

Garreth laughs, shaking his head. "You can't tell an employee to fuck off."

"My restaurant," the grumpy chef retorts. "Anyway, I just wanted to check and see how Cameron is doing. Walker said last night—or I guess this morning—was pretty rough. Have you talked to her?"

Garreth turns his complete attention to me, waiting for my reply. "I texted her a bit ago, and she said all is good."

"How long is she going to be staying with you?"

I shrug, reaching for a bottle of Bud Light and sliding it down the bar to replace an empty. "I'm not sure. However long it takes. Her place is trashed."

Jasper's jaw tightens. "Garreth said it was a mess. Lyndee volunteered to help her clean. Just let us know."

Garreth nods. "Reagan will help too, I'm sure."

"I bet the other wives would be more than willing to pitch in as well, if they can," Jasper adds, slipping behind the bar and filling a glass with water.

"Definitely. Tell Cam to set something up when she's ready. We've got enough trucks between us; we can haul away whatever is broken or she doesn't want."

I know she's going to have to clean up her place soon, but I'm not sure how quickly she's wanting to go over and start that. She was still pretty shaken up by the whole ordeal this morning. Granted, it's been less than a day since she returned home and found it destroyed. Maybe with a little more time she'll be anxious to return to her house and get her life back to normal.

The thought causes my stomach to drop to my shoes.

"I'll tell her," I reply, pushing those previous thoughts out of my head. I have no business entertaining even the slightest idea of Cameron staying in my house for any prolonged length of time.

None whatsoever.

"It was good of you to offer her your spare bedroom," Jasper says. "Sometimes I forget your house is like a mini fortress."

I nod and swallow over the lump in my throat. Apparently, Garreth hasn't told him about my plans to be her pretend boyfriend. Though, if I had to guess, he's probably going to say something tomorrow when they have their standing Monday afternoon owners' meeting. That would be the time he'd discuss any non-urgent employee matters, so it would be logical for him to bring it up then.

"Yeah, she's pretty safe there."

Everyone knows who my sister is, and she's the reason I have the house I do. I would have been fine finding a small one- or two-bedroom place, but with her always using Stewart Grove as her escape away from the realities of fame, I wanted to ensure I had plenty of room for her visits. I also had a good security system installed, even though this town has always been fairly safe. I'm not taking any chances with my sister's safety.

Not now, not ever.

Same goes for Cameron.

"All right, I better get back in there before my assistant burns my kitchen down," Jasper states, placing his dirty glass in the small dishwashing unit behind the bar. Before he gets too far away, he looks over his shoulder and adds, "Are you coming? Those dishes aren't going to wash themselves."

"Asshole," Garreth grumbles, a big smile on his face as Jasper turns and walks away.

"I heard that!" Jasper hollers.

"I wasn't whispering!" he replies, then follows the chef back to the kitchen.

Shaking my head, I chuckle at their antics. That's one of the reasons I love working here so much. It's a serious place, filled with professionals, but we can all joke and have a good time every now and again.

I check on each patron at the bar and also the few at the pub tables, making sure everyone's drinks are good. One table decides to order food to-go and another requests a round of our specialty shot of the week. The more I move around, the faster the night will go. A quick check of my watch while I'm pouring the mixed concoction into the shot glasses confirms only a little bit longer before I can clock out and head home.

I can't help but wonder if Cameron will still be awake when I get there.

Cameron

What was that?

My heart is trying to beat right out of my chest as I cower in the guest bedroom closet, curling into a ball so tight, praying I won't be spotted if someone is in the house. I don't know for a fact there's an intruder. In fact, I'm almost certain there isn't one. My overactive imagination is hearing things, like a bush brushing against the siding or the creak of the wood on the front porch, and it's driving me crazy.

I've never been this person. The one hiding in a closet because she heard something strange outside. Yet, here I am, terrified in a way I've never been before.

Even when I walked into my house last night, I didn't feel afraid, per se. At least not right away. There was so much confusion and sadness, I barely had time to be scared. But now, it's different. For someone who's enjoyed living alone for the last year or so, I'm suddenly petrified to be by myself, and it's worse because I'm in unfamiliar surroundings. Even with the fancy alarm system and the fact this is a great neighborhood, I'm frightened.

I've tried to calm myself.

I've checked the alarm an obscene number of times.

I've verified the doors are locked.

I turned on the security light in the backyard I just happened to find when I was turning on all the lights in the house.

And yet, I'm still hiding in the closet, gripping my phone like it was a lifeline. Kellen's name is pulled up on my screen, one touch away from connecting us, but I haven't found the courage to push the button. Why? Because deep down in the reasonable part of my brain, I know there's no one outside, and the last thing I want to do is look like the scared loser I am in front of Kellen.

While I haven't hit the button to call him, I haven't exactly been brave enough to get out of the closet yet either. All I've managed to do is watch the clock and keep my breathing somewhat manageable, so I don't hyperventilate. I haven't even changed into pajamas yet, for fear I'd have to run outside in something less than my presentable shorts and T-shirt. I mean, no one wants to be interviewed by the cops wearing a cute little tank and short set with dancing avocados on it.

However, as the time inches closer to when Kellen should be home, I know I need to make my move. I don't want to be this girl. I don't want him to find me hiding out, afraid of my own damn shadow. My hands are shaking as I reach for the knob and slowly turn the cool metal in my hand. The overhead bedroom light blinds me, thanks to leaving it on before I secured myself in the small, dark space.

My legs are a little wobbly, but I hurry out of the room, my eyes scanning everywhere around me as I go. I know Kellen will be home very soon, and I don't want him to find all the lights on the way they are. Switch after switch, I flip them off, making my way to the back and allowing the darkness to resume in the backyard once more. I make sure to leave the light above the sink on, as Kellen did the night before. As I'm leaving the kitchen, I hear the sound of his truck pulling into the driveway and the garage door going up. A squeal slides from my mouth as I race back to my bedroom.

No, not mine. His guest room.

I don't have time to change. Flipping off the light, I dive under the covers and pull them up to my neck so he can't see I'm still in my street clothes. I can hear the back door open and the alarm being deactivated, only to be reactivated moments later. A calm feeling settles over me, and I realize how extremely grateful I am he's home.

Even if I'm about to pretend to be sleeping for the sake of not having to explain myself right now.

Keeping my back to the semi-closed door, I lie completely still and listen. Heavy boots walk around the kitchen, and I can tell he's trying to do it quietly. The fridge opens and closes before he moves again, heading this way. My heart is thumping an erratic beat as his footfalls slow, eventually stopping.

Did he go into his bedroom?

I keep my ears peeled for the sound of his door closing, but that's not what I hear. My door moves, opening very slowly, the hint of a squeak echoing off the walls. It's in that moment I realize he's peeking into my room. Checking up on me? Seeing if I'm asleep? I'm not sure why, but I freeze still and hold my breath.

He stands at the doorway without saying a word for what feels like minutes, though in reality was probably only a few seconds. Then, as quietly as he opened the door, he pulls it closed, leaving it cracked just a bit. I hear him walk across the hall and eventually close his door, and only then do I release the breath I was holding.

I flip around and try to get comfortable, but it doesn't come easily. Especially because I can hear the sound of water running in his bathroom. Just the thought of him being naked, wet, and soapy is doing things to my body. Dirty things I have no business picturing, yet are now parading through my brain like a porno.

It's worse when I close my eyes. Those images are so real, so lifelike, I can practically reach out and touch him. My hand slides over my breasts, my nipples already pebbled from desire. Slowly, I move my other hand beneath the waistband of my shorts and panties and find my clit. It's hard, my wetness coating my fingers. Pleasure races through my veins as those naughty images of Kellen in the shower play out. He reaches down, stroking his incredibly hard cock, the water and soap helping it slide from root to tip.

I muffle a moan as I tweak my nipples. My hand moves faster over my clit, and I picture it's him. His hand. His mouth. His cock. He's all I feel as my orgasm builds, threatening to detonate like a bomb at any moment. I think about his eyes on me as he swipes his warm tongue over my clit before burying two fingers deep inside of me. When I come, it's with his name whispered on my lips. I have to clench my mouth shut to keep from being heard. Thankfully, I can still hear the water running in his bathroom.

Sated, I quietly climb out of bed and head for the Jack and Jill bathroom, stopping at the doorway only long enough to confirm he's still in the shower. Then, I quickly slip inside to use the restroom, clean up a bit from my orgasm, wash my hands, and brush my teeth. By the time I'm done and reopen the door, the water is shut off in Kellen's room, so I tiptoe back to bed, praying he doesn't hear me moving around.

I slide beneath the covers once more and relax just as a door opens in his room, letting me know he's finished in the bathroom. His bed squeaks, and I can imagine him getting inside and curling against his pillow, his hard body still wet from the shower.

I mean, if this is my imagination at play, I might as well go all out, right?

Even though he was wearing shorts early this morning when I slid into his bed like the coward I am, I picture him naked again. Kellen McGregor just seems like the type of man to sleep in nothing, his body on full display, and proud of it. Hell, if I had his hard muscles, I'd show them off too. Instead, I have a little extra softness around my midsection, thanks to my love of all things carbs, and flabby underarms. But I also have no desire to actually go to the gym to help eliminate both of those flaws, so I'll just continue to bitch about them, yet embrace them completely.

Weird, right?

I lie there for what feels like forever, but in reality, is only an hour. The last thirty minutes or so has been quiet again. Kellen tossed and turned for a bit until eventually falling asleep, the occasional light snore filters through the doorway, but I still hear every little sound imaginable. Kellen must live on a fairly busy street, because I've been alerted to a handful of cars driving by after two in the morning.

My brain just won't shut down, despite the fact I'm desperate for a little sleep.

Deciding to get up and move around a bit, I head over to the small bookshelf by the reading chair. It's decorated with a small bouquet of artificial flowers, a wax tart warmer, and a framed photograph. I'm not sure why I didn't notice it before, but I instantly realize it's a picture of Kellen and Kinsley. Picking it up, the photo appears to be fairly recent. The love between brother and sister is evident, even through a photograph.

Placing the frame back in its spot, I scan the books on the two remaining shelves. There are several memoirs for actresses and actors, musicians, and public figures. Kinsley is clearly a lover of non-fiction reads, and I can't help but wonder how much reading she actually gets done with her busy schedule.

The bottom shelf contains a few fiction books too, and while I'm not a huge reader, I'm attracted to the gorgeous covers. The author's name is Kaylee Ryan and judging by the pictures, the books are baseball themed. Finding the first book in the series, *Beyond the Bases*, I scan the blurb on the back of the book and take a seat in the chair. Flipping it open, I start reading the first page, instantly falling into the story of a professional baseball player, Easton, and single-mom, Larissa. Before I even realize what's happening, I'm four chapters in and loving it. I'd keep going, but my eyes just won't cooperate with my brain. It wants to devour the rest of the story, but the sleep that's been evading me is finally winning over.

I grab a receipt from my purse on the floor and slip it inside the book to mark my page. Placing it on the chair, I slide beneath the rumpled covers and close my eyes. It's hard not to think about Easton, the hero in the book, and replace him with Kellen. That man seems to be invading my thoughts continuously, and apparently that doesn't stop when I'm reading.

The bedding is cold against my skin, and I can't stop myself from recalling how warm and comfortable it was to snuggle in close to Kellen. I slept better than I ever imagined with his arms around me, and I'm a little worried I may not be able to sleep again. Being alone in this bed isn't cutting it, despite how mentally and emotionally exhausted I am.

Fortunately, my body's need for sleep finally wins out, and I slowly drift off to a fitful rest.

I startle.

My breathing is labored, and I'm covered in sweat. It takes me a few moments to get my bearings and realize where I am. It's still dark outside, and I hate this feeling of fear that constantly hangs over my head like an unwanted rain cloud. It settles in my chest, leaving no room for argument that it's here to stay.

Great.

I run shaky fingers through my tangled hair. I used to hate the color. When I was little, everyone made fun of the redhead in school. I was called everything from Carrot Top to Little Red, thanks to my smaller size, and even Gingersnap. When I lost my virginity to Michael Foster my junior year, his friends called me Fire Crotch for weeks afterward. It wasn't until the end of high school when all that changed. Now, everyone wants my hair color, dyeing it different shades of auburn or strawberry blonde with at-home kits or expensive trips to the salon, and for the first time since I was younger, I love my hair color.

Flipping over, I try to get comfortable again, but it's no use. My brain won't shut off, replaying the nightmare that woke me. Cage was in my house, waiting for me. Everywhere around him was chaos. My belongings broken. But it's the look on his face I feared the most. It wasn't a look I've ever seen before. It was malicious, and the evil intent was evident in his eyes.

I was afraid.

Now, I as I lie in bed, the sheets tangled around my sweaty limbs, all I want to do is escape. Get away from the nightmare, from the reality surrounding me. My feet are moving before I even register the movement. My door is still cracked open, and I'm out and in the hallway within a few seconds. My palm rests against the smooth wood of his semi-opened bedroom door, and it's the tremble I see in my hands that has me pushing and stepping forward.

Kellen's room isn't dark the way it was the night before. Instead, I find the bathroom light on, the door angled toward the bedroom to allow only a little light out. Did he do that for me? Tears fill my eyes at the prospect, which only pisses me off. There's no reason to cry, no reason for my mind to imagine him doing it for me. He probably just forgot to turn it off when he fell into bed, exhausted. I know I've felt that way plenty of times after working a late shift.

Movement in his bed catches my attention. He's on his side, facing the doorway I'm standing in, and without so much as cracking open his eyes, he pulls the covers down, exposing the other side of his bed. Just like he did last night.

Without a word, I scamper toward him and climb inside, enveloped in the warmth of his blankets, his arms, and his scent immediately. The erratic heartbeat I've had since awaking from my nightmare finally starts to calm and my breathing comes a little slower and easier.

I want to say something, but what? Do I thank him for allowing me into his bed, even though it's not for the reason I'm sure he'd prefer? What man welcomes a scared, crying woman, not only into his bed, but his arms? I never would have expected it from Kellen, that's for sure. I've seen his easygoing, carefreeness at work plenty of times, and I didn't picture him as one to offer comfort to a freaked-out woman.

Yet, here we are.

He's holding me against his chest—bare chest, mind you—and just holding me while I work through the mess of emotions in my brain. And believe me, there are plenty to choose from. Not only am I frightened, but physically and emotionally drained on top of it. I'm the worst combination of woman to a man like Kellen. I just pray he doesn't look at this as me being clingy and using his hospitality to my advantage.

"Shhh," he whispers, warm breath tickling my ear as he pulls me even closer to his chest, "I've got you."

I sniffle, not even realizing I started to cry, and that just angers me even more. I *hate* crying, yet that seems to be all I've done today. Hell, for the last year or so since Cage left me to deal with his problems alone.

I don't reply. I'm not sure I could speak, even if I could find the words. My throat is raw with emotion, a lump the size of Rhode Island lodged in my esophagus, but what really surprises me the most is the sense of relief I feel to be here, in his bed. In his arms.

Like a homecoming.

And that's how I know I'm completely losing my mind.

Being in his bed, having his arms wrapped around me, is only because of my situation. Any other night, there's no way I'd be here, and if I was, I'm certain it wouldn't be to cuddle. He'd be demonstrating exactly how proficient he is with using that hard club in his shorts I felt pressed against my ass last night.

"Close your eyes, Cam. You're safe here," he whispers the exact words I didn't even realize I needed to hear.

My body sags against him, the tension I've been carrying all night finally ebbing from me. My eyes grow heavy as I focus on the strong, steady heart beating against my back and the warm breath peppering my neck. If I wasn't so damn exhausted, I might get a little excited at the way my nipples pebble against my nightshirt and the apex of my legs grows a bit wet.

But I'm just too damn tired to fight it anymore. Too comfortable to not follow Kellen as he slowly drifts back to sleep.

Kellen

This time, when I wake with her in my arms, I don't get up. I lie still, pretending to sleep and maintain contact with the sleeping beauty in my arms. Of course, my cock is very happy with the connection too. Her ass is nestled against it, ensuring he stays hard and ready for the moment he finally gets the cue.

I give him no such signal though.

Now isn't the time for naked bedroom Olympic Games.

My fingers flex against her stomach. They itch to move, to stroke the softness, to feel smooth skin against my slightly coarser hand. Her scent is everywhere. I noticed it the moment I climbed into bed. Her shampoo mixed with a hint of vanilla floated from the pillow next to mine, and I found myself turning into it.

Inhaling.

Just like now.

After only two days of waking up with Cameron in my arms and I'm already addicted.

I don't really know how long I lie there and watch her sleep like a psycho, but long enough to sneak a few touches of her silky hair and listen to the little mewls she makes while she's dreaming.

At least, I hope it's dreaming and not like the nightmare I suspected she had last night. I was just about to get up, to go to her, when I heard her climb from her own bed and make her way toward mine. As if a total body reflex, I pulled back the covers, inviting her into my space. Partly because she's a friend in desperate need of comfort. Partly because she's gorgeous and my body craves having her there.

Either would be a total new revelation for me.

I don't do snuggling.

When she starts to stir, so does my dick. Oh, he was hard before, but now that she's wiggling against me, he's porn-star ready. As if all cameras and mouths were angled toward him, he's ready for his moment to shine.

But again, I ignore his needs, because that's not what this is about.

But it could be...

No.

Clenching my eyes shut, I count to ten, keeping my breathing steady in hopes she stops her torturous moving. She doesn't, however. If she didn't understand what her body does to me before, she definitely does now, because her sweet ass cheeks have shifted, my cock nestled between them like a fucking hot dog and bun, despite the fact we're both wearing clothing.

I have to bite my tongue to keep from groaning.

This is what hell feels like.

I should get used to it. That's definitely where I'm headed, thanks to the dirty thoughts parading through my brain.

Slowly, she turns in my arms. I want to hold her there, enjoying the heck out of my big spoon status, but don't fight it when she moves. She's now facing me, her green eyes open and cloudy from sleep. Cameron looks fucking adorable in the morning light, and I have to remind myself not to get too cozy with her here—with seeing her in my bed.

She doesn't belong here.

Not long term.

"Hi," she whispers, keeping her head resting on my forearm.

"Morning," I reply, wishing I had gotten up earlier to brush my teeth. Well, at least I won't be tempted to kiss her.

She averts her gaze as she softly says, "I'm sorry for...this. I shouldn't have come in here again."

Needing to touch her soft skin, I lift my hand and swipe my fingers across her cheek. "It's okay. A pretty woman is always welcome in my bed," I quip with a wink, hoping she knows I'm speaking of her and not a general observation.

Though, old Kellen has definitely fallen into the latter category a time or two.

I receive the smile I was hoping for, but it doesn't last long enough. Tension and worry mar her eyes, creating wrinkles around those emerald orbs. Even then, she's stunning. "I, umm, had trouble sleeping."

I nod, making sure to hold completely still. "I figured, and that's okay. You had something scary happen to you."

She swallows hard and closes her eyes for a brief moment before returning them to mine. "I wasn't expecting to have this overwhelming sense of vulnerability follow me around. It's unnerving."

"I'm sure it is, and the nightmares are normal," I say, hoping my assumptions from early this morning and what brought her to my bed are correct.

She sighs. "Yeah, I suppose they are, but not for me. I'm not used to them."

"Well, you're welcome in here whenever you're scared, okay?" When she nods in understanding, I expect her to extract herself from my embrace, and since that's not what I want to happen, I decide to speak again. "When I was seven or eight, I was plagued with nightmares."

Her eyes widen as she lies perfectly still, waiting to hear more. "Really? Why?"

"I witnessed a bad accident on our way home from school. My sister was too little to remember, but I can still picture it as if it had just happened. We were sitting in front of the post office near an intersection, when a big truck ran through it and plowed into a minivan."

"Oh my God," she mutters, her small hand covering those plump lips.

"It was terrible. I was arguing with my mom, wanting to go to the DQ for ice cream after our stop at the post office. I remember her being frustrated with me, but only because I wasn't listening to reason. It was near dinnertime, and she didn't want to ruin our appetites. I told my sister Mom wouldn't let us have ice cream, and Kins started to cry, demanding she get the treat, the only way a four-year-old can. I heard the squeal of the tires and looked up from the back seat just as the truck slammed into the van. My mom yelled at me to look away, but I couldn't. He hit it directly into the driver's side. The door was scrunched in so bad, practically peeled away from the frame. The woman driving was covered in blood. I didn't realize it at first, but when it finally registered what all the red was, I freaked out."

Taking a deep breath, I continue, "I remember hearing screaming, only to realize it was coming from me. Mom jumped out of the car but didn't run toward the crash. There were already tons of people over there. She came around to where I was sitting—where I was screaming—and pulled me into her arms. I recall her trying to shush me, but every time I'd feel myself starting to calm down, I'd see all that red and start again."

"My God, Kellen. I'm so sorry that happened to you."

"The worst part was the van was full of kids. The boy sitting behind her was a classmate of mine. It was an older van, before airbags and all the safety perks on vehicles today, so when that truck plowed into them, it..." Deep breath. "It killed him. I remember the mom being in a coma for a few days and the other kids all had minor injuries. But every time I closed my eyes, I saw all that red."

Her hand cups my jaw, the soft pads of her fingers lightly caressing my coarse skin.

"I had nightmares for weeks. It wasn't until I went to see a therapist that it started to get better," I confess my weakness and share with her something I've never told a soul.

"Are you suggesting I go to therapy?" she asks, the corner of her mouth turned upward.

"No, I was just telling you I knew a thing or two about nightmares, but if you think it would help you to talk about it with someone, then yes, you should see a therapist."

She nods in understanding. "I'll think about it," she whispers, and I'm not about to push the envelope with her. "When I was moving here the summer between my sophomore and junior year, I was terrified. My dad was transferred, and even though it was an amazing opportunity, I didn't want to go. I had friends and a *life*, as I called it. I didn't want to leave that and move to Nowhere, Ohio," she tells me, the hint of a smile on her full lips. "I made a complete ass of myself, including running away for a whole night."

"Of course you did. Running away is like a rite of passage for teenagers," I joke, even though I know it causes fear and worry for the parents involved.

"Yeah, but I ran away to my grandma's house. I was too chicken to go to a friend's place, and there was no way I was actually going to rough it on the streets. I'm pretty sure my grandma called my dad too, even though she swore she didn't, because Dad never called her freaking out. All night, she just listened to me vent about having to move and never once chastised me for the anguish I most certainly caused my parents, but she didn't need to. I felt so guilty, I ended up calling my dad around four in the morning, crying. He told me it was okay and came to pick me up at eight. The moment he walked in the door, I threw my arms around him and bawled. He never yelled or grounded me for running away. He just told me he understood and loved me, and then took me and Grandma to breakfast. In fact, he thanked me for going to my grandma's house. I never complained about moving again."

"So you were a good girl, huh?" I tease, already knowing she is.

She blushes and averts her gaze, her face sobering. "I don't know about that," she whispers, and it's that moment I realize she really is a good girl. No matter what she's done or what she thinks of herself, Cameron Wright has a good, pure heart.

Even though I don't want to move, I know it's time to get up. Not only does she work today, but she agreed to go to the police station to obtain the order of protection, and I'd like to feed her before we go. "As much as I enjoy lying here with you in my arms, you work soon."

The blush returns with a vengeance, as if she just remembered she's cradled in my arms. "Oh. Yeah." She pulls back, using the covers as a shield to stop me from seeing her pajamas with the avocados on them.

"Go shower," I tell her, throwing back the comforter and getting up. Thankfully, my dick is under control and not saluting her, but then her eyes drop to my bare chest, and I can feel the fucker getting excited by her scrutiny.

Now it's my turn to cut tail and bolt from the room, heading straight for my bathroom. Without turning my body, I glance back and add, "Breakfast in an hour. Then I'll run you to the police station and work."

"You don't have to—"

"Don't argue with me, love. I'm taking you to get that order of protection and then to work," I state pointedly, throwing in a wink before slipping into my bathroom and taking a deep breath.

Having her this close is bad.

Very bad.

I glance down at my rapidly growing erection.

I can practically feel his response vibrating through my veins. *I regretfully disagree.*

Pulling into the back of Burgers and Brew, I go ahead and park in a spot. Cameron gives me a curious look, obviously thinking I was just going to drop her off at the door and leave. However, after having to relive everything while filing the OP, I want to make sure she's okay.

"I've gotta confirm my hours for this week," I tell her, the lie almost getting lodged in my throat as I say it. I already talked to Garreth last night about my hours, only filling in for Kallie one night this week. Max is taking the other remaining shifts, and then she's planning to return for the weekend.

"Oh," she replies, releasing her seat belt and climbing out of the cab.

I follow behind her, casually looking around the near-vacant lot for trouble. Not that I expect to find Cage Bronson lurking in the shadows, but you never know. I want to be prepared, just in case.

I key in the code and pull open the door, stepping back to allow her to enter first. The building is still somewhat quiet, thanks to the doors not being open to the public yet. Most of the activity is in the kitchen, where Jasper is preparing for the lunch shift. Since he got married and had a son, the grumpy chef works only five days a week, relinquishing control of his kitchen to highly trained staff. And even though I'm not part of the kitchen staff, I know how incredibly hard it was for him to cut his hours back to only one meal shift and only work five days a week.

However, as much as he loves his domain in the kitchen, he loves his family more. He works Monday days, because the owners all work on Mondays prior to their weekly standing meeting, as well as Friday and Saturday night. The other two days depend on where he's needed to fill in the scheduling gaps with the rest of his grilling staff.

"Thanks again for the lift," Cameron says, a faint blush on her cheeks.

"You're welcome." I shove my hands in my pockets to keep from reaching for her.

Cam walks away, heading down the back hallway that leads to the kitchen. However, she turns left before she reaches the door and enters the employee break room, my eyes trailing her the entire way.

"What are you doing here? I have Jillian on today."

I turn toward the voice, finding Walker standing near the restrooms. "I dropped Cam off."

He nods in understanding, but then waves me over. "You got a minute?"

"Sure," I reply, meeting him over at the end of the bar.

"Jillian quit."

"Wow, really?" I ask, surprised by the news. Jillian has worked here since it opened, serving as the main bartender during the day shift throughout the week.

"Yep. Going to help her husband run his construction business," Walker adds, shaking his head. "Gonna be weird not having her here during the day."

"Probably. So we're hiring someone else?"

"Actually, no," he states, sliding the case of bottles toward the cooler. Together, we work on filling it, even though it was done the previous night. I know he places vendor orders today, so he's making as much room as he can in the walk-in before the delivery. "Kallie's gonna move to days."

That surprises me. "Seriously?"

"Yep. She hinted about it not too long ago. She's wanting to be home more in the evenings with Leo and her dad, so when Jillian turned in her notice at the end of last week, I called her and talked to her. She's gonna finish out the schedule as is this weekend, but next week, she'll be our daytime bartender."

I nod in understanding, happy she's able to make the change. Originally, she preferred evenings because tips are usually better, especially on Friday and Saturday nights. But now she's married and her husband works daytime hours as a mechanic, I can understand them wanting to be on the same shift schedule. Plus, there's no weekends, which means she has more free time at home with her father, as well as Leo's. "Good for her."

"Max is going to pick up more shifts, going from three days a week to five, and Dalton wants any remaining hours, so it'll be just you three, plus Garreth and me behind the bar. You're already at five, so the only changes for you would be who you're working with from time to time."

"That's fine," I assure him, having worked with both Max and Dalton plenty. When Max first started, he was as green as a golf course, but over time, he's grown into one hell of a bartender and server for this side.

Walker stops what he's doing and gives me his full attention. "How's Cameron doing?"

I exhale, but not dramatically. "All right, I think. I'm not sure she likes being alone right now."

He seems to consider my words. "That's understandable. She had a pretty good scare."

"Yeah," I say, picking at invisible lint on my T-shirt. "It's hard watching out for her when we work different hours, you know?" I add, mostly to myself.

"What if we could change that?"

His offer shocks me a little, but I don't hate the idea. "What do you think?"

Crossing his arms over his chest, he says, "Well, we'd have to talk to Garreth, but we could move her to evenings. I know she likes the days better, but for at least a little while, she could work the dinner shifts, coming in with you, and then only being alone for a couple of hours at the end of the night instead of all night."

His suggestion has merit, and I realize I don't hate it. Having her here when I am would give me more opportunities to watch her—and not in a creepy fucker way. Plus, with her car currently out of commission, giving her a ride would be easier.

And that reminds me, I need to figure out how to get her back to my place after work...

"You think Garreth would go for it?" I ask, even though I know he would. If G knew Cameron was terrified to be alone, he'd make sure someone was with her twenty-four seven, and this might be the easiest solution to that problem.

"I'll bring it up during our meeting this afternoon."

I nod and slap him on the back. "Sounds good. Tell G to make it sound like her idea when he talks to her."

Walker chuckles. "Spoken like a true man who knows his woman."

His woman?

Is that what he thinks?

And why does that thought not freak me the fuck out like usual?

I don't contest his statement, mostly because now that I've heard it, I have this weird desire to make it happen, which is stupid because a relationship—and I say that word loosely—wouldn't work out between us. For one, I don't believe in them, and two, work entanglements are the worst idea in the history of all ideas.

Just ignore the fact it worked out for Walker.

And Garreth.

Focus on me here, will ya?

"See ya at four," I tell him, turning to leave, but before I make it too far, my eyes automatically scan the restaurant side, where I spot Cameron stocking silverware bundles in the bin. She gives me a warm smile that makes my balls tingle, and I find the one I offer her is as genuine as they come. Throwing a wave as I go,

I leave the building with thoughts of her and the potential of working the same shift. Seeing her all day and then all evening is probably a terrible idea, but I hope Garreth can make it work. Then, I could keep an eye on her more.

I'm sure that's the main reason.

Her safety is top priority.

The way she makes me feel when she's near is a distant second.

Ha.

Keep telling yourself that.

Cameron

"Got a minute, Cam?" Garreth asks as I'm finishing up my shift.

"Sure thing," I reply, closing out my receipts and handing everything over.

I follow him into his office, taking a quick second to check to see if Kellen is behind the bar yet—he is, by the way—and step inside the small office. "Everything okay?"

"Of course," he replies immediately, allowing me to take a deep breath again. Ever since last summer when he called me in to talk about what I did, I've always gotten a little sweaty in the pits at these impromptu meetings. "Take a seat." When I do, he continues, "How's everything going at Kellen's?"

"Fine," I respond a little too quickly. Clearing my throat, I add, "I mean, it's going well. He's a good host."

Garreth nods. "Okay, listen, there's been some employee changes, and I wanted to run something by you."

I sit up a little straighter in my seat. "Shoot."

"Well, Jillian is stepping away to work with her husband, and Kallie is moving to the lunch shift. Meredith was looking to adjust her shift because she signed up to take night classes at the community college. I'm trying to see if anyone was interested in switching lunch and evenings shifts with her."

I swallow hard, my throat suddenly tight. "Umm," I start, but he keeps going.

"Ideally, I'd like to swap two employees, you know? We have a great team in place right now, and everyone works hard. I don't want to cut back to try to squeeze another lunch server in. That's not fair to anyone."

I nod, my mind reeling.

When I first started here, I trained on both shifts and worked both, but lately, I've stuck to the day shift. I like coming and going during the sunlight hours, especially since my car has always been unreliable. And while I make great tips working the current shift I'm on, I'm aware the dinner crew tends to make more, and that's not a bad idea right now. Considering I'm going to be replacing pretty much everything I own, a little more cash would definitely come in handy, and even though I haven't been able to fix my car yet, I could possibly catch a ride with Kellen on the days we work similar hours.

It sounds like a win-win.

"I might know someone."

His eyes light up. "Who?"

"Me."

He seems a bit taken back. "Really? You'd be interested in working the dinner shift?"

I give him a shrug, averting my gaze. "Well, yeah. I mean, I'm going to have to buy a lot of stuff, and I still have a little money owed to you and Reag."

"That's not a priority, Cam. You'll pay it back when you do."

I'm already shaking my head. "No, I have to keep the schedule we set. I don't want to drag this out any longer than it is. I have a little money saved up, and was hoping I'd be able to pay you guys off early, but now..." I swallow hard. "Since I have to get a new mattress and a few other things, I may not be able to do it as early as I thought."

His eyes soften, and I swear, every time he gives me this proud, big brother look, my eyes start to burn. "You're doing great, Cam. We're very proud of you."

"My point is, that money I've saved is probably going to be used to get a couple of necessities for my house, which means I'll have to stick with our original payment plan."

"I don't want that to cause any worry for you, okay? You'll pay us when you do. If you stick to the original plan, great. If not, we won't hold it against you. And if you're interested in the dinner shift, it's yours. She works four days a week, with the possibility of a fifth."

I already know this is the right step for me to take, and not just because of the extra money or the convenience of working with Kellen, but because I won't be stuck by myself as much, and that thought makes me want to cry with relief. "Sounds good. You know I'll take whatever I can get."

He smiles softly. "I do know that, Cam. You're a helluva worker."

"Thanks," I whisper, my voice small and meek. "I'll let you get back to work," I add, noting it's past time for me to clock out.

"Oh, here," he says, handing me a set of keys. My throat goes dry as I look down at the single key fob and a house key in my palm.

"What's this?" I ask, knowing it's not the one to my POS car parked behind the auto repair shop.

"Kellen asked me to give it to you. It's for his truck."

My eyes widen. "What?"

"He asked me to drop him off at his place after work tonight so you could take his truck home," Garreth states almost too casually as he stands up behind his desk and walks around to where I sit.

"I can't do that," I argue. "Aren't guys territorial about their trucks? What if I wreck it?" I demand, my voice high and pitchy.

He laughs, going to the door and pulling it open. "Are you going to wreck it?"

"No!" I insist.

"Then you have nothing to worry about," he says, his smile sobering as he meets my gaze. "Be careful, Cam, and I'm not talking about you driving the truck. Vehicles can be fixed or replaced. *You* can't."

I move my head up and down, understanding exactly what he's meaning. He's still worried about me, about Cage, and what happened before I got home early Sunday morning.

"I will," I reassure him, reaching out and squeezing his arm. Not because I'm flirting or anything, but because I want to show him how much I appreciate the support.

I step out into the hallway, but before I can move any farther, he adds, "You best go see your goddaughter soon. She's on the verge of rolling over by herself." His smile beams with fatherly pride, and I can't help but flash my own happy grin.

"That's because she takes after me," I quip, knowing I've heard both Garreth and Reagan use that line when their daughter, Evangeline, is doing something amazing.

He barks out a laugh and heads for the kitchen. Instead of going toward the back exit, I decide to walk to the bar. The keys are burning my hand, and I need to address them. I wait at the end of the bar for him to finish pouring drinks for one of the servers, and even though he seems focused on his task, I can still feel his eyes stealing glances at me, so I busy myself with retrieving my phone from my pocket, even though it doesn't have a ton of fancy features. It's a basic monthly prepaid jobby that ensures I can check basic email, make calls, and send texts.

"Hey," he says, stepping up to the counter in front of me. He's wiping his hands off on a towel.

Have his hands always looked that...big?

"Cam?"

My eyes fly up to his face, and I swear my face catches on fire from embarrassment. "What?"

"I said hi," he replies, dropping the towel and placing both hands on the bar top in front of him. He gives me a wide grin, one I know he uses when he's behind the bar, begging for a bigger tip.

"Hi," I squeak out, my throat Sahara dry.

"What's up? Not that I'm not happy to see you," he says, leaving the door cracked open.

"Oh!" I state, shaking my head a little to dislodge the picture of his big hands. "I wanted to give you back your keys. I don't need to use it. I don't mind walking," I insist, holding them out for him.

He reaches forward, closing his hand around mine. It's warm and sends zaps of electricity up my arm. "I insist. There's no point in it just sitting outside in the lot. Take it home, and Garreth can drop me off when we leave."

"That seems unnecessary," I argue, noting his hand is still firmly wrapped around mine.

"Cam, what's unnecessary is you walking home alone, especially when we don't know where Cage is."

A lump forms in my throat.

"I'm not trying to freak you out, honestly, but I think until he's moved on, it's best to be safe than sorry. So take my truck. You don't even have to park it in the garage if it makes you uncomfortable to pull it in."

My voice is weak as I counter, "I don't mind walking."

His sexy little grin curls his lips. "And I don't mind you taking my truck. I insist. Besides, I wouldn't be the best fake boyfriend in the world if I let you walk home."

Kellen winks before releasing my hand, and I feel the loss instantly. "Fine," I grumble, slipping the key fob into my front pocket. "We have something else to talk about, but you're working."

Even though a server has approached the bar again for another drink order, he props his hip against the top and says, "I am, but that doesn't mean you have to leave. Stay. Have dinner."

"Oh—"

"Why don't I call Reag and see if she wants to bring my baby girl up to have dinner with you?" Garreth asks, interrupting the conversation, but I don't mind.

"I'm sure she has other things going on," I counter, as he brings his phone out of his pocket and fires off a text.

Kellen just smiles, probably knowing as well as I do Reagan will probably be here in no time. I could slip out, jump in the truck in the lot and head to Kellen's house, but if I'm being honest, the thought of being there by myself doesn't settle well in my stomach. Plus, I haven't seen Reagan in a while, and I'd really love to catch up with her and see my goddaughter.

Evangeline isn't my goddaughter in an official church capacity. The declaration was made by her tired mom, mere days after giving birth, when I stopped by to meet their new baby. Reagan happily told me I was her godmother, and that was that. End of story.

"Okay, it's all set. When Reag closes down the boutique, she's going to pick Evangeline up from her grandma's house and come here for dinner." He glances at his watch. "Should be about an hour."

I want to argue with him, but it's fruitless. Besides, I'm really excited to see Reagan and Evangeline. "I'll go wait in the employee break room."

"Take the pub table," Kellen states.

"I don't want to waste a spot for paying customers," I counter.

"Look around, love. There's plenty of open tables. Besides, that particular one is reserved for the VIPs of the business," Kellen says before he winks again and walks away.

I try not to think about how easy it is to swoon every time he does that, because I've never been *that* girl.

"He's right, you know. The wives often come in and take those far tables. You might as well go ahead and have a seat. I'll bring you a drink," Garreth says just as a server from in front waves to get his attention.

"You will do no such thing. I can get my own damn water," I insist, giving him a grin before he heads to deal with whatever is happening up front.

I slip behind the bar to grab a glass, feeling Kellen's eyes on me the entire time. I scoop a bit of ice inside before filling it with water and walking over to the far corner pub table. I know the wives and kids come in and use these tables, so I don't feel completely bad for taking up residence here, but then I start to worry about them coming in for dinner. What if they need this seat? I know Reagan will be here, but what if the rest show up too? I've seen it before where the wives will all gather, sometimes with kids, sometimes without, and if that happens, I'll move. I don't belong in their small, intimate group.

Pulling my phone out of my pocket, I key in my passcode and stare at the blank screen. I don't have apps. No games. The social media accounts I have are old, not posting on them since well before my life imploded with Cage. And what would I say now anyway?

Sorry I've been absent on here. My boyfriend left me, dropped seven grand in drug debt in my lap, and trashed my home. Oh, and I stole from my employers too. But the good news is I have a fake boyfriend and we're living together. Go me!

Yeah, definitely not posting that.

Knowing I only have so much data for internet each month and not wanting to waste it, I turn off the screen and push my phone away. I sip my water and watch the late afternoon crowd in the bar. Some are here for drinks, while others take the booths around the sides of the room and enjoy a meal. They all seem happy, content, and I can't stop the tinge of envy that bubbles in my chest. Where did my life go so wrong? Am I not a good enough person to receive a little bit of good too?

I already know the answer to that.

Good people don't steal.

I swallow over the thickness clogging my throat and look away. Suddenly, a phone appears on the table in front of me. The screen unlocked and there's an open folder labeled games. My confused eyes pull up, meeting Kellen's. "You looked bored."

I glance down again, still seeing the phone. "What?"

He backs away but doesn't take the device with him. "I've got tons of games on there you can play to kill time, but if you lose my top ranking in Sudoku, the gloves come off."

Sudoku? Kellen is a puzzle guy? I don't know why this surprises me, but it does. Maybe because he seems more like the Chapters type. You know, the game where you pick what happens in your character's life? I hear there's one with threesomes. Not that I know firsthand or anything, but I've heard customers as well as employees talking.

I tap on the Sudoku app and watch as the game pops up. I almost snort out loud when I see his score. Of course the high number is set on the hard version of the game. I click on a few settings, changing the game to expert, and then I get to work. I know he's still standing behind me, watching, as I make several plays to fill in the squares.

"This is better than porn." His words are hushed, private, and make me laugh. When he meets my eyes, he offers me a wide grin. "I love a woman who can work over...puzzles."

My face flames red as he throws me that trademarked wink and walks away, returning to his post behind the bar. I look down and keep my focus on the screen, slowly weeding my way through numbers and filling in the blank squares to complete the puzzle.

"Hi!"

I startle, looking up and finding Reagan standing beside me. Phone forgotten, I jump up and throw my arms around my friend. The moment she lets go of me; I turn my attention to the smiling baby in the carrier in her hand. "Little princess," I coo, taking the carrier from Reagan and placing it on the ground. With expert fingers, I release the harness buckle and carefully lift the happy baby girl into my arms. "Look at you! I swear you've grown a foot since I saw you two weeks ago," I insist, holding her tightly against my chest and inhaling her clean baby shampoo scent. "I've missed you."

Reagan takes a seat, placing the diaper bag on one of the empty stools beside her. "We started jarred baby food the other day. We're working our way through green vegetables," Reagan boasts, smiling down at her happy daughter.

"Yum," I coo, sounding like one of those crazed women who use baby talk when speaking to a child.

"There's my princess," Garreth announces as he approaches the table. Evangeline, hearing her father's voice, turns in his direction, seeking him out. "Come see Daddy."

I can't help but smile at the exchange of father and daughter. It's evident the sun rises and sets in her little eyes, his love beaming for his child so brightly it makes me tear up a bit.

"Sorry we're late," Madelyn announces as she approaches the table with her daughter, Rose.

"Oh. Hi," I mutter, surprised to see another wife join us.

"Hope it's okay I crash your dinner. Reagan called me when she was leaving the boutique, and I sort of invited myself and Rose along," she notes with a chuckle.

"It's fine. I'm happy you're here," I insist, realizing how true that statement is. I enjoy visiting with all the wives, even if it doesn't happen often.

We visit, eat, and I listen as the two women, cousins by blood, catch up on the ages and stages of both baby girls at the table. Garreth hovers and makes numerous visits to the table, stealing kisses on the cheek from his daughter and always seeming to find his hand on his wife somewhere. Jameson joins us too, holding his own daughter while eating a burger and mountain of fries. Isaac comes down and joins us for a bit too before heading home to be with his wife and son. The entire meal shows a small family unit, a big loving group of those related by blood, as well as united by friendship. It's amazing to watch, and even more spectacular to be drawn into the mix, and that's how they've made me feel sitting here.

Kellen comes by the table, his hand continually landing on the back of my chair, brushing his fingers across my back. With each touch, a shiver sweeps through my veins, and I know it's noticed by the women I'm sitting with. If Reagan knows about our plan to fake a relationship, she's not letting on. In fact, she seems quite pleased by the way he's giving me subtle attention.

When it's time for everyone to leave, I look for the bill for our table, not seeing one. Everyone throws money onto the table in what I assume is the tip for Kellen, and that's when Reagan leans in and whispers, "We eat for free."

"I'm not a wife though. I can pay for my meal," I insist.

She just gives me a small smile, handing over her daughter so I can say goodbye. "They'll never accept your money. Just leave a little for a tip, Cameron. That's how we do it. Don't argue," she replies with a smile.

I run my nose against the baby's head, committing the scent to memory, before returning my goddaughter to her mother to be secured in her carrier once more. "Thanks for joining me for dinner."

She pulls me into a hug. "Stop by soon."

"I will," I confirm.

"And bring that guy who can't keep his eyes off you." When she pulls back, there's mischief in her eyes.

My cheeks burn as I mutter a quiet, "What?"

Reagan chuckles and shakes her head. "Play coy, that's fine. We have lots to talk about. I can tell."

And then she's gone, leaving me standing by the table, my mouth gaping open as she goes to tell her husband goodbye. Am I that easy to read? Can she tell I've been fantasizing about Kellen, especially after falling asleep in his arms? But what I don't get is the part about him not being able to keep his eyes off me. He's a good actor, I know it. I can tell he's playing his part of the boyfriend to a T.

That's all it is.

Has to be.

Seventeen 17

Kellen

I watch as she moves away from the table and disappears down the back hallway. I can't help but wonder if she's slipping out and heading home, and what's more alarming is the fact I wish she would have come over to say goodbye first. But then I see her return with her small wristlet purse she uses and pull cash from within, and I'm on the move.

"There's no charge for dinner tonight," I maintain, collecting what's left of the dishes, even though Garreth already taken care of the majority of them.

"Oh. This is a tip."

"Not necessary," I state, refusing to take the cash she places on the table.

"Please, Kellen, I insist. I'd rather pay for my entire meal, but something tells me that's not happening. Please let me put money toward your tip."

I turn my attention to her and get lost in those gorgeous green eyes. I seriously could stare at them all day long and never get tired of them. They make me want to dive into the deep pools of green and do the backstroke. I also realize by the slight lift of her chin and the firmness swimming in those eyes, she's not about to let me get away with some bullshit excuse to not take her tip. She'll leave it on the table, even after I've cleaned it off.

Choosing to ignore the whole thing, I pick up the remaining dishes and ask, "Heading home?"

She doesn't call me on the fact it's not *her* home, it's my home, and I'm ignoring the bubbles of excitement I feel when I don't get all panicky at the statement, because the last thing I've ever expected or planned was to share my space with someone else. At least long term.

"Yes, are you sure you don't want me to just walk?"

I narrow my eyes, letting her know I'm getting annoyed at this conversation rehash.

She sighs. "Fine, but if you want me to come back at closing and pick you up, I'm more than willing."

"I'm good, Cam. Go home and relax. Garreth will drop me off."

"All right," she mutters softly, looking everywhere else but at me.

It's on the tip of my tongue to ask her if she'll be waiting for me in my bed tonight. She's slipped into it twice now, and the prospect of finding her there when I get home causes my cock to twitch with anticipation. Needing to move away from her before I completely embarrass myself, I start to move toward the kitchen. "Hey, let me know when you get home, okay?"

She nods, making sure she has everything and heads for the back exit. I notice she slips inside the bathroom first, which gives me time to drop off the remaining dirty dishes in the kitchen. When I leave, she's exiting the restroom and stops in front of me. We're suddenly close in the dimly lit hallway, and this overwhelming sensation to take her in my arms and kiss her is almost overpowering.

I step forward, invading her personal space, my eyes locked on hers. I can feel this invisible pull, this tug from a string no one can see, and I'll be damned if I'm strong enough to fight it. My hands lift, pushing a strand of her beautiful auburn hair off her forehead. The touch is...intimate, one I'm not accustomed to making. My hand, while steady, is usually a little rougher where women are concerned, but for some unknown reason, I find myself moving with a delicacy unfamiliar to even myself.

"Oh, sorry, didn't mean to—Oh! Hey, you two!"

Cameron jumps back as if we were in a much more compromising position than we were, and while I would much rather keep my gaze locked on her, I slowly turn to face Jenna, one of the servers. "Hi, Jenna. Sorry we're blocking the restroom," I state, giving her an easy, carefree grin as I step back, gently placing my hand on Cameron's arm to shift her out of the way.

Jenna's eyes bounce between Cameron and me, and I can practically see those wheels in her head spinning. Oh, the gossip mill will be churning wildly within an hour. Most likely a group text message will go out with accusations and speculations over what she just witnessed in the hall.

I won't confirm or deny anything, however, because at the end of the day, we want people to believe we're dating. All it will take is a few people to see something and share it, and it will get back to Cage in no time. Small towns and gossip go better together than Jack and Coke.

"You better get home, love. See you when I get off," I whisper just loud enough for Jenna to hear, especially since she's made no move toward the restroom. Then, I lean in and press my lips against Cam's. The kiss is gentle, tender, and somewhat chaste, but surprisingly, packs a hard punch.

When Cameron whimpers the sweetest sound, I pull back, knowing I'm two seconds away from throwing her over my shoulder and ravishing her in the first available office I can find. Not needing to take this gossip quite that far, I run a finger across her cheek as I whisper, "Have a safe drive home."

She mumbles something I don't understand, her eyes still closed. Her lips are plump and ripe for kissing, and I have to dig down deep to physically step back from where she stands. I throw a wink at Jenna before turning and walking back to the bar. Only when I get there do I glance back at the hallway and see Cameron standing there, her fingers pressed to her mouth.

Good thing I walked away when I did, or I'm liable to kiss her all over again.

Cameron says goodbye to Jenna before practically running out the back exit.

There's a big smile on my face for the rest of the night, and not because I'm flirting and raking in the tips hand over fist. Because I'm thinking of Cameron, of kissing her, and knowing she's at my place, waiting.

This night better hurry the fuck up.

There's a handful of lights on when Garreth pulls into my driveway, and while the overhead kitchen light flips off immediately, the rest seem to stay on. I'm going to have to get to the bottom of this. If she's scared, I want to help. I think her working the same shift as me will aid in overcoming that fear, since she won't be here by herself as much, but it's more than that. I want to help her slay whatever dragons are lurking in the shadows.

"Thanks for the lift," I state, releasing my belt and opening the door.

"So, it's already all around about you and Cam. Apparently, Jenna caught you two making out in the hallway?"

I fight the smile threatening to spread across my lips. "Well, it wasn't quite like that. I didn't kiss her until we had the audience. I knew as soon as it happened, the dirt about us would spread like wildfire."

He nods slowly, his throat working to swallow. I can tell he has something to say.

"Just say it." I want to get into the house and see Cameron.

"There's been a lot of negative gossip about her already," he states matter-of-factly, a hint of regret in his eyes. "This is going to cause more. I didn't think that through," he adds, almost to himself.

"I won't let it affect her negatively, G. She doesn't deserve that."

"No, she doesn't. She didn't deserve it before either, but sometimes shit happens and it's out of your control."

Now it's my turn to have difficulty swallowing. "I'll do my best to keep her from getting dragged into more bullshit drama."

He nods. "Thanks."

I hop out, and before I close the door, add, "Have a good night."

"You too," he replies before backing out of the driveway and heading for home.

I walk quickly to the back door, even though my body is worn down from being on my feet all night. Sliding the key into the lock, I disarm the alarm, only to relock the door and arm it once more. My cock is already getting hard at the thought of her being somewhere in here, my eyes searching for any sign of her. I plan to stop by the fridge to grab a bottle of water, but I detour to the living room where I find Cameron sitting behind my drum set.

Not at them.

Behind it.

On the floor.

"Hey," I whisper softly, crouching down beside her.

Her eyes are wide as she looks up at me, and as if I were to snap my fingers, she flinches and shakes her head. When she doesn't respond, I ask, "Why are you on the floor?"

Cameron looks around, seeming as surprised as I am, but then she looks at me once more and humiliation fills her features.

"I, umm...well, I was sitting here for a moment, looking at your drums when I...heard you at the back door. No matter how much I tried to tell myself it was you, I just couldn't escape the voice in my head telling me to hide."

My heart hurts just a little more than anticipated as I look at her pained eyes. "It's okay. It's normal to be scared, remember?"

She nods, placing her hand in mine as I gently help guide her to standing. Only, I don't move us out of the alcove in the living room. Instead, I take a seat at the drums and pull her onto my lap.

"I just don't like this feeling of weakness," she whispers, her fingers reaching out and tracing the edge of the snare drum in front of us.

"That I understand. We're hardwired not to show it, especially with something that causes us pain."

She nods, her finger tapping on the drum and filling the space with a soft sound.

An idea hits me. "Come here," I instruct, shifting her body so she's straddling my legs, facing forward. I grab the set of drumsticks from the basket beside the stool and take them in my hands. "Let's play."

Cam snorts. "I don't know how to play!" she bellows with a laugh.

"I'll show you. Hold the sticks like this," I instruct, helping her position them properly in her hands. With my hands wrapped around hers, I move them into position above the drum. "Ready?"

"If you say so," she mutters, her chuckle vibrating her back against my chest.

Hands poised, I bring the tips of the sticks down on the drum and slowly tap out a beat. I adjust my foot to add in a little bass, and even though I'd love to bring the tom into it, I opt to keep it simple.

By the time I've helped her play for a few minutes, I stop, unable to take my eyes away from her smile. "Is your whole family musically inclined?" she asks, her eyes on me.

"Just me and my sister. I taught her everything she knows though," I say, the long-standing joke easy to spout off, knowing it's complete bullshit. I've already told Cam how my sister taught me to play the drums. I'm so glad I did too, because it's one of the few things I'll always cherish from our childhood not tainted with anger and hatred.

"I'm sure you did," she replies with the shake of her head, clearly not believing a word I said.

"Sometimes playing helps me relax," I tell her, lightly beating the sticks against the drum once more.

"I can see that. There's something about music that's soothing," she whispers, a hint of exhaustion in her words.

We play in silence for several minutes, and when I start to pound out the melody to my sister's most popular song, Cameron hums along. She leans her head back against my shoulder and closes her eyes, letting me control her hands as she hums. I turn my head slightly, my mouth and nose angled into her neck. It would be so easy to brush my lips across the delicate skin, then kiss behind her ear, to make her moan.

But I don't.

Now isn't the time, despite my dick disagreeing.

He has a compelling argument, but I don't want to push her into doing something during a moment of weakness. I refuse to take advantage of her while she's vulnerable, so instead of placing my lips against her, I commit the feel of her body and the scent of her vanilla and lavender shampoo to memory.

It'll come in handy later when I'm jacking off in the shower.

Pervert.

When I reach the end of the song, I contemplate starting another, but I know she's tired. I can feel it seeping through her pores, ebbing from her body. As if knowing this is the end, Cameron stands up, her lean legs straddling me. To keep from reaching for her hips and pulling her back down to my lap, I drop the sticks in the basket and push back on the wheeled stool. She shifts, walking around to the front of the drum set and giving me a small grin. "Thank you."

"Anytime you want to play, just let me know," I tell her, adding in a flirty wink because I can't help myself.

The tips of her ears turn red before her cheeks, as she nods. "I can't wait. We'll definitely play again soon."

And I'll be fucking damned if my cock doesn't try to claw its way out of my jeans to get to her. The insinuation was clear, the flirty banter so unexpected and welcomed. It's something I haven't experienced much from her, especially since she moved into my guest room.

And now?

Now I want to hear her flirty comments nonstop, wondering how far she'll take it.

Not that I'll find out tonight, but maybe someday down the road. Actually, the thought of flirty banter turning into more, perhaps even getting naked with her, has a lot of merit, and not just because I'm a horny guy. The thought of *her* whispering dirty innuendos is enough to make my dick hard for days.

I suppose that's a bridge I'll cross if we ever get there.

Until then, I won't take this any further than the friendship I've offered, because that's exactly what she's expecting from me. I'm her friend and coworker, and I'm helping her out during a trying situation.

My dick could do wonders to remember that.

As if on cue, I hear her door creak open and her soft footfalls pad across the hall. Like the last couple of nights since her arrival, I've left my door cracked open in case she needs me. For a third night in a row, she's creeping into my bedroom, and I'm pulling back the bedding in invitation.

This time, she doesn't face away from me when I draw her to my chest. She remains facing me and wraps her arms around my midsection. The sweetest little sigh slips from her lips as she moves her head, wedging it between my neck and my jaw. It amazes me how well she fits against me.

"I'm sorry I keep invading your bed," she whispers, yet makes no move to leave or adjust her position.

"Don't apologize, Cam. You're welcome here anytime." I'm shocked by how right it feels to confess that. I enjoy having her in my bed, and the fact I haven't even gotten busy with her while in it is pretty startling.

I remain quiet, hoping she goes to sleep quickly. I know she hasn't had the easiest time catching ZZ's in the guest room, so if having her beside me helps her rest peacefully, then I'm fine. My bed and my arms are tribute for the cause.

She sighs, her warm breath tickling my skin. "I switched shifts with another server, so starting next week, I'll be working the dinner shift with you."

"Yeah?" I ask quietly, having to refrain from running my finger across her shoulder just to touch her skin.

"Yep. Garreth said Meredith is starting night school, and she asked about switching to days. Since we're both going to the same place, I figured it might be easier for us to catch a ride together. Or at least until my car is fixed. I'll pay for gas too. I don't expect you to just give me a ride every day without contributing," she insists, her words coming out in a big rush.

"I'm not worried about it," I tell her, knowing what's coming next.

"You might not be, but I am."

And that's one of the things I respect about her. She's not taking advantage of me and wants to make sure she's pulling her weight in regards to everything.

"How about on the nights we work together, you don't worry about it. I'd be driving there anyway, right? The other nights, you can just take my truck."

"And put gas in it," she insists, making me smile. Mostly because I've already talked to Garreth about making sure we're scheduled together for the time being. As long as she's here because of Cage, I'm sticking to her like a shadow.

After a few minutes of silence, she murmurs, "Night, Kellen."

Instinct has me shifting my arm and casually drawing her closer. "Night, Cam. See you in the morning."

She drifts off a few minutes later, her body sagging in my embrace. I could—and probably should—carefully roll her over and keep my distance. Finding so much pleasure just holding her in my arms is the last thing I want—and need.

Yet, I make no move as I close my own eyes and feel the heaviness of the long work night start to drag me under.

If anything, I hold her a little tighter.

Cameron

My body is warm. I rock my hips, trying to put a little separation between me and the heat, but then I reach for it to bring it closer. It's a weird cycle of push and pull, and it's oddly addictive.

Fire spreads through my veins as I gyrate, the pleasure slowly increasing. My legs spread farther apart, and the pressure on my clit intensifies. Pushing back, I grind against the steel length behind me, letting it glide between my ass cheeks, despite the fact there's material between us.

My hands move to my head. No, not my head. Another head. My fingers grip hair, tugging and pulling strands as the euphoria continues. Warm breath and a hot mouth lick and nip at my neck, kissing my fevered skin. A single hand slips beneath my pajama top and cups my breast, pinching my nipple and driving me absolutely wild. The other hand works its way into my bottoms, immediately contacting wetness and gliding between my lips.

A moan fills the stifling air around me, as I continue to rock against big fingers. I squeeze my eyes shut as an orgasm builds, praying this dream doesn't end before I cross the finish line. My body tenses, the hard cock at my ass presses against me more, gliding faster and faster, creating glorious friction.

My fingers dig at the scalp, clawing at flesh, as firm hands work me over. Two fingers press inside of my pussy, which instantly clenches down. "Let me in," a voice whispers. It's deep, husky, and laced with desire. It's also recognizable, and not surprisingly so. Kellen McGregor has starred in every sexual fantasy I've had in the last few weeks, so why would tonight be any different?

I whimper as my legs relax enough for two fingers to glide inside. They go all the way too, buried to the knuckle. His thumb brushes across my clit, and it's the magic trigger that detonates this bomb. I come hard, my muscles clenching around his fingers as waves of pure bliss race through my veins. "Kellen," I moan, his name the only one my brain will entertain in a moment like this.

Even O's in this dream are proving to be better than any I could give myself.

My ass moves, rolling against his erection until he pauses and groans, moving his own hips in small pumps. I've never had a man come against my ass like this, especially with a clothing barrier, but I like it. A lot. It's incredibly erotic and makes my pussy spasm with more building desire.

He continues to toy with my nipple, pinching it harder than before and causing little tinges of pain that's most definitely turning to pleasure. He keeps moving his fingers, my release coating his hand as he cups my pussy and thrusts his digits back inside. "Oh God," I whisper, feeling a second release building even faster than the first.

I hold on tight, my hands gripping the sides of his head as he thrusts his cock against my ass in time with his fingers. "Give me another, Cam. I want to feel you come on my hand again." He grunts, biting down on my neck.

Then, suddenly, his pinky is there, gliding around my back entrance in a way I've never experienced. The intimate and slightly forbidden touch is enough to trigger my second orgasm. This one steals my breath, my ability to see, and my sanity. It's so intense, I wonder if I blackout from the pleasure.

"Someone's a naughty girl," he whispers against my ear as my legs shake and my hips move entirely on their own. "The thought of you being dirty makes my dick so hard, Cam. I want to see you riding it from every position. I want to see you swallow it until I come down your throat. I want to hear you cry my name so many times you're hoarse for days, your pussy sore from taking my cock a million times."

I whimper at his words, shocked to like them as much as I do. I've never been one to experiment with sex, the men I've been with being more focused on getting themselves off, but dreaming about trying new things with Kellen might be the best thing to ever happen to me.

"Best fucking dream ever," he mutters against my neck, nuzzling against my sweaty skin as he removes his fingers from my body, his other hand still cupping my breast.

It's in that moment I realize my eyes are open.

Not closed.

And they have been for a while.

This wasn't a sex dream.

This was real.

"Kellen?" I whisper.

I feel him go rigid behind me, and I'm not talking about his cock. His masterful hands still, and it's as if all the air is sucked out of the room. "Cam?"

"Yep," I croak out over a suddenly dry throat and mouth, my mind replaying what he did, how I felt, and what he said. Embarrassment hits with the force of a thousand semis, but I realize quickly it's not because of *what* we did, but because I really liked it.

A lot.

He still hasn't moved. I'm not sure he's breathing at this moment. "I...uh..."

"Thought you were dreaming," I finish for him, releasing my hands from his hair.

"Yeah," he mumbles. He must realize where his hands are too, because he lets go of my breast and carefully extracts the other from my sleep shorts.

"Me too," I confirm.

I can practically feel him distancing himself from me, even though he hasn't done it physically yet, and the last thing I want to feel is regret right now. "Listen, Cam—"

"Wait," I interrupt, needing to say my piece first before I'm unable to. Maybe it's the double orgasms talking, but he needs to hear what I want to say. I sit up and turn around, cradling the sheet to my chest, even though I'm wearing my sleep shirt still. Call it an emotional shield, if you will, just in case this backfires on me.

Taking a deep breath, I meet his gaze. "I admit, I thought I was having a dream, but it was a pretty good one. Best dream I've ever had, in fact," I say with a small grin on my lips. "But I don't regret it. I'm not embarrassed we did what we did, as long as you're not." I swallow over the lump in my throat, over the fear of him not agreeing with me, as I ask, "Do you regret it?"

His eyes don't give any indication of what he's thinking. They're wide and a little hesitant, and I can definitely tell he's blaming himself for having his hands all over me, despite the fact I had mine all over him. I don't know who made the first move, but to me, that doesn't matter.

He inhales loudly as he mutters, "No, I don't regret it, but I'd never take advantage of you, Cam, and that's what I did."

"But did you? Because in my dream, I clearly remember pressing back against you and loving the way your cock got hard."

Kellen McGregor blushes.

Yes, ladies and gentlemen, his face turns as red as a tomato.

"What?" I ask.

He doesn't avert his gaze as he says, "Quit talking about my cock and getting hard. It's making me hard."

A bubble of laughter slips from my lips. "Okay, then. My point is, I may not have been looking to ride your hand until I came twice, but it happened. And I'm not sorry. Are you sorry?"

He seems torn with himself, as if he doesn't want to like what happened, but unable to deny it either. After several very long seconds, he states, "No. No, Cam, I'm not sorry."

"Good," I reply, throwing the blanket off and sliding from the bed. "I'm going to go shower," I add, heading for the door. As I reach the doorjamb, I pause and glance over my shoulder. "Oh, and, Kellen?"

His wide eyes look at me, but he doesn't say a word.

"Thanks for the orgasms."

And then I leave the room, cross the hall to the guest room, and head straight for the shower. Not because I need to wash him off my skin, but because I feel ready to start my day. For the first time in a very long time, I feel rejuvenated, alive, and ready to tackle whatever comes my way.

With a smile on my face and a buzz still zipping through my veins, I step into the bathroom with a bit more confidence than I had before.

I like it.

My phone buzzes in my pocket as I pour myself a cup of coffee, and I automatically smile when I see my friend's name on the screen. I take my first sip, enjoying the fact Kellen makes enough for two, before I click on the screen and her message pops up.

Reagan: Hey, how's your Tuesday going?

Me: Fine. Enjoying a cup of coffee before work.

Reagan: I was just talking to some of the wives and we're all off Sunday. We thought we'd meet you over at your place and help you start to get it cleaned and sorted.

Like a bucket of cold water, my high from the early morning bedroom activities is doused away. I know I need to return to my rental house and start sorting through the shambles of my life, but I've been enjoying this Kellen bubble I find myself in. Despite being afraid to be alone when the darkness falls, I'd rather be here than at my old place.

And that alone is a big problem, which is why I fire off a response.

Me: I'm off Sunday, so that works. And starting Monday, I'm switching to the dinner shift, so my days are free.

Reagan: Perfect! Lyndee says she'll bring pastries. Mallory has lunch with Walker's family at noon but will come by afterward. She said she'd see if her mother-in-law will watch the kids so Walker can help with the heavy stuff. Garreth is working, but Madelyn said Jameson will come too and help keep the kids busy.

A smile spreads across my face. Jameson Tankersley was the last person on earth I suspected would love kids like he does. He's gruff and intimidating, but when he's around kids, he turns into a big teddy bear.

Me: Sounds good. I think Kellen works, but maybe he'll let me borrow his truck to haul away the broken stuff.

Reagan: I'll have Garreth's truck too, so between the two, we should be good.

Me: Okay. What time works for you all?

Reagan: Is 10 too early? You don't work Saturday night, do you?

Me: No, 10 is good.

Reagan: Perfect. See you then!

I set my phone down and stare at it as I reach for my cup of coffee.

"Morning," Kellen says as he strolls into the kitchen looking freshly showered. He heads straight for the coffee pot and pours himself a big cup. "Hungry?" he asks, taking a sip.

My eyes betray me completely and automatically drop to his crotch. I recall the feel of it pressed against me and the noises he made while he came.

"Knock it off," he growls, drawing my eyes back up to his.

Instead of blushing the way I expect, I shrug and casually take small sips of my coffee, peeking at him over the mug. "I could eat."

He moves with ease around the kitchen, pulling a small waffle maker from the pantry, as well as a box of mix, then goes to the fridge and grabs a pint of blueberries. He gets to work mixing up the batter, while warming the small, round device that'll cook the waffles. I'm oddly fascinated by watching him work, especially because each day brings something new. I've only been here a handful of days, but each one has been an adventure of sorts.

"I didn't even think to ask. You like waffles, right? I can make yours with or without blueberries."

"Who doesn't love waffles?"

He flashes me a grin. "Weirdos."

I bark out a laugh before heading to the fridge. I grab the butter and syrup, placing them both in the middle of the table before going to the cabinets to retrieve plates and silverware.

Kellen places the first waffle on my plate and waves me to the table to get started. By the time I have my waffle doctored up, he's got one on his plate too. He cooks a third one while piling butter on his breakfast and dousing it in enough syrup to feed a small country.

As we eat, he shifts in his seat. I can tell something's on his mind, but I don't want to pressure him into talking. We're friends, in a fairly loose form of the term, but after what we experienced together this morning in his bed, I feel like we're also more than that. It's a weird place to be in, and I can't help but wonder if he feels the same.

"So, I was thinking," he says, his mouth full of food as he chews. Once he swallows, he nervously adjusts himself in his seat again, which suddenly makes me a little nervous. "This Saturday, I'm off. Kallie is back and she's working with Max and Walker. I know you work days, but I was thinking...we need to be seen out all coupley in order for it to get back to Cage we're dating, right? There's this movie in the park thing, and it would be a good place to be seen. And we can grab a pizza beforehand, if you want."

I fight the smile threatening to spread across my lips, because nervous Kellen is cute as hell. He's slightly fumbling with his words and his body language is nothing like what I've witnessed while he's working. This version of the confident, cocky man I know is much more endearing, and I really like it.

"If you think you'll be too tired, that's fine. No obligations. I was just thinking—"

"I'd love to," I interrupt with a little too much eagerness.

He seems to relax a little as he offers me a friendly smile. "Yeah?"

I nod. "I haven't been to one of the movies in the park since I was in high school." I leave out the part about Cage thinking they were stupid, even though I loved the idea. "Do you know what's playing?"

"Umm, *Ferris Bueller's Day Off*."

"Are you kidding me? I'm there!" I proclaim, super excited to see the cheesy eighties teen movie I used to love watching growing up. My parents had tons of DVDs, so I'd watch all the classics like *Pretty in Pink, Breakfast Club, Footloose, Sixteen Candles, Goonies,* and my personal favorite, *Steel Magnolias.* They were all made well before my time, but I didn't care. I loved them all and would watch them repeatedly.

"Do you have a big crush on Matthew Broderick?"

"Totally. I probably won't even realize you're there Saturday night," I quip, surprising even myself by my flirty comment.

He awards me with one of his panty-melting grins. "Oh yeah? I'm pretty sure I can make you forget all about him. By the end of the night, it'll be Matthew Broderick who?"

I giggle, pushing my plate aside, too full to eat anymore. "Will there be popcorn?"

He tsks. "Of course."

I consider my options for a few moments before replying, "Popcorn will get you public hand-holding. If you're looking for blanket cuddles, I'm going to require some Twizzlers too."

He leans forward, his eyes glued to my mouth. "And what about kissing? Is there a kissing option on the menu?"

My tongue slips out, quickly licking my dry lips. I didn't even mean to do it, but his reaction is instantaneous. His eyes widen as he bites down on his own bottom lip, as if picturing more than just stealing a few kisses in the park under the night sky. "Kissing, huh? It's a menu option. I'm thinking one of those Coke freezes and some nachos."

"Nachos, huh? That's all it'll take to kiss you in public? I'll buy out the entire concession stand of chips and cheese," he quips with a wink.

Clearing my throat, I decide to mention the text I received earlier. "Reagan messaged me. She and a few other wives are willing to help me clean my rental this Sunday."

Kellen studies me closely, and even though we've really only known each other a short time, I feel like he can already read me like a book. "Are you ready for that?" he finally asks, the concern evident in his voice.

"I think so. I mean, I have to do it at some point, right?" I ask, offering a small smile I'm sure doesn't reach my eyes.

His eyes assess me before giving me a nod. "Yeah. I have to work at four, but I can help before that."

"Okay, thanks."

After several long moments of just staring at each other, he finally pushes away from the table and stands, collecting our plates and taking them to the sink. "I have an idea," he says, turning around, leaning his backside against the counter.

"I'm washing and you're drying?" I ask, earning me a bark of laughter.

"Nope, the dishes can wait. Let's go for a ride."

"A ride? In what?"

He just smiles a wide, mischievous grin, and something tells me I'm in for quite a ride.

Scary part is, I don't seem worried about not knowing.

I trust him.

That's the main reason I reply honestly with a simple, "Let's go."

Kellen

She jumps on the bike and gives me a smile. "Ready," she announces after adjusting the gears on my sister's ten-speed bike.

I flash her a grin and push off, aiming my own bike down the driveway and toward the street. I check the rearview mirror attached to my handlebars to make sure she's close or if I need to adjust my pace but am surprised to see she's hanging right with me.

I take us on my usual route to the bike path through the park. Once we arrive, I'm pleasantly surprised not to see a lot of other bikes. It is a weekday morning, which thankfully means we won't be dealing with extra riders on the trails like you would in the evenings or weekends.

We make it through the park, and when we reach the end of the trail, I pull over beside a picnic table. We both disembark from our bikes, Cameron taking a seat on the top of the table as soon as she has the kickstand down. I silently berate myself for not bringing water, even though I knew it would be a shorter ride. I'm fine, but I should have some to offer her, since she may not ride nearly as much as I do.

"Do you know how long it's been since I've been on the bike trail?" she asks, swinging her legs and leaning back on her hands. She looks so casual, so carefree.

So fucking beautiful.

I walk over and take a seat on the bench beside her, and even though she's close enough to touch as she relaxes on the picnic tabletop, I don't. If I touch her, I may not be able to stop myself from taking it further than it should go. "A while, I'll assume?"

She turns and gives me a small grin. "My former best friend, Aneeka, used to ride all the time after school before we'd go home to study or do homework."

"Former?" I ask, knowing I haven't heard her refer to an Aneeka before now.

She looks away, staring off into the trees as they lightly blow in the breeze. "We're not friends anymore. When I started dating Cage, she wasn't a fan of his. As his manipulation of me grew, she tried to tell me he wasn't good for me, but..."

"But you didn't listen," I deduce.

Shaking her head, she whispers, "Nope. I didn't listen, which is why she pulled away from our friendship. Looking back now, I regret letting that happen so much."

I stay quiet, even though I'm unable to keep from reaching for her now. I place my hand over hers and give it a gentle squeeze. "If you only knew then what you know now, right?" I give her the hint of a smile.

"Yeah."

"But, on the bright side, if all that shit wouldn't have happened, you might not be living with a sexy beast of a roommate, letting him fix you gourmet breakfasts every day, and teaching you how to play the drums at night," I josh, winking the moment she looks my way.

A wide smile spreads across her kissable lips, making my dick twitch in my pants. All I've been able to think about since she

189

left my bedroom this morning to go shower is what that mouth would feel like wrapped around my cock, and thinking about it right now, in this moment, really isn't a good idea. "So far, he's proving to be a great fake boyfriend."

I bark out a laugh as my phone rings. I pull it from my pocket and spot my sister's name on the screen. I always get a little worried when she calls, mostly because she doesn't usually call me during the morning. She performs at night, meets fans both before and after a show, unwinds and decompresses afterward, and then sleeps while traveling to the next location. Usually when she calls, it's in the evening, when she's getting ready for the upcoming show.

"I gotta take this a minute," I tell Cameron, holding up the phone. She nods quickly as I stand and press the connect button. "Hey."

"Good morning, big brother."

"Everything okay?" I ask, pacing back and forth beside the picnic table.

"Yeah, why?"

I take a deep breath. "You never call me in the morning, Kins." I notice Cameron take notice of the name I say, so when I look up and meet her gaze, I offer a small grin.

"I'm fine, Kel. I'm at home, getting ready to go to the studio. Mom wants to have dinner with me tonight."

"Yeah? You going?"

"Probably. We usually have dinner at least once a week."

"How's she doing?"

"Good. Staying busy with her reading club."

I decide to ask the loaded question. "And how's Dad?"

Kinsley snorts. "Same as always," she grumbles, and I'm certain she's referring to the fact he's shacked up with a woman barely older than his youngest child. I wish I could say she was even the woman he cheated on our mom with, but there were many over the course of several years. Aleshia is just the latest in a long list of indiscretions our dad seems to gravitate toward.

Just when I open my mouth to smart off something I probably shouldn't say, Cameron swings her arms in front of her face and squeals loudly. I watch as she swats at the bee buzzing near her head before she jumps off the picnic table and dances around.

"Who was that?" my sister asks, a mixture of worry and humor in her question.

"What?"

"That woman. She sounded close," Kinsley states.

I glance over and smile as Cameron finally calms down, the pesky bee no longer swarming her face.

"Kellen? What's going on?"

"Nothing, Kins. Just a friend."

"Oh my God! You have a friend? Who is she?"

I roll my eyes, as Cameron sits back down, her eyes apologetic. "A friend."

"What's her name?" my sister hedges, clearly not going to let this go.

"Cameron."

"Cameron? Can I talk to her?"

"What? No, you can't talk to her," I argue, turning my back to the beauty sitting on the table.

"Yes. Otherwise, I'll tell Mom at dinner tonight you have a girlfriend."

I swallow hard.

"And it's serious. She'd love to hear all about your quest for babies—"

"Fine, but behave."

My sister giggles. "Who, me?"

"Yeah, you," I grumble, pulling the phone from my ear and turning to face Cameron. "My sister wants to talk to you."

Her eyes go comically wide. "What?" she hisses as I take a step her way.

I wave the phone in front of her and add, "She won't let this go, so you might as well say hello."

"To your sister...the country music superstar," she mutters, as if she can't believe it herself.

"She's just a person. A complete pain in the ass, annoying, bratty sister, but still a person," I say as I hold the phone toward me.

"I can hear you!" Kinsley bellows through the phone line.

I bring the device back to my ear as I state, "I know." Then, to Cameron, I hand over the phone and add, "Say hi."

Cameron takes the phone and with shaky hands brings it to her ear. "He-hello?"

My pacing gets worse than it was when I first answered that call. And why the hell did I answer it anyway? I should have just let her go to voicemail, which is exactly what I'll do from now on.

"Oh, umm, we work together." She turns wide, panicked eyes my way. "Y-yes?" Before I can just rip the phone away from her and tell my sister to kick rocks, Cameron busts out laughing. "Really? He did that?"

My heart drops in my chest as I groan. "Give me the phone," I demand playfully, holding out my hand.

She shakes her head and turns away from me. "Keep going." She gasps, giggling like she's talking to a long-lost friend. My sister, the traitorous woman she is, is probably sharing every embarrassing story she can think of about me.

"The phone, Cam," I state, heading her way and reaching for the device.

The woman moves quickly though, easily deflecting my blocks and grabs, trying to get her off the phone with my sister before she kills any chance I have at stealing more kisses from Cam because she'll know all of the mortifying stuff from my past.

"My sister is a liar with a drinking problem. You can't believe anything she says," I argue, even though Kinsley doesn't.

Cam just rolls her eyes at my blatant lie. "She says stop making up lies about her, or she'll tell me all about the sixth-grade field trip."

I groan, snatching the phone away from the woman holding it. "I hate you," I state bluntly the moment I have the device back to my ear.

She's laughing, as is Cameron, who returns to her sitting position on top of the picnic table. "You do not. You love me."

I refuse to concede, even though she knows I do.

"I like her."

Me too.

But I don't speak those words aloud. Instead, I let her talk, because she's going to do it anyway.

"There's a story you haven't shared, but that's okay. It's not the right time to talk."

She's like a dog with a bone, and I know she'll be bugging me later for the details I haven't given her yet. "She's a friend from work. She needed a little help."

"And you were more than willing to help her," she derives.

"How's the tour going?" I ask, changing the subject.

I can hear the smile in her voice as she replies, "Amazing."

"I'm thinking of catching the Philly show."

She gasps and squeals in delight. "Really? That would be so...I don't even have a word for it."

I smile at her excitement, making a mental note to get the night off when I go into work later. "It's not guaranteed, but I'll try. Work has been a little crazy lately."

"You best not let me down, Kellen McGregor. I'll have tickets waiting for you at will-call. If I look out into that crowd and don't see your ugly face, I'm going to post all your embarrassing photos on my social media accounts, and I recently just hit seven million followers. That's seven million sets of eyes seeing you in your Batman underwear and a pillowcase cape, my friend."

"You're a terrible person," I tell my sister, smiling as I speak the bullshit words. She's the best person I know, even when she's blackmailing me.

She snorts a very unladylike noise. "You better be there, Mister. I'll have two tickets waiting."

"Two?" I ask, my throat constricting as I try to speak.

"I want to meet the woman who's finally cracked through that hard wall surrounding your heart."

"Okay, Dr. Phil. I better go."

"Fine, but I better see both of your asses in the seats I'll reserve for you," she says.

"I'll see what I can do," I reply casually. Mostly because I can't say for certain when this thing with Cameron will end.

"Love you, Kel."

"Love you more, brat."

She's giggling as I hang up, and like always after speaking to her on the phone, I feel lighter. Slipping my phone back into my pocket, I spin around and give Cameron a sheepish grin. "So, that was Kinsley."

Cameron nods. "I can't believe I just talked to *the* Kinsley McGregor. That might be the highlight of my year."

My eyes narrow just a bit. "I'll try not to take offense to that."

She gives me a coy little grin that makes my balls tingle. "She's kind of a big deal."

I point at her. "She's a menace. And a liar. What did she tell you?"

Big innocent green eyes stare back at me. "Nothing, I swear."

Now it's my turn to bark out a laugh. "Yeah, whatever." Glancing over at the bikes, I add, "You ready to ride back?"

"Yep," Cameron says eagerly, jumping off the picnic table and heading toward my sister's bike.

As I reflect back over the last hour—hell, the last several—I realize I'm having a great time. I don't ride bikes often, but when I do, it always helps me clear my mind. Inviting Cameron to join me on this short ride only enhanced the experience. I enjoy spending time with her outside of work. I enjoy having her in my space. In my bed.

I'm walking on a very slippery slope here. I need to remember she's temporary, the relationship we're portraying is fake, and she'll eventually go back to her home. To her old life. She's not permanent here, despite the fact she fits in so easily.

The fact remains she's not mine to keep.

Even though for the first time, despite her being with me mere days, I'd like to think perhaps I'd be willing to explore the prospect of more with her. She's just so easy to be around.

And that's the craziest thought I've ever entertained, because I don't want that life. I don't want forever. I don't even like to think past tonight.

That will never change.

"So," she says, breaking through the turmoil in my brain. Cameron pushes up the kickstand with her foot with a wide smile spreading across her lips, "Tell me about Pink Puppy."

"Hey, gotta minute?" I ask Garreth, who's behind the bar when I get to work.

"Sure, what's up? Everything okay with Cameron?"

"Yeah, she's fine," I quickly say, watching the worry lines around his eyes disappear. "I was actually hoping I could get a night off in two weeks. Actually, both me and Cam."

Those worry lines are back as his eyebrows draw up in confusion. "You and Cam?"

I clear my throat, suddenly a little nervous.

What the hell?

"I talked to my sister earlier, and she has a concert in Philly two weeks from this Saturday. I'd like to go, and she invited Cameron to attend as well."

He nods slowly, reaching into a chest cooler to pull out a bottle of beer and place it on the tray. Once the server walks away, he props his hip on the cooler and gives me his full attention. "So, you two are going to Philly?"

Finding my usual bravado, I cross my arms over my chest and reply, "Well, I haven't asked her yet, but it's a possibility. If she wants to go, she's welcome. My sister extended the invitation, and it's up to her if she accepts."

He sighs. "Fine. Shouldn't be a problem. Walker will be here, and I'll make sure Max is on that night. Anything else?" he asks, and I have to fight from smiling at his annoyance.

"Actually, yes. We're going out on a date this Saturday, and I might need a little gas money, Dad."

Garreth spins around, holding up his middle finger as he walks away. It's the sound of my laughter carrying him from the bar to the restaurant side, where he stays for the majority of the evening.

Later that night when I get home, I find Cameron sitting at my drums. She's holding the sticks, but makes no sound, and I can't help but wonder if she's tried playing them at all. She looks a little scared, but nothing like the fear I've seen in her eyes over these last few days. She's acting as if the sticks were snakes, ready to bite.

Without saying a word, I move in behind her and grin when she immediately stands up and allows me to sit on the stool first. Then, like she did the night before, she takes a seat on my lap and holds out her hands. Wrapping mine around hers, I bring the sticks down to the snare drum and tap out a slow beat. She seems to relax against me, her arms suddenly a little heavier than before, and I realize she is scared.

She's just trying to overcome it.

If sitting here, staring at my drum set and building up the courage to hit the sticks against them is what she needs, I'll let her have them and take as much time as she wants. It's a hell of a lot better than knowing she's turning on all the lights and cowering in a corner because she's afraid to be alone.

We play together for a while, neither of us speaking, and when I finally lower the sticks in our joined hands, she gazes over her shoulder at me. Her lips are so kissable and plump, it takes all the strength I possess not to take them with my own and kiss the hell out of her until we're both breathless.

And then maybe take her to my room and continue what happened early this morning.

Unfortunately, that's not what *should* happen.

It's what I *want* to do, but not what I need to do.

When she stands up, I take her hand and lead her down the hallway. I pause between the open doorways, turning and facing her room. Her eyes meet mine, and I can't help but release her hand and slide my fingers into her hair, cradling her head in my hands. Instead of kissing her lips, I place mine on her forehead and inhale like the creeper I am, drawing in the scent of her shampoo.

"Night, Cam," I whisper, pulling back and holding her gaze.

She swallows hard, her fingers gripping and flexing against my arms. "Good night, Kellen."

Then, she's gone, moving into the guest room and shifting the door between us. She doesn't close it completely, though I wish she would have. Seeing it cracked open is way too tempting.

With heavy legs, I make my way across the hall to my own room, knowing there's a very good chance she'll be joining me in my bed at some point during the night. Consistency tells me she'll be there when the weight of her inability to sleep in the guest room becomes too much for her.

And the bastard I am is ready for that moment.

My bed and my arms are waiting.

Cameron

"Are you nervous?" Meg asks, her eyes sparkling with the prospect of gossip.

"What? No," I insist, placing the last glass of water on my tray before delivering them to my new table.

She shrugs as she reaches around me to grab a clean glass. "A Saturday night date is a big deal."

When I arrived to work this morning, Meg was her normal chatty self, so when she asked about my weekend plans, I found myself telling her about my date tonight with Kellen. Ever since, she's been beaming with excitement and anticipation for all the juicy details. I don't tell her the only juicy details happened in the early morning on Tuesday when we both thought we were dreaming and took things a little too far. Since, he just holds me, but there's definitely an intimacy there that wasn't present before that fateful morning. We have yet to actually put our mouths on each other, but I'll admit, I'm anxious for that to happen. Something tells me Kellen McGregor with his mouth between my legs will be even better than just his fingers.

"If you say so," I tell her before heading off to take care of my new table.

The truth is, I'm not nervous. Yes, perhaps if this was a normal first date I would be, but this is anything but. We're not really dating. This dinner and movie are for appearance purposes only, in hope it'll get back to Cage and he'll officially leave me alone. The good news is, since we saw him in the back parking lot here last Saturday, I haven't seen him since. Of course my house being trashed could have very well have been his doing, but as far as physically seeing him, I haven't.

I'll chalk that up in the win column.

As my shift draws to an end, I head for the computer system at the servers' station and get ready to clock out. Meg is there, as are the three night servers. "Have a good night, ladies," I tell the three newcomers as I officially end my shift.

"You too," they reply in unison, leaving me to walk back to the break room with Meg.

"Are you excited? Freaking out a little?" she asks the moment we're alone in the room.

"I'm not either, really," I insist, grabbing my wristlet from the locker I use to store my personal belongings.

"Liar!" she bellows, pulling her own bag from a locker two doors down.

"I'm really not, Meg. I mean, I'm staying with him," I tell her, even though what I really want to say is it's not real. But I also understand Kellen's point that it must be believable to as many as possible so the story gets back to Cage.

She slams her locker closed and faces me. "Did you shave your legs?" My mouth hangs open, ready to defend myself, but she interrupts. "I knew it! You're gonna get freaky tonight. I'm so jealous," she adds, linking her arm with my own and leading me toward the back exit. "Not because it's Kellen, even though I'm a little jealous there because he's totally hot and has the most amazing ass, but because I don't even have any date prospects on the horizon. The last dick to go anywhere near my vag had batteries, Cameron. Batteries!"

Before I can even laugh, a throat clears off to our left. We both turn to see a very red-faced Isaac at the foot of the stairs coming from his office. "Ladies."

"Isaac," Meg mutters, her face as red as his.

"Have a great evening," he replies, practically running from the stairs to the kitchen.

"Oh my God," I blurt out with a laugh.

"So embarrassing. He's probably going to tell all the other hot owners I've been on a dick dry spell for the last three months."

Three months? Try fourteen months.

We step outside and I spot Kellen's big truck in the same spot I parked it in when I arrived. I still find it weird he's letting me drive his truck, but I suppose I won't complain. Sure does beat the alternative of walking.

My car should be fixed middle of next week. I called Otto and was able to work out a payment plan with him to get my car back on the road and make manageable payments over the next several weeks. As long as I bring in extra tips working the evening shift for a while, it shouldn't be too long before it's paid off. One of the good things about living in a small town. Everyone knows everyone else, and they're more likely to help when you fall on hard times.

"You better text me tomorrow and tell me all the juicy deets," she hollers at me over her shoulder when she reaches her car.

"There won't be anything juicy to share," I assure her, even though deep down, I'm secretly hoping for a few juicy tidbits. Not that I'll share them with her, of course, but a few private details I keep locked away in my mind wouldn't be so bad.

"Whatever!" she bellows as she slides into her car and shuts the door.

With a smile on my face, I unlock Kellen's truck with the key fob and get ready to climb in. Just as I step up on the running board, a dark SUV catches my attention. It's at the far back corner of the lot, way over away from where the rest of the staff park. It's backed into a spot, the window's tinted so I can't see inside. A shiver sweeps up my spine. Is that Cage? It sure looks like the SUV he was driving the day at the grocery store.

It can't be.

It's probably one of the owners' wives' vehicles.

Shaking thoughts of Cage out of my head, I climb inside the truck and fire it up. I have less than two hours to go home, shower, and get ready for our night out. The very public night out, but one, nonetheless. The last time I went out on a date—real or otherwise—was with Cage, and even that was early on in our relationship. Once he convinced me to move in with him, the date nights dried up and the nights in by myself amped up.

That's how he slowly started to isolate me from my friends.

Pulling from the lot, I vow to forget everything that happened before now. I won't let Cage or the toxic relationship we once had put a damper on the evening. Kellen is nothing like the man who came before him, and that's what I need to focus on, because I'm really excited about dinner and a movie.

Even if it's for appearances only.

At exactly six, there's a knock on my bedroom door. I could open the door, but I opt to take a few moments to get my erratic heartbeat under control, as well as dry off my sweaty palms. Taking a deep breath, I release it slowly and pull the door open. What I find is something straight out of a romance novel. Kellen is wearing a pair of dark jeans that fit him to perfection and a nicer black T-shirt that's molded to his upper body like a second skin. Throw in his ever-present smile that makes panties wet all over the world, and you have a recipe for disaster to my lady parts.

My mouth waters at the sight.

"These are for you," he announces when it appears I'm just stuck here, staring.

I finally notice the flowers in his hand. "Oh my gosh, they're gorgeous," I tell him, reaching for the red roses and yellow sunflowers bouquet. The fragrant scent of the blooms hits me even before I bring them to my nose. "Thank you."

Kellen winks, leaning casually against the doorjamb. "Every first date deserves some romance, right?" He leans in just a bit as he lowers his voice and adds, "Plus, I figured flowers would only help my chances for some extra PDA at the park later."

I can't help but laugh as I set the vase down on the empty dresser. "I think I'm ready," I state, grabbing the sweater I placed on the end of the bed. I know it'll get cooler as the sun goes down, and I want to be prepared.

Though, if the heated look in his eyes is any indication, I'm sure Kellen has other ideas on how to keep me warm.

Without saying a word, he places his big hand on my lower back and guides me through the house. We don't stop until he's setting the alarm and locking the back door. I head for the passenger door, which he politely opens, and climb inside. A quick glance in the back seat confirms there's a large blanket folded up, with a smaller one on top of it.

We chat about my day as we make our way to dinner, which happens to be the pizzeria down the block from Burgers and Brew. He finds a parking spot along the street and is out of the truck moments later. We walk in together, the place already buzzing with Saturday night activity.

Moving through the crowd of what is clearly a large family waiting by the front door, we stop at the hostess stand. "Two, please," Kellen says after greeting the hostess.

"Right this way," she replies, grabbing two menus and leading us into the heart of the pizzeria.

I keep my eyes straight ahead and not on the those sitting at the booths and tables around me, even though I can feel their eyes on me. When we stop beside a booth, I quickly slip inside the booth and take the offered menu. Kellen sits across from me and smiles, his eyes only on me as we're left alone.

"Good evening. Name's Maci. What can I get you to drink?" the young high school student says as she reaches our table.

"Just ice water for me," I reply.

"Same."

"Want me to put in an appetizer for you?"

Kellen holds my gaze as he asks, "Breadsticks, please."

"Sure."

Maci writes it down and disappears in a flurry to take care of her next table.

"What do you say, Cam? You gonna split a Hawaiian pizza with me?"

My stomach chooses that moment to growl. "Sounds good."

"Salad too?"

"Sure." I'm not sure I'll be super hungry, thanks to the breadsticks we've already ordered, but something tells me I need a little salad to combat the thousands of calories I'm about to consume with pizza and soft, garlicky breadsticks before we hit the concession stand at the park.

Maci returns with our drinks and breadsticks, and while Kellen orders the salad and large pizza, I place a warm, fluffy stick on two plates and set the cheese dipping sauce between us. My mouth waters as we dig in and chat. Our conversation moves from work to Garreth and Reagan's daughter, who is an easy topic because she's so cute and loveable.

Our salad arrives next, and even though I should probably fill up on the healthiest option placed on the table, I only eat a small helping. The impending Hawaiian pizza is too tempting to pass up, so I'll be eating my weight in that pineappley deliciousness.

Just as our main entrée arrives, movement across the room catches my attention. It only takes a fraction of a second to recognize the woman standing up from a far table and heading this way. She's laughing at something another woman says, and the sound of her laughter is like a punch to the gut. While I've seen Aneeka around Stewart Grove, it's not very often and we've never actually spoken.

When she readies to pass our table, I want to avert my gaze, but something tells me not to. She looks down at that moment, surprise reaching all her pretty features. Her legs seem to stutter movement, and perhaps maybe that's why I choose to speak words aloud and not just running through a pretend conversation in my head. "Hi, Neek," I say, barely able to cover the tremble in my voice.

"Cameron, hi," she says, turning to her friend and saying, "I'll be right out."

As her friend walks away, I notice the way her touch lingers on Aneeka's arm in silent support, but also in another way too. It's a very intimate touch, one that threatens to bring a smile to my face, but I'm able to school my features, because her relationship status isn't my business anymore.

"How have you been?" I ask, really hoping she gives me more than just a cut and dried answer.

"Really good," she replies, glancing over to the man across from me. He's watching our exchange, though has kept quiet up to this point.

"Aneeka, this is Kellen McGregor. Kellen, my...this is Aneeka King." I almost said my friend Aneeka, but the truth is, she's not my friend anymore and hasn't been for a couple of years now.

"Aneeka, nice to finally meet you," Kellen says politely, holding out his hand for her to shake. "Cam has mentioned you on a few occasions," he adds without elaborating.

My former friend seems a bit surprised by this news. She flashes him a small smile as she says, "I hope it was all good."

"Of course it was," he replies with a grin.

She turns back to look at me as she asks, "So, you two are dating?"

"We are. I was a lucky guy when she finally agreed to go out with me," Kellen announces proudly, reaching over and squeezing my hand. The unspoken support means more to me than he'll ever know.

My heart skips a beat, and I have to remind myself his gushy words aren't real. "I don't know about that," I mutter, feeling my cheeks heat and hating having their eyes on me to witness it.

"I do, sweetems," he coos, bringing my hand to his mouth and kissing the knuckles. "I'm sorry, I've monopolized the conversation. I'm going to go use the restroom and let you two catch up." With one more kiss to my hand, he slips out of the booth and walks toward the back of the pizzeria where the restrooms are located.

"So," she starts, seeming to notice the sudden awkwardness surrounding us both.

"So," I say at almost the exact same time.

Suddenly, we're both laughing, and the worry and heaviness I've felt in my chest the last few minutes seems to fall away.

"You look good, Cam. Happy."

My smile doesn't fall away. "I'm working on it. On me."

"I'm happy to hear that," she replies genuinely. "Truly. And Kellen? He's good to you?"

That familiar tap dancing in my chest starts again, beating steady and fast. "He is." Even if the relationship aspect is fake, he's been a good friend—and man—to me throughout this entire ordeal.

"Good. I'm glad. You deserve some happiness, Cam," she whispers, a hint of emotion clogging her throat.

"Thank you," I reply. "It hasn't been easy, but I'm getting there."

Aneeka smiles and glances toward the door, and that's when I realize our time is up. She has someone waiting for her outside, and it's rude of me to keep her here any longer. I'm about to open my mouth to wish her well, when she surprises me with her next question. "Would you like to catch up some time? Maybe have coffee or dinner?"

My throat is so tight, I'm not sure how I manage to get words out, but I do. "I'd love to do that." Tears fill my eyes.

She smiles. "Good. I'm glad I ran into you, Cam."

"Me too, Neek."

"I'll text you. Is your number the same?" she asks innocently, but all it does is remind me of how my life has changed so drastically in the last year.

"Oh, uh, no. I have a new number." Again, cue the blush.

"Here," she says, pulling her phone from her purse. "Give me your number and I'll text you so you have mine, in case you don't remember it."

I do as instructed; trying to ignore the way my fingers tremble slightly. When I hand back her device, she replaces it in her purse and gives me a smile. "I'll let you get back to your dinner."

"Okay. I'm glad you stopped by."

"Me too." Before she walks away, she adds, "I'll text you when I get out to my car."

I nod, spotting Kellen heading back this way. "Have a good evening, Neek."

"You too, Cam."

And then she's gone, leaving me stunned at the table.

"You okay?" Kellen asks, reaching out for my hand and giving it a squeeze.

Giving him a watery grin, I reply, "I am. We're planning to make arrangements to meet for coffee or something."

"I knew it," he replies, reaching for the spatula and scooping a slice of pizza up and placing it on my plate. "I'm happy you're reconnecting with an old friend, Cam. Now, what do you say we eat this pizza and get to the park? If we don't hurry, they'll get all the good spots, and we'll be stuck in the back by the shrubbery without a clear view of the screen. That means all we'll be able to do is make out. That's not on the itinerary until the second half of the movie, love."

With a chuckle, I lift my slice of pizza and take a hearty bite. I realize I'm enjoying the first part of this date so far and can only hope the next stage goes as well and as comfortable as this portion.

And heaven help me if it does because I already like Kellen McGregor. Knowing he's the full date package might just put me firmly in the in-trouble category.

I'm not sure I'll survive once he walks away.

He may very well take a small piece of me with him when he goes.

Twenty-One 21

Kellen

"Okay, I have all the necessary movie snacks," I announce, dropping onto the blanket and placing the flat box down in front of us.

Cameron's eyes are wide as she takes in the feast. "How can you still be hungry after eating all that pizza?"

"This isn't for nourishment, Cam." I hold up the tub of popcorn. "This is to ensure I get hand-holding." Placing that back on the cardboard tray, I reach for the Twizzlers. "These are for the snuggles I still hope to get while the movie is playing, and the rest of this," I state, waving my hand over the Coke freezes and nachos, "is for the kisses I plan to steal throughout the night." Of course I punctuate my statement with a killer smile, one I've regularly used as a secret weapon that tends to bring women to their knees.

"Awfully confident," she says with a cheeky grin before reaching for a chip and dipping it into the nacho cheese.

"Not really," I retort with a chuckle. "You tend to keep me on my toes."

She chews her chip, her eyes crinkled in confusion. When she swallows, she asks, "What do you mean?"

"Well," I start, reaching for my own chip and coating the end with cheese, "My go-to flirting, while you seem to appreciate a bit, isn't as effective on you. Not that I want to use my usual lines, but when I flash you a smile, you're not just falling at me feet. Honestly, I like that better. You've made me have to work at getting to know you, even the little details about your life. I actually want to know them, and knowing you trust me enough to share each one is better than any reaction I could ever get by throwing you a few innuendos before we jump into bed."

She blushes at my honestly. Or the reference to jumping into bed. Either way, I can't get over how adorable she is, blushing or otherwise. The fact I've gotten to know her on a whole different level than any other woman is astonishing. Not just because of what she's shared, but because I actually want to learn it. All of it. Everything about her. And it's been a fucking week. That's how long she's been rooming with me, but that doesn't seem to matter. It's more than just some hero complex I might have or hero worship on her part. There's a friendship growing, and I really like it.

More than I ever expected.

"I like talking to you too," she whispers, glancing up at me from beneath her eyelashes. But it's not in that flirty way women do at the bar, hoping for an invite back to my bed. It holds a touch of insecurity, as if she's not sure she wants to share that confession. "And as far as your bed goes, obviously I've enjoyed that part too."

And cue the raging hard-on.

Just by her mentioning my bed, my dick is ready to jump to that portion of the night.

Not that it'll lead there, but he's an eager bastard, that's for sure.

The movie comes to life on the screen in front of us, and while the crowd in the park quiets down, I lean over and lightly tap her shoulder with my own. "For the record, I really like having you in my bed. Best snuggle partner ever," I reassure her, adding a wink just because. "Come on, let's get comfortable. My favorite part is when Ferris and Cameron go to pick Sloane up from school."

She slips her legs beneath the second blanket and pulls the food closer. When I stretch my own legs out and lift the tray, she throws the blanket over mine. Placing the food back down, we both look up at the screen and watch the opening scene unfold, our hands occasionally touching as we share our feast of snacks.

This part of the night has barely begun, but I'm already having the best time.

Who knew I could actually enjoy spending so much time with a woman without getting her naked.

At the intermission, I pick up the trash and take it over to the nearest can. I spot a dozen people I know, the questions evident in their eyes or in the way they greet me. I don't stop to chat with anyone, mostly because I want to get back to Cam.

When I reach our blanket, I find her lying down on her side, facing the paused movie screen. My hands instantly tingle to touch her skin, my arms anxious to wrap around her. Taking a seat beside her, she looks back and says, "I figured we could skip the hand-holding and jump straight to the blanket snuggles."

Smiling, I take my position behind her, much like I do every night when she slips into my bed. "Who am I to turn down snuggles?"

"Well, you *did* provide the proper movie snacks."

"Damn right I did," I reply, lying on my side behind her. I can just see the movie screen over the top of her head, and even though it's not quite as comfortable without my pillow, I'm willing to overlook that slight discomfort in favor of having her in my arms.

"What do you think? Have enough people seen us on our public date?" she asks quietly so the nearest group doesn't overhear.

"I had lots of eyes on me when I went to the trash can. I'm guessing we'll definitely be the talk of the town tomorrow."

She snorts. "I'm sure. Doesn't take much here," she concedes.

"Unfortunately, that's correct."

"We'll probably be dating, engaged, and had public sex under the blanket by noon."

I bark out a laugh, mostly because she's not wrong. Rumors have a way of spreading in this town, and what could have easily been something innocent will no doubt be scandalous by the time it's shared. "So you're no stranger to the gossip mill in Stewart Grove."

"No, definitely not," she mutters, and I can't help but wonder if she's referring to all the things being said about her regarding Burgers and Brew, but even though I'm curious, I won't ask. It's not my place. Besides, I want her to come to me with anything she wants to share, and I know that's one of the big secrets she's still harboring.

The movie continues, but my attention isn't there. My hand rests on her hip, my fingers slowly drawing lazy circles across her side. Even though my hand is outside of her shirt, I can feel the heat of her skin, which makes me antsy. I prop my head in my hand and look around at those nearby. There're people of all ages here. Older couples enjoying the warm fall night, younger groups of friends, and even some small families. But as my eyes roam the crowd and land on one individual not watching the movie, I pause.

"What's wrong?" she asks, glancing back over her shoulder.

"Hmm?"

"You just tensed and did this little gasp thing."

"Oh," I reply, my eyes quickly moving to the man across the park, as if to confirm they're not playing tricks on me. "I spotted someone."

"Who?" she asks curiously.

Taking a deep breath, I whisper, "Cage."

Her green eyes widen in shock. "What? He's here?"

"Don't look," I instruct as she starts to turn her head away from me. "Just lie here and keep those pretty eyes on me, okay?" When she nods subtly, I add, "He's over by the row of pine trees off to the right. No blanket, just standing over there. He has a clear view of us."

She exhales slowly, closing her eyes as she does. "So, we're being watched?"

I nod. "We are."

When she reopens her eyes, there's no hint of fear or worry. Those gorgeous eyes are full of resolve and determination. "Then, we better give him a good show, huh? I mean, the whole reason we came here was to show him—and everyone else—that we're together, right? Let's show him, Kellen. Kiss me."

You don't have to tell me twice. She rolls to her back, which only brings her closer to my chest, and wraps her arms around my neck. Her fingers dance at the edges of my hairline as I lower my mouth to hers. That first touch of her lips causes a tsunami of desire to build and crash down against me at an alarming speed.

Immediately, she opens her mouth, and my tongue delves inside, tasting and savoring the feel of our tongues gliding. Her nails dig into my scalp, as my own fingers move beneath her shirt and slide against the hot, smooth skin of her lower back. Need races through my veins, my cock hard and ready to get in on the action. She must sense his eagerness because she shifts her own hips, rocking her pussy against my thigh and driving me absolutely wild.

I'm not sure how long the kiss lasts, but it's not nearly long enough. I could kiss this woman all night long and never get tired of it. Unfortunately, thanks to the family-friendly event surrounding us, I force my lips from hers and suck in a greedy breath of oxygen. My desire for her is overwhelming.

Jesus, this could have easily gotten out of hand right here with Ferris Bueller and God watching.

"Wow," she mutters, her lips plump and tempting.

"Yeah," I reply, clearing my throat and slightly pulling back. I look up, surprised to see our audience no longer there. "He's gone."

Like a glass of cold water dropped on her head, the lust clouding her eyes clears and realization fills in. "Oh. Good."

I make a noise of agreement and slowly roll back to my side. Cameron doesn't move, lying on her back and staring up at the stars, and Jesus Christ, I want to kiss her all over again. I want to kiss her lips, her neck, her tits. I want to slide between her spread legs and thrust inside her pussy. I want to make her cry out with pleasure so many times she can't remember her own name. Not because I'm a guy and I'm horny, but because I've heard how she sounds when she's coming and I want to experience it—I want to be the cause of it—over and over again.

Then I want to do it the next night too.

Her eyes are pure fire, as if she can read my dirty thoughts. Her fingers flex against my side and grip my flesh, but before we can begin round two, the crowd around us laughs at something happening on the screen, which is just another reminder of where we are. Cameron sighs, a slight giggle falling from her lips as she turns away from me, returning to our earlier spooning position. Only this time, when I place my hand on her hip, she grabs my hand, draws it down in front of her, and links our fingers together. I place a kiss on the side of her forehead and snuggle in close to watch the remainder of the movie. I don't even care my cock is hard and pressed against her ass, and since she's not making any movement to put distance between us, she doesn't seem to mind either.

When the ending credits roll, we both sit up and start to gather our stuff. I take the remaining trash to the can, while she folds the blankets. I take the bedding in one hand and her hand in my other and slowly lead her toward the lot where my truck is parked. We pass many local people, all who seem to notice us. One woman I slept with in the past zeroes in on our joined hands and seems shocked by what she's witnessing. I just give her a slight nod and look away. I'm not about to explain myself to her or anyone else here.

Cameron's the only one who matters.

There's a heavy sexual tension riding along with us back to my house. I'm very familiar with it, though not necessarily from Cameron. I've experienced plenty of anticipation for sex, but never this extra layer of friendship on top of it. It's unusual and exciting all at the same time, and all I want to do is find out if she feels it too.

But that's not what we are.

We're friends, yes, but we're in a very unique situation. A gray area, if you will. We didn't meet at the bar and are heading off for a night of mutual satisfaction. We're coworkers and friends. Two people who are attracted to each other, but also have a lot riding on the unique situation they find themselves in.

I pull into my driveway and garage, climbing out of my truck as soon as it's off. My feet carry me to the passenger side, opening the door for Cameron and helping her down from her seat. She gives me a small grin in appreciation and quickly slips her hand inside of mine. The contact is familiar, and I didn't realize how much I needed it until right now.

We're secured inside with the door locked and alarm reset a minute later. I drop the blankets down on the table, but neither of us make any other pause in the kitchen. We walk through the living room and down the hall, finally coming to a stop in front of the open doors.

She turns to face me, placing her non-linked hand on my chest and says, "You know, I've been thinking."

"Yeah? About what?" I ask, wanting to wrap my hands around her waist and draw her closer, but refraining.

"Well, since I end up in your bed every night at some point, I thought maybe…" I hold my breath, waiting. "Perhaps, it would make more sense for me just to start out there."

My heart is trying to pound from my chest, my cock threatening to claw from my pants. "That does make sense," I reply, finally giving in to the urge to touch her. Placing my hand on her side, I slowly work it around to her lower back, drawing our bodies closer.

"You wouldn't mind?"

My eyebrows pull together in question. "Mind having an unbelievably gorgeous woman lying in bed with me from start to finish? No, I can't say I mind that at all."

Giving me a coy smile, she gazes up and says, "Okay. I'm going to go put on my pajamas and use the restroom."

"Don't put on pajamas on my account," I quip, unable to keep the naughty innuendo from flying.

There's a giggle as she releases my hand and takes a step back. "I'll be back in a minute."

I nod, my throat suddenly dry. It's not until she walks away and I hear the click of the bathroom door that I finally move from the hallway and into my own bedroom. I make quick work of grabbing a pair of shorts and slipping into the bathroom to change. Once I'm wearing the shorts and have my teeth brushed, I head for the door. Honestly, I should probably slip in the shower and take care of the ache in my balls and the hardness of my cock, but all I want to do right now is get into bed and wait for Cameron.

I don't have to wait long. The moment I slip beneath the covers, I hear her bathroom door open across the hall and the soft footfalls of her bare feet against the hardwood floor. My door is standing wide open, so she just enters, this time with a lot more confidence than what she's had when slipping over in the middle of the night in the past.

Then, I see her pajamas.

If you can call it that.

It's a fucking nightgown.

Yes, it's cotton and has not one provocative feature, but just seeing it hit midthigh and hang loosely off one shoulder makes all my blood race straight to my dick.

There's a different posture in the way she walks toward me, and I know I'm in trouble. Big fucking trouble. No way will I be able to keep my hands off this woman with her wearing that nightgown. All I'll want to do is slide it up her silky thighs and bury myself between them. First, my mouth. Then, my cock.

I don't have time to pull the covers back for her, since I'm too busy gawking and fantasizing about all the dirty things I'd like to do, so when she does, it just seems that much naughtier. Like she's taking control and entering my bed on her own, even though we just had a conversation about doing just that.

Cameron is facing me and scoots forward until she's in my personal space. Usually, she keeps her back to me and allows me to hold her, but tonight, she's different. She's taking control, being more assertive, and my God, I really fucking like it.

She places both hands on my bare chest, her fingers dancing across my skin and burning me with their heat. "I've been thinking," she starts, holding my gaze as she nibbles on her bottom lip. It's not in seduction, but in nervousness.

"What's up, love?" I ask, holding still while she runs her hands across my chest.

"Remember the morning we both thought we were dreaming? You were touching me."

My tongue is thick, words difficult to speak, but somehow, I manage. "I remember."

I remember every second.

"I've been thinking a lot about that," she says, holding my gaze.

"Yeah? What about it?"

217

"I have questions, like what would it feel like to do that again, and what if we took it a step farther, and you actually put your mouth on me?"

I can feel her blush more than I can see it, thanks to the dark room, and my brain latches on to not one, but both of her questions.

My hand moves, starting at her hip and snaking around to her back, slowly dropping down to her ass. "You want my mouth on your pussy, Cam?"

She nods insistently, her breath catching. "Yes, please, but only if you do too."

A wide grin spreads across my mouth in anticipation. "Oh, I want. I want bad, love, so lie back, and hold on tight, because I've been dreaming about eating your pussy since the first morning I woke with a hard dick, and your tight little body pressed against me."

She rolls onto her back as I get to my knees. This woman is absolutely stunning, and as if she took a page out of my own spank-bank playbook, she's asking me to eat her. This is better than Christmas, my birthday, and every other fucking day, all combined.

This is going to be fun.

Cameron

I'm not sure I'm breathing as I lie back on the pillow and stare up at Kellen. There's a hunger in his eyes, one I feel clear down to the apex of my legs. I've never been on the receiving end of this type of desire, at least not one I've stared down. I'm not thinking about my ex right now, but Cage definitely never looked at me like he was a starving man, and I was a juicy steak.

A shiver of anticipation runs down my spine.

Kellen reaches down and grabs the bottom of my sleepshirt. It's not sexy, but it was the closest thing I could find in the bag of stuff Reagan dropped off for me. It was either this or one of the few top and short sets, and there's nothing sexy about those.

"May I?" he asks, holding up the hem of the shirt.

I nod insistently, which makes him grin.

His eyes drop down as he slowly lifts the shirt up, exposing my core. He groans, clearly noticing my lack of panties. I knew where I was hoping tonight would go, therefore left them off when I got ready to come over here. "Jesus, your pussy is beautiful."

I wish I could say I don't blush, but I do. Bad. No one has ever talked so...bluntly to me. Kellen McGregor's mouth is dirty, and the anticipation to see what other mad skills it possesses is driving me mad.

"Can we take it off?"

"Yes, but can we take off your shorts?" I ask, sitting up so he can lift the sleepshirt over my head.

"Not yet, beautiful. We'll get there. First, I want to worship your sexy body and make you come," he replies, hovering over me when I lie back down.

My hand reaches down and cups his very hard erection. "I want to do that too."

He closes his eyes and shudders as I slowly stroke the tip of his cock. "We will, love, but if you touch me right now, I'll explode."

Giving him a slight smirk, I reply, "That sounds like fun."

He pulls back so I have no choice but to drop my hold on him. "Oh, I have no doubt it will be. But first, let me worship you. I know you have two, maybe even three orgasms in you. I plan to extract every single one."

My eyes widen at the thought. Two has only happened once, and that was Tuesday morning by his hand. The thought of three seems preposterous, but if he wants to give it a shot, who am I to deny him?

He drops his mouth and licks my nipple. "If you're not comfortable with any part of this, you tell me, okay?"

I nod, unable to speak as he draws lazy circles around my right nipple with his tongue.

"Say the words, Cam."

"Yes. Yes, I understand."

"Perfect," he replies, and then gets to work. His mouth is heaven as he licks and sucks at both breasts. My body is moving to a silent beat only it can hear, a song Kellen orchestrates himself.

Just when I'm about to beg for more, he slowly kisses down my abdomen and lies between my spread legs. His mouth trails open-mouthed kisses across my pubis. Shivers sweep through me, causing goosebumps to erupt across my entire body. Again, I'm ready to beg for more, but before I can open my mouth, his mouth is there—right where I ache for it.

The first swipe of his tongue is pure bliss. He must think so too, because he moans, the sound vibrating through my clit. He inhales deeply before flattening his tongue against my core and slowly licking from bottom to top. Sensations flood my body, just as wetness floods my core.

"Fuck, you taste like honey," he mutters without removing his mouth.

Then, he goes to town. Like a man possessed, he sucks my clit into his mouth, causing me to cry out in pleasure. He slips his tongue inside me, mimicking exactly how I'd picture he'd use his cock. Deep, sure thrusts that drive me closer to the edge of oblivion. He works me over like an expert, showering attention to my clit and making my internal muscles tighten with the building release. He knows I'm close and pushes my body easily past the breaking point and straight into an orgasm.

My hips rock against his mouth as I cry out his name, riding the waves of my release. He never lets up on the pressure either, drawing out every ounce of pleasure he can. Just when my body is sated and ready to rest, he moves his hand between my legs and runs two fingers across my swollen clit. The contact causes me to jolt in a mixture of pleasure and pain. He shifts those two fingers downward and presses them inside my pussy.

I gasp at the tightness, at the fullness.

"Again, Cam."

Shaking my head, I whisper, "I'm not sure I can."

"Oh, you can, love, and you will. Just feel."

He adjusts his hand so his fingers are curled upward. He strokes the inside of me, hitting that magical spot inside a woman that drives them wild. "God," I mutter, trying to relax enough to allow his fingers more room to move, but at the same time, craving the fullness those two fingers offer.

His tongue moves across my clit once more as he continues to make shallow thrusts with his fingers. I reach down, grabbing on to his head, gripping his hair, as he drives me right back toward another orgasm. This one builds with a speed I've never experienced, my body still humming from the one only minutes ago.

I rock my hips, my body taking over as it gyrates and grinds against the blissful friction. My nipples pebble hard, and with one hand, I reach up and squeeze a single nipple.

"Fuck, do that again. I can feel your pussy squeezing my fingers when you do that," he demands, looking up at me without removing his mouth from my clit.

I do as instructed, using both hands now to toy with my nipples. Closing my eyes, I just feel. Feel his fingers stroking my G-spot. Feel his warm mouth sucking on my clit. Feel the euphoric pleasure of nipple play—something I wasn't even aware I'd enjoy, mind you. It's the combination of all three that has my body so hot, so ready to come once more it only takes the slightest vibration of his mouth as he whispers, "I love eating you," and I detonate like a bomb.

This release is almost painful, the onslaught of sensations too much for me to take, but he doesn't let up. He draws out every part of my orgasm, making sure I'm completely boneless and spent before finally withdrawing his mouth and fingers.

I crack open my eyes to see him bringing his hand to his mouth and sucking on those two fingers. The heat in his eyes sends more shivers through my limbs. Now that I've been on the receiving end of that passion, I know I'll never be the same. And the crazy part is, we haven't even slept together yet, but I guess it doesn't matter. No one has ever shown me so much hunger with the simple act of oral alone.

I hate to admit it, but I'm going to want more.

Eventually.

Right now, my body is humming with satisfaction.

However, that's the moment I look down and see his hard, long cock pushing his shorts straight out. Suddenly, I'm no longer tired. In this moment, I'm ready to give as good as I got. The thought of wrapping my lips around his cock and taking him deep in my throat is all-consuming.

It's all I want and exactly what I need.

I scramble up and point to the spot I just lay on. He moves, but his actions are very slow, as if he's going to give me an out. He's going to suggest we snuggle and fall asleep. I can see it, and that's not happening. If I don't have him in my mouth right now, I might die.

Dramatic, yes, but still true.

I crave it.

I crave him.

"Don't say a word, Kellen," I tell him, getting onto my knees beside him.

"How do you know what I was going to say?" he asks, his voice tight.

Splaying my hands on his chest, I run them down toward where his cock is trying to claw his way out of his shorts. "Because deep down, you're a good guy, Kellen, and you don't want to do anything to hurt me."

"Never," he insists through gritted teeth.

"Then let me do this, not because it's a thank-you for what you just did, but because I want to do it. I want to suck your cock, and I need to do it right now."

He releases a shuttered breath, and he shivers. "Then I will not stop you from taking what you want."

I give him a smile as I cup his balls through his shorts and give them a gentle squeeze. "Good."

When I finally release my hold on him, I grab the waistband of his shorts. He lifts his hips so I can tug them down, his cock springing free and landing with a thump on his stomach. Holy shitballs, I've never seen a dick so magnificent. Long, straight, and thick, with trimmed dark hair above his groin and smooth, shaved balls below it.

"Oh, I'm definitely putting my mouth there," I mumble, not meaning to say it out loud.

He barks out a laugh as he kicks his shorts off his ankles and onto the floor. "I promise you I won't mind at all."

Reaching down, I grab his erection and give it a slow stroke. "Did you do that for me?" I ask, referring to the shaved part.

"I do it every day," he grinds out through gritted teeth. "Having no hair there heightens the sensations."

"I've heard that about piercings too," I tell him, recalling a conversation I overheard one night between BJ, who is a tattoo artist and piercer, and Reagan. BJ discussed in great detail the sexual benefits of having piercings, something I've always kept in the back of my mind.

"You've been talking to BJ." He gasps as I gently twist my hand as I move it down his shaft.

"I've overheard a few things."

He meets my gaze and asks, "Would you ever get a piercing?"

Shrugging, I confess, "I've thought about getting my nipple done."

Kellen groans, and I'm pretty sure it's not entirely because of what I'm doing with my hand. "Yes, do it. As sensitive as your nipples are while you come, I think having a piercing would make it even better."

"Maybe I will," I reply with a coy grin, wrapping a second hand around his erection.

"Fuck, love," he grunts out, his hips flexing upward. "You're driving me wild."

"Good," I confess, dropping down and running my tongue across the vein on the underside of the head. "Turnabout's fair play."

Then, I do what I've been dying to do since the first time I woke in his arms and felt his erection pressed against me. I wrap my lips around the head of his cock and suck him in deep. "Jesus, Cam," he mutters, gasping for air.

I adjust my position above him and do it again, drawing him a little farther into my mouth with each stroke. Kellen makes noises as I pick up the pace. I reach down and cup his balls, loving the feel of the smooth, soft skin in my palm. He grunts, thrusting his hips upward in time with my movements. He never forces it, just seems to ride along with my pace.

I release the suction of my mouth, letting his cock go with a pop. My hand strokes his cock as I lower my mouth farther and taste his balls. A hiss fills the room, encouraging me to take it one step farther. I open my mouth wide and gently suck one, then the other into my mouth. His hands grip my hair, but he doesn't pull. It's as if he's using it to just hold on.

"My God," he mumbles, his head falling back on the pillow as I continue to lightly suck and lick his balls. "That might be the best feeling in the world, having your mouth on me."

"Yeah?" I ask, running my finger across one while sucking on the other.

"Fuck, yes."

After a few moments of showering them with attention, I lift back up and prepare for the big finish. I poise my mouth directly over his cock, spreading my knees a part a little for leverage. Just as I lower my mouth and draw him inside, he slips his hand between my legs. I jolt at the contact, as he slides his fingers across my pussy using the wetness from my earlier releases.

"You're still soaked, Cam. Do you like sucking my dick? Does it turn you on and make you horny?" I groan in response as he presses a finger up into my pussy. "Oh, yeah. I think you like it a lot," he adds, fucking me with a finger and cupping my clit against his palm. "Show me how much you like my cock in your mouth, beautiful."

I do. I bob my head, taking him deep. I cup his balls, loving the feel of them as they tighten. And I move my hips, fucking his hand. I can't believe I'm going to come a third time, but there's no stopping the build. It makes my movements more frantic, is the driving force behind my need to make him come.

"Are you close?"

"Yes," I whisper.

"Me too. If you don't want me to shoot my load down your throat, say so now."

I groan at his dirty words. "No, I want it."

"You sure?" he asks in confirmation, his own words getting tight.

"Yes. Come down my throat, Kellen."

He moans loudly, dropping his head back on the pillow again, but he doesn't let up on the assault with his finger. He thrusts into me at the same moment I grind down on him, my mouth maintaining the same pace. His thumb comes up and presses into my clit, causing me to explode a third time. When I cry out, he pauses before pumping his hips upward, filling my mouth and throat with his release. I swallow everything he gives me, lapping at his flesh to make sure I've consumed every drop. I've never been a big fan of blow jobs, but then again, I've never experienced one with Kellen McGregor.

Something tells me he's on a whole different level of oral gratification.

"Come here," he mutters, reaching for my arm and pulling me down on top of his body. He claims my mouth with his, uncaring I probably taste like him. But then again, he tastes like me still, and it's a heady mixture. "That was...wow."

"Mmm," I mumble, snuggling into his neck. "And we haven't even gotten to the sex part yet."

Running his hand across my back, he turns and kisses me on the side of the head. "We won't be having sex tonight, love."

I lift up and meet his gaze. "We won't?"

"Nope. You're not ready for that."

"I'm not?" I ask with a smile.

"No," he says, pulling me back down to cuddle against him. "Soon, Cam. When—and if—I get you naked and beneath me, there won't be anything hanging over us. It'll be because you're free from the bullshit going on and living your life again under your terms. Then, and only then, love. Until then, you can have my mouth and my hands on you as much as, or as little as you want, and that's not contingent on the status of our relationship, real or otherwise. It's not just because you're sexy as fuck and in my bed, either. Frankly, I *like* you and couldn't deny you if I tried."

My heart is pounding, and I'm certain he can feel it's erratic beat against his own chest. If he does, he doesn't say a word.

"Sleep, Cameron," he whispers, kissing my forehead once more.

I should slide off his chest, but I don't. It's too comfortable here, his strong arms wrapped around me. I feel content. I feel cherished. Most importantly, I feel safe.

Is it too soon to have feelings for him after only living here a week? Absolutely! I'd be silly to hang all my hopes and dreams on things that have transpired in the last seven days, but do you know what? I'm adult enough to look at the entire situation with both eyes wide open. I have come to care a great deal for him in a short amount of time. He's funny, caring, and a genuinely good guy. Sure, he may have been a bit of a player over the years, but he hasn't appeared to be engaging in extracurricular activities since I started staying in his guest room.

What does that mean for us? I have no idea. We're friends who dabble in the benefits side of a relationship, but most importantly, I trust him. With my safety and, yes, my secrets. I've shared a few with him in the early morning hours of lying in bed over the last week, and I haven't regretted it once. He's done the same, which speaks volumes for a guy who hides behind his confident smile and flirty come-ons.

But the big question is, do I have it in me to tell him my biggest secret—my greatest regret—of them all?

Twenty-Three 23

Kellen

Holding her like this is better than I ever expected. I've never been a cuddler, so why now? Why am I not pushing her away, gathering my clothes, and making a break for it like normal. Because of her.

Cameron.

There's something that calls to the very depth of my soul. She lights a fire inside me I didn't even know I wanted to feel burn. I want to make her smile. I want to make her breakfast in the morning. I want to help her release her stresses and fears by playing the damn drums, and that's fucking crazy, because I've gotten to know her more over the last week. Eight nights of her sleeping across the hall, before ending up in my bed. Most of those nights were innocent, but even those were good.

What the hell is wrong with me?

This isn't me, but I don't seem to have the gumption to fight it.

Watching her mouth wrap around my cock was something I'll never forget, not because of the way it felt—though, that part was fucking epic—but because of the way she made me feel. My entire world was on fire in a way I've never experienced before. Mindless sex with faceless women? Who could ever go back to anything remotely close to that when you've experienced what we shared tonight. And the craziest part of all was the fact there wasn't even sex.

It was better.

I know she's not asleep yet. I've watched her enough over the last few days to know when she's legitimately snoozing or pretending to. Though, I'm not sure she's pretending right now either. I just know she's not out.

Cameron shifts a bit, just doesn't slide off my chest. Probably because I'm still holding her tightly, refusing to let her go. She fits too perfectly in this position, and I'm going to hang on to it as long as I can. "Have you ever done something you regret with every fiber of your being?" she whispers, her fingers curling into my arm as if she's trying to hold on to me.

"Of course. We all make mistakes. Some are bigger than others."

She exhales, and I start to wonder if she's going to continue or if she was generally asking. "Last summer, I made a big mistake. I'm sure you've heard all the rumors."

My heart starts to pound. Is she actually going to talk about what happened at Burgers and Brew last year? "I've heard a few, but I chose to ignore them."

She lifts her head, those stunning green eyes full of question. "Why?"

I shrug my shoulder and pull her head back down against me. "Because I didn't know any facts, and it's not fair to you or anyone to make judgements based on rumors."

She's quiet again for a few long moments before she whispers her truth. "I stole money from Burgers and Brew."

It's weird that my initial reaction is one of respect, not anger or disgust. For her to speak those words just proves to me how good of a person she is, because, clearly, she's remorseful. I can hear it in her words, feel it ebbing from her body.

"Tell me about it," I whisper, stroking her back and arms, doing everything I can to show her support. There's a drop of moisture on my neck, and it breaks my heart a little to know she's crying.

"Cage and I lived together, and when he up and left, stealing a whole bunch of drugs and money in the process. A man showed up and demanded I pay Cage's debt. I didn't have the money, of course, so I had to use my paycheck and tips each week to make the payments. Each week, I had nothing left to pay my own bills, so I slowly started to lose my utilities. I couldn't call my parents and ask for help. I was too embarrassed, too ashamed at what was happening in my life."

She takes a deep breath and continues. "One night, I was counting my tips at the end of my shift and realized I was short. My landlord had given me a short extension on that month's rent, but because of the extensions he'd given the previous months, he wouldn't budge anymore. It was pay it in full by noon the next day, or he was starting the eviction process."

She reaches up and wipes her eyes, but keeps her face buried in my neck. "It was ten dollars. I was ten dollars short, Kellen, and had nowhere to go. I had already sold anything worth any value and felt like the walls were closing in around me.

"Ten dollars. I took it from the cash register, vowing to put it back the next shift. But then it kept snowballing, and before I knew it, I had taken one hundred forty dollars over four shifts. I was so angry with myself, so disgusted to look in the mirror. Working at Burgers and Brew was the best job I'd ever had, and I was essentially stomping all over it, over them. I was so ashamed, and when Garreth called me into his office to let me go, I was relieved. I hated lying, hated myself for living that lie, so when he called me out on it, I was just overwhelmed with relief. I expected to be taken to jail, but that's not what happened."

She lifts her head and meets my gaze. "Garreth helped me. He paid off the debt I owed to Cage's dealer and allowed me to keep my job under the stipulation I never stole again, and I'd come to him if I needed help again. He was...a friend. When I didn't feel like I had anyone in my corner, he offered me an olive branch, and I've made sure to make my payments and keep my nose clean so he never regrets helping me out."

My arms tighten around her as I just hold her close. "You're the strongest person I know."

She adamantly shakes her head. "I'm not. I'm weak. I should have asked for help instead of doing what I did."

"But you're righting that wrong, Cam. That takes guts and determination."

"I'm paying seventy-five dollars a week out of my tips to Garreth, which boils down to two years to pay it off. I've been able to maintain it for more than a year, but then my house got trashed. I can't imagine what it'll cost to replace practically everything in my place. It wasn't much, but it was enough I was comfortable."

I run my hand over her forehead and tuck her back against my neck. "Don't worry about that, okay? Let's see what we can salvage tomorrow. I don't want you to stress over that stuff, because at the end of the day, it's just stuff. You're safe, and that's all that matters. You're working toward the day you can go back home and feel comfortable and free to live your life without looking over your shoulder. That day is coming, love. Have faith."

We lie together, just feeling. I can feel her breath against my neck. I can feel her heartbeat in her chest. I can feel her worry slowly fading from her body. Then, all too quickly, she tenses. "Do you want me to leave?" she whispers.

"What? Why would I want you to go?"

She wiggles against my body, and even though I'm sure she's not doing it to get a sexual reaction out of me, my dick doesn't get the memo. He's suddenly getting hard and raring to go for another round. "Because I'm a thief," she insists, lifting her head and meeting my eyes head-on. "I stole from my bosses and yours."

"I heard all of that, and I understand your reasonings for doing what you did. I also am not worried about having you here in my house, even after hearing all of it. I trust you, Cam, just like you trusted me enough to share what happened."

I wipe away a single tear falling from her eyes and pull her back down against me. When we're situated once more, she mutters a simple, "Thank you."

"No, thank you," I insist, running my hand over her hair once again. "Thank you for trusting me. That means more to me than anything else."

No other words are spoken because they're not needed. I stand behind everything I said, including the fact I'm not worried about having her in my house. She'd never steal from me. I know deep in my heart she's learned her lesson, the guilt from what she did before weighing too heavily on her mind. She'd never put herself in that type of position again, and I only hope she understands she has me too. In addition to Garreth and Reagan, I'm in her corner. Not because of some sense of obligation I feel, but simply because I want to be there.

As I drift off to sleep, my arms wrapped around her, I realize I'm not afraid.

For more than a decade I've feared this. I've been afraid of opening myself up and letting myself feel, but all it took was one week with Cameron Wright to completely wreck my life in the best way possible. For the first time, I'm considering the possibility of having more.

It's terrifying, but so is the thought of not having her in my life.

In such a short amount of time, she has come to mean a lot to me.

Now, I just have to figure out what to do about it.

"What about all of this?"

I glance inside the bedroom where Cameron, Reagan, BJ, and Lyndee are clearing out the broken or trashed items and find Cameron sitting in the middle of the floor, surrounded by her stuff, an overwhelming look on her pretty face.

Stepping inside the room, I realize Lyndee is asking about the dresser. The drawers were all pulled out and tossed, the clothes that were once strewn all over the room somewhat cleaned up. I wait to see if Cameron is going to reply to her, but when she doesn't, I decide to step in and help.

"That doesn't look too bad," I say, walking over to the first drawer and the broken back. Picking up the broken piece, I realize it's cosmetic and can easily be fixed. "Actually, it's fixable. I bet Walker can slap a new piece of wood here," I tell her, indicating with my hand. "See how the tracks are still in place? That's a good thing. We'd have to ask him when he gets here, but I'm certain this dresser is salvageable. Even the nightstands."

Her green eyes dance with a little hope, probably in light of the fact we've thrown out quite a bit of stuff, and it makes me want to throw my hands up in victory. "Really?"

"Definitely," I reassure her with a smile. "Let's put these pieces in the living room and have Walker look at them when he gets here," I state, earning me a nod from everyone in the room. Lyndee, Jasper, and I carry the pieces into the living room, where, unfortunately, there aren't many other salvageable items.

"Knock, knock," Garreth hollers at the back door, entering before anyone yells for him to enter. "Hey, guys. Can you help me?"

Jasper and I follow him outside and instantly notice the back of his truck loaded with stuff. "What's all of this?" I ask, taking in the mattress, chair, and other small pieces of furniture.

"Some older stuff donated to Cam to get her back on her feet," Garreth says, opening his tailgate. "There's some bags in the back seat too."

"Come on, muscles. Let's grab that mattress and box spring," Jasper says, slapping me on the back while Garreth unstraps the load. I climb up into the bed and help move the large pieces as Jasper asks, "Why did Jameson get voted to watch the kids? I think next time we vote on who gets to hang with the babies and who has to come do manual labor."

I snort a laugh and hand him the mattress before jumping down and grabbing the other end. We carry it inside, setting it down against an empty wall in the living room, just as the girls come out of the bedroom.

Cameron stops and stares at the mattress, a look of uncertainty on her face. "What's that?"

"A mattress," Garreth says, entering the house with a small television.

She swallows hard and asks, "Where did it come from?"

"From our house," Lyndee announces. "We turned the guest room into Elsa's room last winter and weren't sure what we were going to do with it. It's been in the basement ever since, and I thought you might be able to get some use out of it."

"And that?" Cameron asks Garreth, who's still holding the television.

"And old one from the shop," BJ informs, her hand resting on her pregnant belly. "We upgraded to a bigger one, and since there was nothing wrong with it, I offered to take it for you instead of just throwing it away."

I can tell Cameron's on the verge of crying. She's fighting tears, at a loss for words. After a few long moments, she finally says, "I can't accept this. I can't afford it all right now."

Lacey Black

Reagan moves to her friend before I can get there, so I just stand back and watch, ready to step in if needed. "You don't owe anyone anything, Cam. This is stuff we've all had lying around or were going to throw out. It's not a lot, but it's something to help until you can buy your own stuff."

"I can't," Cameron says again, and this time, I can't stand across the room.

She steps into my arms immediately, which makes me want to roar and pound on my chest in victory. "This isn't a handout," I whisper, knowing where her mind is at.

"No, honey, it's not," Reagan reassures her, moving closer. "This is stuff we had lying around. Some of it isn't even really nice, but it's better than nothing, right? You're our friend, and friends take care of each other. That's what this is."

She turns to Reagan, as BJ and Lyndee walk up. The girls place their arms around each other, and suddenly, I'm being pushed out of their circle. I watch as they wrap arms and hold Cameron. It's as if they're showing her she's a part of their group, their family.

"You're one of us now. We help each other out," BJ insists, resting her purple-haired head against Cameron's auburn one.

"I don't know how to repay you guys," Cameron says between sniffles.

"You don't have to. Just pay it forward someday to someone who could use a little help too," Lyndee replies with a big grin.

We hear the back door open and close. "Okay, what'd I miss?" Mallory hollers, her belly protruding from her front as she enters the living room and finds the girls all hugging. "You made her cry?" Mallory hollers, her own eyes filling. "You know I can't handle tears," she mutters, sniffling as wetness leaks from the corners of her eyes.

"Which one of you assholes made her cry?" Walker asks the group, but his eyes have me pinned against the wall.

I hold up my hands. "We didn't do this. You guys did with the stuff in the truck."

Realization hits him, and he turns his attention to Cameron. "This is what family does, Cameron. You're part of that family," he says, offering her a small smile.

"Yep. Family." This from Lyndee.

Cameron looks around and returns their grins. "Thank you," she whispers, wiping at the wetness on her cheeks. "I promise to pay it forward."

"Good," Mallory says, reaching over and squeezing her arm. "Now, why are the guys standing around? Go get that truck unloaded," she adds, clapping her hands together.

Jasper, Garreth, and Walker turn and exit the house to start bringing in another load, but before I go to help, I want to check on Cameron. I'm ready to pull her into my arms once more, but Mallory is there.

"Listen, Cameron, when I first moved to Stewart Grove, I didn't have hardly a thing to my name. I left my old life with as much of Lizzie's stuff as I could take and barely anything else. I worked hard to provide for me and my daughter, but I can admit now, it wasn't really enough. I had to accept help from Walker and the guys, and that was hard for me. I had pride and didn't want to rely on another man, but he made me see what it was like to have real friends. He and the guys. They always considered my position and input, which I hope is how you see us. We don't want to take over. We just want to help." Mallory gives her a watery smile and pulls her into a hug.

"Okay, enough of that. I have to pee again," Mallory states, wiping her cheeks and scurrying off to the bathroom.

"You okay?" I ask, wanting to pull her into my arms, but giving her a little space to get her emotions under control.

"I'm...perfect," she whispers, a small grin playing on her lips.

"Good. Now, let's get the rest of the mess out of your bedroom so you can set up the new stuff. Then you'll have an idea of what you have and what you still need."

She moves, stepping forward and pressing herself against me, wrapping her arms around my waist and squeezing. "Thank you, Kellen."

I return the gesture, inhaling subtly the scent of her shampoo. "I didn't do anything. This is all you."

Cameron rests her cheek on my chest as she whispers, "You've done more than you'll ever know." She looks up and meets my gaze. "I know it isn't quite the right time for me to move back in here, but at least I'll have a place to come home to once this Cage mess is sorted out."

"You have a place to stay as long as you need it, but now you also have your home ready and waiting for your return." I try not to let my face show the nasty taste I suddenly had in my mouth while saying those words. They are exactly what she needs to hear. She's not ready to move back home yet, but I can tell she's getting stronger and less afraid with every passing day. Soon, she won't be in my bed at night, and that thought makes me want to hurl.

The back door opens again, and a flurry of activity enters the house as all of the used furniture is hauled inside.

Garreth steps inside first and notices us standing in the living room. "Come on, you two. Let's get back to work."

Twenty-Four

Cameron

Kellen grips my hand a little tighter as we weave through the people milling around the hallway backstage. Most people look our way, the women clearly checking Kellen out, while the guys seem more interested in watching the women. Everyone's just trying to figure out who we are, being led through the crowd by security.

I still can't believe I'm here.

A Kinsley McGregor concert!

The large man leading us down the hallway stops in front of a door and knocks. A loud "enter" comes through the door, indicating the man can open it. He pokes his head in and says, "Your guests are here, Ms. McGregor."

A loud squeal is heard, making Kellen laugh. The door opens widely, and a short woman reaches out, grabs Kellen's arm, and pulls him inside. "I can't believe you're really here!" Kinsley bellows, throwing herself at her brother and holding on tight.

He releases my hand so he can return her hug, and I can't help but smile at their exchange. Clearly, they're very close, and that makes me happy to know they have that relationship.

"Zander, look! Kel is here," Kinsley says, turning her attention to her husband. He's sitting on the couch, his nose in his phone as he types feverishly on the device.

Zander Houston barely looks up as he mutters a quick, "Hey."

I quickly look back at Kellen, taking note of his brother-in-law's brush-off, who doesn't miss it either. His jaw tics, but he schools his features enough in front of his sister so she can't see the annoyance he tries to hide. I see it, though. It flashes through his eyes, as does the guilt at having it. He wants to like his sister's husband, but it's clear he doesn't.

"Cameron."

I look up and find Kinsley staring at me, a wide, friendly grin on her face. Extending my hand, I prepare to shake Kellen's sister's hand, but she bats it away. Before I can even process the action, she wraps her arms around me and pulls me into a big hug.

"I can't believe I'm finally meeting you."

I can't help but laugh as I return the hug. "What? You can't believe you're meeting me?"

"Of course. I've been dying to meet the woman who changed my big brother," Kinsley announces, stepping back and patting Kellen on the chest.

"Oh, I don't know about that," I reply, doing this weird, unnatural chuckle at her comment.

Zander gets up off the couch, his face still plastered on his phone screen. "I'm gonna go meet Jimmy. He wants to talk about...stuff."

Kinsley doesn't look happy he's leaving, but says, "Uh, all right. Is everything okay?"

Slipping his phone into his back pocket, he gives her a pacifistic smile and replies, "Yep. Everything's gonna be great. Enjoy the visit with your family."

Then he's gone, leaving us to hang out before her concert.

"Jimmy?" Kellen asks.

"Come on, have a seat. I have to finish getting ready," Kinsley announces, pointing to the couch her husband just vacated and returning to the chair where a woman patiently waits. "Jimmy is our stage manager, the one who makes sure everything is ready to go before the show. Zander takes care of any last-minute details after my soundcheck. And this is Amber. She's a magician with my hair and makeup."

The stylist waves quickly before getting back to work on Kinsley's hair. "I've heard a lot about you both. This one has been chomping at the bit for the better part of two weeks in anticipation for tonight's show."

"That's because I'm the awesome one, and she couldn't wait to see me," Kellen says in a teasing tone, his sister sticking out her tongue.

We spend the next hour chatting while she gets ready. Even when the opening act goes on stage, we hang back. Kinsley is so easy to talk to, drawing you into the conversation. Never once have I felt out of place, even when they tell stories from their childhood. I do notice most of them involve just the two of them. There's very little mention of their parents, and I'm sure that has a lot to do with the fact their parents' marriage, and eventual divorce, was rough on both of them. From what I understand, the divorce happened while Kellen was in late high school, and when Kinsley decided to pursue her music career, their mom opted to go with her. Not wanting to be left out, their dad decided to go too, taking his then-girlfriend along for the ride.

When she's completely dressed in a stunning rhinestone tank top, jeans that were made for her body, and black sparkly cowboy boots, it's time for us to head to our seats for her show. We're in the front row, off to the right. She says this is a better place, considering all the fans tend to gather right in the middle of the stage.

"May I use your restroom quickly?" I ask, hoping we have a few minutes before we need to leave. Not that I mind using the public restrooms out in the concert venue, but I know the lines will be a mile long, especially since it's the intermission, and I'm not sure I can hold it that long.

"Absolutely," Kinsley says, placing dangly earrings in both ears.

As soon as I close the door, I take care of business. I don't know how tight of a schedule we're on, but I know she's going to need to go to the stage very soon. Just when I start to wash my hands, the sound of voices carries through the wall. I'm not trying to eavesdrop, but there's no way to *not* hear their conversation.

"I like her," Kinsley says.

"I like her too," Kellen replies.

My heart starts to pound a little bit harder, and considering I've been hanging out with a country superstar for the better part of an hour, that's saying something.

"I can see why you love her."

"What?"

What?!

"I'm not in love with her," Kellen argues. Just when I think she's about to say something else, he adds, "I do really care about her. I like her a lot, actually, and…it's complicated, Kins. She's only with me because we're in a pretend relationship."

"That wasn't pretend anything I saw in her eyes, Kel. She likes you too."

"You think?"

"I know, my friend. I can tell when a woman is into you, and she's most definitely into you."

"Relationships aren't my thing," he replies, making my heart drop down to my stomach. Not because it's new information, but because he has just confirmed exactly who he is. While I've enjoyed spending time with him, my time is running out. I've known that all along, despite the fact my heart has started to hope for more.

"Maybe they weren't in the past. Maybe you were just waiting for the right one to come along and make you see."

"See what?"

"That love is amazing when you find the other half of your soul."

"And let me guess, you found it with Zander," he states, a hint of sarcasm I can hear even through the door.

She doesn't reply, not right away, and I wish I could see her face. "There are different levels of love, Kellen," I hear her whisper, making my heart break just a bit.

"What does that mean?" her brother asks. "Besides, I'm too young to fall in love."

"Oh my God, you're ridiculous," Kinsley replies.

"Whatever. You're dumb."

"Cameron is amazing, and if you don't realize it soon, you'll lose her, big brother." There's a knock on the door, and suddenly the conversation is over. "Showtime!" she yells.

I step away from the door and give myself one quick glance in the mirror. I'm wearing my own navy-blue tank top, basic skinny jeans, and comfy ballet flats. My hair is down and my makeup subtle. I'm nothing special, but I'll never forget the way Kellen's eyes lit up with something that felt like appreciation as I stepped out of my bedroom earlier.

Exiting the bathroom, I find them both standing in the middle of the room, smiling. "Ready?" Kinsley asks.

"Are you?" I can't help but ask.

"I'm always ready," she states proudly, reaching for a necklace. She hands it to Kellen, and asks, "Do the honors?"

He grins widely. "Of putting Nana's cross around your neck? Abso-fucking-lutely," he states, securing the chain and gorgeous silver cross around her neck.

"Now I'm ready." She turns to me, fingering the delicate piece around her neck and bringing it to her lips to kiss. "Nana wore this necklace daily when I was younger. When she passed away, it was the only item I wanted. I've worn it at every show I've ever performed. It's like having her with me."

"It's beautiful," I tell her.

A second knock echoes through the room. "Kins, time to go!"

We step out into the hallway and find Zander there, waiting. He looks completely put together in a different outfit than the one he had on when he went to meet up with Jimmy, which strikes me as odd. I would have thought they'd share a dressing room, considering they're married. Perhaps one of them is a diva and requires separate digs, but after spending an hour with Kinsley, I would doubt it to be her. She's the least *diva* of anyone I've ever met. She's gracious and humble and makes her brother smile, which in turn, makes me smile.

We follow behind them as they walk down the hall toward the stage. Someone hands Kinsley a bottle of water, which she takes small drinks out of. "I'm going to have security grab you both after the show, okay? I want pics for my social media accounts."

I'm unable to school my surprised response, which makes her laugh. "I have to show off my brother, and I definitely want you a part of that," she says to me.

We reach the side of the stage. I can see the arena, and it's full. My heart is beating wildly in my chest with excitement and nerves for her, yet she seems so casual and unaffected by the thousands of people all here to hear her sing.

"All right, we're going to our seats," Kellen says, stepping forward and giving her a hug. "Break a leg, kid."

She beams at her brother, returning the gesture and squeezing as tightly as she can. "I'm so glad you're here."

"Me too," he mumbles, kissing her forehead and stepping away.

Then, she turns to me and pulls me into another hug. "I'm so happy to officially meet you. Be good to my brother," she adds with a whisper so no one can hear. "He's kinda stupid sometimes so be forgiving when he messes up, okay?"

I can't help but giggle. "Yes, ma'am."

Kinsley gives me the biggest, best smile and turns toward the stage. She looks at the guy I assume is Jimmy and says, "Let's do it."

Kellen takes my hand and follows a security woman around the stage and to our seats. By the time we get there, everyone is standing in anticipation. The entire place is electrically charged, and I can feel it course through my body. When the music starts, I'm pulled into the excitement with those around me, my hands in the air as I cheer for Kinsley's arrival. The entire time, Kellen has his arm around my waist, holding me closely.

We never sit down. We stand, sing, and dance the entire time, even when she acknowledges her family in the crowd. We're not put under the spotlight, thankfully, but the entire arena cheers for us without knowing who and where we are.

By the end of the show, my throat is raw and my legs tired, but I've never felt this amazing. My first concert experience and it did not disappoint in the least. Of course it doesn't hurt I got to go backstage and meet the headliner before the show too.

As the crowd starts to thin out, Kellen takes my hand. "How was it?"

"The best night of my life," I tell him, not realizing I'm yelling until he laughs. "Oh, sorry. I probably won't be able to hear for two days."

"The downfall of a live concert when you're near the speakers," he states with a tired smile. "I went to see the Crüe last summer at their stadium tour and was fortunate enough to be seated near some speakers."

"Fortunate?"

"Or unfortunate, depending on how you look at it. I definitely had hearing trouble for a few days post-show, but it was one of the best performances I've seen."

"I bet that was amazing."

"Mr. McGregor, if you'll follow me, I'll take you backstage to see Ms. McGregor."

We follow the same female security guard who led us to our seats before the show. Instead of going down the hall toward the dressing rooms, we're taken to a large room, which is set up with food and drinks and several dozen people. We wait until Kinsley finishes speaking to a small group of fans, and the moment she sees us, she heads our way. "What did you guys think?"

"Ehh," Kellen replies, shaking his hand from side to side as if to say so-so.

"Oh, shut up!" Kinsley bellows with a laugh. She takes a long drink of water before she turns to me. "What did you think?"

"It was amazing. Of course I don't have any other show to compare you to, but it was the most amazing experience, and I'll never forget it."

"This was your first concert?" Kinsley asks, her mouth falling open.

I feel heat creeping up my cheeks as I nod in confirmation.

"Oh my goodness, I didn't realize that. Hold on!" In a flurry of rhinestones and electric energy, she spins around and disappears across the room. Kellen squeezes my hand as we watch her grab a guitar and move from band member to band member, including her husband. He's over talking to two women and barely acknowledges his wife as she approaches and asks him to sign the guitar. He does quickly before handing it back to her to resume his conversation. Kellen must notice how he brushes her off too and lets a small growl fly.

When Kinsley reaches us again, she writes on the guitar and signs her name before handing it to me. "Here. To commemorate your very first concert experience."

My hand is a little shaky as I take the guitar from her and look it over. The entire band signed it, as well as Kinsley herself. She even wrote a message. *"Cameron, here's to following your passion. Love always, Kinsley McGregor."*

It's suddenly hard to swallow over the lump lodged firmly in my throat. "Oh, wow. Thank you so much," I whisper, blinking repeatedly to keep the tears at bay.

"I've never gotten a guitar," Kellen grumbles, breaking through the heaviness surrounding me with humor. Something he seems to do so easily.

"That's because I like her more than you," the woman of the hour announces with a laugh.

"Yeah, yeah," Kellen says, unable to fight his grin. We hang out backstage for about thirty minutes until Kellen catches me yawning. "Hey, Kins, we're gonna head to the hotel."

His sister nods, waving at the man we know as Jimmy. He walks over and pulls out his phone, as if knowing exactly what to do. With Kellen in the middle, he wraps an arm around each of us as we pose for a picture. I smile, hoping it looks natural and not like a goon. I'm floating on a bubble at this point, unable to believe this is my life. Hanging backstage with a country superstar.

"Cameron, send me your phone number. I'd love to keep in touch," Kinsley says once the pictures are taken.

"Not happening. You'll tell her all my embarrassing stories," Kellen counters, keeping his left arm around me.

"Too late. Besides, it's my right as little sister."

Her brother grumbles before adding, "Hey, send me that pic."

"Will do. Jimmy, text me that photo, please?"

"Already done, Kinsley," the older man says before reaching out and shaking Kellen's hand. "Nice to meet you both."

"Same." Kellen turns to his sister and engulfs her in a big hug. "I love you, Kins, and I'm so fucking proud of you."

"Thanks, Kel. I'm proud of you too," she whispers, her eyes finding me. "You better be good to this one."

I swallow tightly.

"I will be. Promise you'll be careful out on the road, you hear?"

"I will," she confirms, her eyes filling with tears. Then, she spins to face me and gives me another hug. "Thank you."

"For what? I haven't done anything," I insist, confused as to why she would be thanking me.

Kinsley just gives me a knowing smile. "You've done more than you'll ever know," she says softly, glancing over her shoulder to her brother. "He's changed, and that's because of you."

My throat burns with emotion as I glance down at my shoes. "I've only really known him on this level a few weeks. I don't think I've done anything."

When I look back up at her, she winks. "You've brought him to life. Don't ever forget that."

Kinsley takes a step back. Kellen grabs my signed guitar in one hand and my hand in the other. "I'll talk to you soon."

"Love you," Kinsley says with a smile so similar to her brother's. Not the flirty one, but the genuine one he seems to share more and more lately.

"Love you more, kid." He looks over his sister's shoulder and adds, "Tell Zander we said goodbye."

Something passes in Kinsley's eyes, but I'm not sure what it means. She's smiling, but the grin doesn't quite meet her eyes as she replies, "I will."

Then, we're gone, exiting the back room and worming through the mostly empty concert venue on our way to the parking lot. We reach his truck easily, thanks to the lots being mostly vacant, and he stores my new guitar in the back seat. Just as he climbs inside the driver's seat, his phone rings. Considering it's after midnight, my heart skips a beat at the thought of something being wrong.

Worry etches his features as he pulls his phone out of his pocket. "Hey, G, everything okay?" he asks, and my heart starts to pound double-time now.

Why would Garreth be calling him so late?

And why does the overwhelming feeling of dread make it so hard to breathe?

Nothing good comes from a phone call at this hour.

Nothing.

Twenty-Five 25

Kellen

"Hey, sorry to call so late. I took a shot you might still be up from the concert," Garreth replies.

"We're still up. Getting ready to leave the show and head to the hotel."

"Okay. Well, I thought you'd want to know now instead of in the morning, but Cage was arrested tonight."

"What?" I ask, turning and looking at Cameron. She looks like she's ready to have a panic attack, so I reach across the console and take her hand in mine. "What happened?"

"Stupid fucker tried picking his business up where he left off. I guess they set up a sting operation and got him for selling to two undercover cops. Had enough product on him for distribution, but, apparently, he also had a book on him. It contained dates of sales, amounts, dealer names and contacts. Basically, he handed his entire operation over to the police because he's stupid enough to put it in writing. He's going to jail, man. For a long fucking time."

I close my eyes, just trying to absorb what he's telling me. An overwhelming sense of relief washes over me, and as I squeeze Cameron's hand, I hope to pass a little bit of that relief to her. "That's amazing fucking news, G. I can't wait to tell Cameron."

"Tell her she's free."

My throat is thick as realization sets in. "I'll tell her," I whisper, my words a little hoarser than normal.

"Talk to you tomorrow." He signs off, leaving me alone with Cameron.

"What's wrong?"

I start the truck and turn and face her. "Cage was arrested tonight. Distribution and selling to undercover cops. He'll be behind bars for a long time, love."

A mix of emotions crosses her face as my words sink in. "It's over?"

I nod in confirmation. "It's over."

That's when my heart sort of cracks a little bit.

"Wow," she replies, as if unable to come up with a better word.

I throw the truck in gear and exit the lot. Thanks to the late hour, traffic is already dispersed, and it doesn't take long to get to the hotel I reserved for the evening. We're both silent the entire ride, as we work through the emotions we're feeling. For three weeks, this woman has been living in my house. She's been afraid to be alone at night. She's cried tears of fear and worry. She's found solace in my bed every single night since the first one. She's found comfort and has learned to trust again.

And now it's fucking over.

Just like that.

Our fake relationship isn't needed anymore.

There's no longer a reason for her to stay.

I park my truck in the lot and jump out. I grab the guitar and her hand and lead her into the building. Her grip is a little tighter, and I can't help but wonder if that's because she realizes we've reached the end of our agreement. Or is she hanging on tighter because she's afraid to let go?

Why do I really hope the latter is the reason?

Using the key card I was given at check-in before the concert, I let us into the king-sized suite I reserved. I probably could have gotten us a room with double beds, but when I called to make the reservation, I didn't even consider it. She's been in my arms every night for the last three weeks. That's exactly where I wanted her tonight too, and despite hearing the news about Cage's arrest, that's where I want her still.

In. My. Arms.

When I secure the room with the extra security features on the door, I set her guitar down on the desk and drop the key card on the dresser.

"Kellen?" she whispers, breaking through the fog in my head.

Even in the dark room, I can see her standing by the bed, her hands wringing together in front of her. She does that when she gets nervous, and the thought of me being the reason for those nerves makes me feel a little sick. "Yeah?" I ask, clearing my throat.

She takes a step forward and another until she's directly in front of me. "Do you remember when you told me I wouldn't be under you until everything with Cage is over?"

I nod, unable to find words.

Cameron runs her hands up my arms, across my shoulders, and around my upper back. "Well, it's over."

My cock is starting to get hard, anxiously awaiting the green light. Is she saying what I think she is? "It is over," I confirm, my eyes dropping to the hint of cleavage on display above her tank top.

Going up on her tiptoes, she leans in, her mouth angled up toward mine. "I'm ready to be under you now."

I groan, my cock kicking against my zipper. "Are you sure?"

She digs her nails into my neck, the bite against my skin like waving a red flag in front of a bull. "I'm very sure."

I take a step back, gauging her, but see not a hint of hesitancy in those green eyes. Running my hand down my face, I take a deep breath and whisper, "Take off your clothes, love. I need you naked now."

Heat flashes in her eyes and her cheeks as she nods eagerly and kicks off the flats on her feet. Her tank top goes first, gently lifting it up and over her head, exposing the dark blue bra beneath it. Her nipples are already hard, begging for my mouth, but they're going to have to wait a few minutes. I intend to enjoy the fuck out of this show first.

Next, she reaches for the button on her jeans. She takes her time, releasing the button and slowly dragging the zipper down. I can see a hint of blue lace, which matches the material covering her delicious tits. She shimmies out of the jeans, the same ones that have given me a chubby all fucking night because of how amazing her ass has looked. Now, I'm about to see that ass without the denim shield, and my cock couldn't be happier.

When she's standing in just her bra and panties, I twist my finger, indicating for her to spin around. The view from the back is just as amazing as it is from the front, and even though I'd love to sit and stare at her all night like a painting in a museum, I want to get her naked and feast on her body more.

I lift my T-shirt up and over my head, my eyes still devouring the sight of her. After I toe off my shoes and pull off my socks, I unfasten my own jeans and lower the zipper. "Lie on the bed," I instruct.

Cameron moves to the bed, pulling back the blanket and lying on the sheets. Her skin is flushed and pink compared to the stark white bedding, and the sight of her just makes my dick harder. "Pull down the cups of your bra, Cam," I say, walking over to the bed but not joining her yet.

She does, exposing those dusty pink nipples. They're hard and ripe for my mouth.

"Now the panties. Pull them to the side so I can see that pretty pussy of yours."

She shivers as she reaches down and slides the blue material to the side. The scent of her arousal hits me square in the chest and the balls.

"Do you want me to make you come, love? Want my mouth on that sweet pussy of yours?" I ask, wishing I had taken off my jeans so I could stroke my cock, but at the same time, glad I didn't so I wouldn't be tempted to just go for the gold right now. I plan to take my time with her and drag out our night together. I don't know how tomorrow will look, so I plan to take advantage of having her in my bed tonight. As much or as many times as possible.

"Yes. Please."

I climb onto the bed and take my position between her spread thighs. Of all the places in the world, this has quickly become my most favorite place to be. I've become addicted to her in the last few weeks. Ever since that date we went on. After making her come three times that night and many more times in the two weeks that followed, she's simply become my addiction. My drug.

One I don't want to think about giving up.

Lowering my head, I swipe my tongue across her pussy, reveling in the taste of her. "Fuck, angel. You're so damn delicious."

She moans in pleasure as her fingers glide into my hair. She grips my scalp, knowing what's to come and trying to hang on for the ride. I take no mercy on her either. I work her over with my tongue like a madman, bringing her to the brink of release and then pulling back. Cameron groans, just as I expected her to, while I place kisses against the soft skin of her thighs.

"You want something, love?" I tease.

"Yes. I want to come, Kellen. Don't make me beg."

"I won't make you beg. Not when you tell me so directly what you want. You want to come, huh?" I lower my mouth and suck on her clit hard. The result is an explosion, just as I anticipated, and I don't let up until I've sucked every ounce of her release from her body.

Her legs and arms drop to the bed boneless as a satisfied smile spreads across her lips. I move, covering her body with my own and claiming that sweet mouth with mine. My tongue delves inside her mouth, tangling with hers and causing what little blood still remains in my body to move to my dick. It's so hard it could pound concrete right now, but I keep my focus on her.

When we finally come up for air and her eyes open, she gives me a coy little grin. "That good?" I ask.

She shakes her head no.

"No?"

Again, she shakes her head no, dancing her fingers down my bare chest to where my cock pokes out of the top of my open jeans. "I want more."

"More, huh? What more do you want?"

"I want to be beneath you," she says, using my own words against me. "Or above you. Or bent over in front of you. Or all of it, really. I want it all."

"All of it, huh? That might take all night," I tell her, running a single finger down the side of her face.

She smiles widely once more. "I kinda hope it does."

I move, getting off the bed and standing beside it. She watches as I lower my jeans and boxer briefs in one push, kicking them off beside me. My cock is so hard and ready, it's seeping for her. She must notice, because my little vixen licks her lips as her eyes devour my cock. "Take off your bra and panties, Cam. I don't want to ruin them."

She does, sitting up and removing the bra before lying back down and shimmying out of her panties. I reach for my wallet, pulling one of the condoms out. I've always carried one or two since I was a horny sixteen-year-old, but when I checked my stash last week, I slipped a third one in there. Not that I had a plan to get naked with Cameron, per se, but I wanted to make sure I was prepared on the off chance we were finally able to take this relationship to that level. Thank God I thought ahead, because I'm certain I'm going to need all three of them before this night is over.

Sheathing my erection, I return to my position between her legs. She instantly hitches her ankles over my hips, opening herself up nice and wide. My eyes are down, glued to her wet pussy. It's open and inviting and ready to be fucked.

I push the tip down, gliding it across her clit. She jerks, groaning as I slowly work my way down to her entrance. "Get up on your elbows, love. I want you to watch me fill you for the first time," I instruct, which she eagerly does. "Watch as your pussy takes my dick."

And then I push forward, inch by inch, my cock disappears inside her until it's completely gone. The warmth and tightness are pure bliss as I close my eyes and just feel. "Open your eyes, Kellen. I want you to watch my pussy take your dick."

My eyes fly open and meet hers. It's right now, in this moment, I know. I've fallen in love with her. As I stare into those green hypnotic pools, I know I've gone and lost my heart. She slowly knocked down every wall I've erected since I was a teenager, trying to ensure I always protected myself. And here I am, balls deep for the first time in the only woman I've ever loved, when I open my mouth to say something, the words just get stuck.

I can't tell her like this.

No woman would ever believe a love declaration while being fucked. Everyone knows the little heads are doing all the thinking right now, and anything that comes out of their mouths while fucking isn't to be believed.

So, instead, I'll just show her.

Cameron looks up at me, a look of wonder and bliss in her eyes. Slowly, I pull back and slide back in, slowly feeling her body start to relax and loosen. I reach down, hitching her leg up higher on my back and changing the angle just a bit. This position allows me to go even deeper, and most importantly, will cause my cock to stroke against her G-spot. Her eyes roll back in her head, and I know I've found the place. My hips start to pick up the pace, thrusting forward, fucking her into the mattress. She reaches up and curls her nails into my back, something I never even knew I'd like until she showed me. Now, I want to feel her nails biting my skin all the damn time.

I'll never get enough of her.

She cries out as I rock forward, rolling my hips and grinding my pubis against her clit. I know she's getting close; can feel the way her pussy is clamping down around me. There's nothing like this feeling, like being inside her body for the first time. To understand the magnitude of the moment and cherish every second of it.

"Kellen," she whimpers, rocking her hips to the tempo I set.

Bending down, I suck one greedy little nipple into my mouth, loving the moan of pleasure that fills the room. Releasing the first one with a pop, I shower the same attention to the second, while making shallow thrusts with my hips and teasing her pussy with only the head of my dick. "Yes, love?"

She groans in frustration, so I suck on her nipple a little hard, lapping at the tip with my tongue. "I want...I need..."

I release my mouth and thrust my hips, causing her to gasp and tense. "I can read you like a book, Cam. What you need is to come, right?"

"Yes." Thrust. "Please," she begs.

"On my dick, Cam. You're going to come on my cock."

She whimpers again, her core gripping me like a vise.

Reaching between us, I glide my thumb across her clit and watch as she gloriously detonates. She cries out, her pussy clenching my dick so hard I can barely move, let alone keep myself from coming, but I'm not ready yet. I want another release from her before I finally let go.

Somehow, I'm able to keep my own release at bay, waiting until she's starting to come down from her high before slowing my pace. Only then do I pull out. "Roll over, sweetness. I want to see that beautiful ass of yours while I fuck you from behind."

I reach down, holding her hips until she spins around and gets up on all fours in front of me. My hands reach out and grip her ass, my fingers itching to delve inside her pussy. I trace the edge of her hole with my thumb, slipping inside for just a moment to ensure she's still wet and ready for me. "Sit back on me," I state, removing my thumb and gripping her hips to help guide her. She takes me all the way inside, leaning back against my legs.

I wrap my hands around her chest, palming her tits and pinching her nipples. She sits up, leaning back on my cock, and threads her fingers into my hair behind her head. "Fuck," I groan, bouncing forward in short thrusts.

She leans her head to the side, exposing her neck. My mouth latches on, kissing, licking, and nipping at the soft skin, as she bounces back against my legs and takes me in deep. "You feel so good," she whispers.

My balls start to draw up, and I know the end is near. I've fought my orgasm as long as possible, but it's barreling down on me. "Reach down and play with your clit, Cam. I'm going to come, and I'm taking you with me."

She makes a noise, and I wonder if she's going to argue with me, but she doesn't. She moves her hand between her legs, her fingers brushing against my cock as it slides inside her pussy. Then, she reaches down and cups my balls.

"Jesus," I bite out, pinching back my release. "Make yourself come, Cam. I'm already there."

Her hand is gone, and I feel her pussy clenching me once more. She's playing with her clit, and I just need to hold off a few more seconds. I roll a nipple between my thumb and first finger with one hand and hold on to her hip with the other. The moment she starts to come for a third time, I blow. I come so hard I see Jesus, emptying everything in my balls into the rubber. It's the most glorious feeling in the world, one I want to repeat over and over again.

But at the same time, not knowing where this will go in the morning light.

We fall together in a heap of sweaty limbs and labored breaths onto the mattress. I know I need to take care of the rubber but am too afraid to move. I don't want to break the spell. I just want to stay wrapped in this blissful bubble we're in.

When we both start to calm down, I know I need to get up and take care of the condom. Placing a kiss on the back of her bare shoulder, I slide from her body and the bed and head for the bathroom. I take a moment to clean up, use the head, and grab a warm washcloth for her. By the time I return to the bedroom, she's curled up on her side, her beautiful ass poised in my direction. My dick actually twitches, ready to prove he's ready for another round, but I ignore his advice. She's going to be sore tomorrow. The last thing she needs is my dick between her thighs again so soon.

She barely stirs as I use the warm cloth to wipe at her sensitive areas. "You didn't have to do that," she mumbles, her face pressed against the pillow.

I can't help but smile as I throw the washcloth onto the floor and climb in behind her. She scoots to make room and nestles her ass against my groin like the naughty girl she is. She wiggles against my growing cock. "Stop that, or you'll get him hard again."

She giggles, pulling my arm beneath her neck and snuggling in. "That doesn't sound like a threat."

"Oh, it's not. It's a promise of a good time, my little vixen." Bending down, I kiss her shoulder once more and wrap my other arm around her. "Sleep, love. There'll be time for that later."

She mutters something I don't quite understand and is out only moments later.

I, on the other hand, lie awake as long as possible, just holding her close. Too afraid to let go. Because I fell in love, and for the first time in my life, have no idea what to do next.

Cameron

There's a heaviness in the truck as we make our way back to Stewart Grove. It's hung over our heads from the moment we woke up this morning. Hell, probably since we received that phone call last night.

I'm still trying to process everything that has happened.

First, with Cage being arrested. I had prayed daily for vindication over what happened last summer, and now it looks like it's finally happened. Add in the fact Kellen and I slept together, and not just when we got back to the hotel room. He woke me around three a.m. and then invited me into the shower with him before we checked out. I'm deliciously sore in all the right places, a reminder of his size and how easily he played my body like a violin.

Now, as we approach his house, I know there's an important conversation that needs to be had. My reason for staying with him is behind me, my house slowly being put back to the way it was before. I'll have plenty to purchase, but I have the basic necessities right now, thanks to good friends.

We pull into Kellen's driveway, and instead of parking in the garage, he stops in front of it. My car is parked in the second bay, where it has been since I picked it up from Otto's shop. Since we've been working the same shift, we've been going to work together. Even though he doesn't get off until after me, I've enjoyed sitting at the bar and chatting with him, Garreth, and whoever else is working that night.

Kellen grabs our bags from the back seat, as well as my signed guitar, and when he notices I don't move to the house, he stops and watches me.

"I need to go home," I blurt out, trying to find the right way to say this, but realizing very quickly I'm coming up short.

He sets the guitar down, leaning it against the bumper of his truck, and places the bags beside it. "Okay," he replies softly, stepping forward and invading my personal space. Part of me wants to step into his arms, while another piece tells me to put distance between us. This is going to be hard despite the circumstances, but if he's touching me, it'll be downright excruciating.

"With Cage being in jail, I just...I feel like I need to do this," I whisper, "For me."

He gives me a small smile and cups my cheek with his big, warm hand. "I understand, Cam. You need to take back your independence. Your life."

Before he can say anything else, I quickly push on. "I mean, this relationship was fake, right?" I state with an awkward chuckle.

Something flashes in his eyes, but it disappears before I can figure out what it is. "Yeah. Right. Fake." He releases my cheek and shoves his hands in his pockets rapidly. "So, you're going to go home." It's not a question.

"Yes," I croak out, my throat dry and tight. "I think it's for the best."

He nods in agreement. "Okay. Let me help you gather your things," he replies, reaching down and picking back up the guitar and the bags.

Somehow, he manages to open the back door and step aside so I can enter. The house feels...familiar. Safe. Like home.

That's probably because when my world felt anything but safe a few weeks ago, he gave me shelter. Solace. Friendship.

I bypass the drums and the familiar throw blanket on the back of the couch that smells like him and head straight to the guest room. I don't have a lot here but have more than what will fit in the small bags I have available. Oh well, I can carry stacks of my clothes out to my car.

While I go into the bathroom to retrieve the dirty clothes I have yet to wash, I hear the dresser drawers open and close, and when I peek out, I spot Kellen pulling the clothes out and placing them on the bed. He looks forlorn as he does it, and the thought of him feeling a little sad to see me go causes me to wonder if I'm reading him incorrectly. But then I recall how he said we were friends and I know we're just not on the same page. He's not a relationship guy, and everything we've shared above that level of friendship wasn't real.

It was for show.

I shove my dirty clothes in the bottom of a bag and set it aside, not wanting to mix in the clean stuff. Then, I return to the bathroom to gather everything from there, making sure to only take the items I brought or bought myself. Everything else is Kinsley's, and it all stays.

When the bathroom is cleared out, I return to the bedroom. Kellen is placing the paperback I've been reading on top of the stack. "Oh, that's not mine. That's your sister's book."

He looks up. "Have you finished reading it?"

I shake my head.

"Then, take it and finish it. She won't mind, and probably won't be coming for a visit until after the tour winds down."

Opening my mouth to argue that I don't need to borrow it, I shut it just as quickly when he walks over and grabs the other book off the shelf I was wanting to read next. He places it on top of the one I'm currently reading and adds, "I assume you haven't read this one yet? It was sitting away from the others so I figured it was next on your to-be-read list."

A smile cracks across my lips, even though my heart feels nothing but sorrow. "How do you know what a to-be-read list is?"

"Kins. If she's not playing music, she's reading. It's one of her escapes, and she always has different stacks of books based on read or not read."

"Well, you're right. I haven't read that one yet, but I don't know when I'll get to it," I tell him, grabbing the book to return to the bookshelf. "I don't want to take her books."

"She's read all of these. She'll bring whatever she's reading or plans to read while she's here."

"Still, I don't feel right about it," I tell him, placing the book on the shelf.

"Well, I don't feel right about you not taking it if it's a book you'd like to read, Cam," he counters, taking the book from the shelf and placing it back on the pile of clothes.

"You're being difficult," I argue, even though I'm smiling.

"Perhaps, but so are you," he counters, narrowing his humor-filled eyes at me.

"Fine, but it may be a while. I don't read very fast," I whisper, turning away in hopes maybe he didn't hear my confession.

"Like I said, she's already read these, so take your time." He looks around the room, making sure we haven't forgotten anything. I notice how surprisingly void it now is of my stay, as if my time here was nothing more than a memory. "Is that everything?"

I nod, my throat thick with emotion again. "That's it."

He walks out of the room, surprising me a little by his hasty retreat, but returns a minute later with a large duffel bag. Without saying a word, he starts to carefully place my clothes inside the bag. It's incredibly heartbreaking to watch him pack up my belongings, and I don't really understand why. This was always the plan—for me to return home when the threat of Cage was somehow taken care of. Now that it has, the thought of leaving Kellen's home is just as hurtful as the reason I had to move into it in the first place.

To keep my hands busy, I help shove the rest of my stuff into the small bags I have, and when it's all packed up, I give the room one last glance. It's all here, which means it's time for me to go.

As if knowing this is it, Kellen picks up the larger bag and takes my hand in the other. I grab the smaller bags in my free hand and allow him to lead me from the room I've called home for the last three weeks. In the hallway, I have to force myself not to look into his bedroom. Seeing his bed will break me. Knowing I'll never be in it again, wrapped in his arms and feeling the safety they provide, causes tears to well in my eyes once more, but I refuse to let them fall.

Not until I'm back home and alone.

Then, they can fall freely, which I'm certain will happen.

Probably a lot.

Because leaving Kellen is going to be the hardest thing I've ever done, and despite taking all my belongings, I'm leaving something behind.

My heart.

When we reach the kitchen, he releases my hand and takes the bags. "I'll get this stuff loaded up," he says, grabbing the things in my hand and exiting the house.

I look around and find the signed guitar and smaller duffel bag I used for our overnight trip to Philly and head outside. With one last look over my shoulder, I take in the bright kitchen that holds so many memories for me a final time. I'll miss the breakfasts, the chats, and the time we spent in here.

I'll miss *him*.

Everything is placed in the back seat of my car, and although not ready, it's time for me to go. Before I get inside the driver's seat, I turn and face the man who now means more to me than I ever expected someone could. "Thank you, Kellen," I whisper, unable to fight the onslaught of emotions.

He wraps his arms around me and pulls me against his chest. It's familiar and comfortable and makes the tears seep from my eyes. "You're welcome, Cam. Anytime you need me, I'm a phone call away."

I nod against his chest and sniffle. He doesn't seem fazed at all by the fact his shirt is getting wet.

"If you need me, call. Text. Just come over. Whatever," he says, pulling back and meeting my gaze. "I'll always be your friend, love, and that's what friends are for."

My heart breaks in two.

Friends.

There's that term again. At least now I know the truth. We'll never be more than just friends. Friends who shared an amazing few weeks together. Friends who know what the other sounds like when they're coming. Friends who have seen each other naked. I'm the one who let my heart get involved, despite trying not to, and now I'm going to have to live with that hurt.

Love sucks big monkey balls.

"Anytime you want to come over and jam with me, just stop by," he says, flashing me that sexy grin I can't seem to get enough of.

"Oh." I pull back, realizing I have something else that's his. I pull my keys out and retrieve the one for his house. "Here," I add, carefully trying to extract it from the key ring.

"Keep it, Cam. At least for a while, so you know you always have a safe place to go if you need one," he says, wrapping his big hand around mine to stop me from removing his house key.

I nod, my throat so thick I can barely draw oxygen into my lungs. Then, I throw my arms around him one last time and just breathe him in. His arms go around me too, holding me a little tighter than normal. He drops his nose to my hair and inhales, and if I wasn't so out of sorts with emotions, I might tease him about his creepiness, despite the fact I often do the same thing. Instead, I pretend he's doing it to commit my scent to memory, much like I'm doing with the feel of his arms wrapped around me and my cheek pressed against his pec.

He's the first one to pull back, and there's no missing the sadness in his beautiful eyes. "I'll see you in a few hours at work, right?"

I nod, wondering how in the hell I'm going to get through a shift tonight, especially with him in the other room. "I'll be there," I tell him. I don't have a choice. I have debts to pay, which means there's no chance I can call in sick and sulk at home for a night or two. I'm going to have to put on my big girl panties and pretend like I'm not affected by his nearness, because that's not what *friends* do.

He lets go of me, and I feel the distance immediately. A cold chill sweeps through my body. "Do you want me to follow you home and help you unload?"

No, definitely not. I need to sulk and have a crying fit in peace.

"No, I'm good. It's not a lot of stuff," I reply with a chuckle and a forced smile.

Kellen nods and takes another step back. He walks over to the wall and presses the button to lift the garage door, and I know that's my cue to go. There's no reason for me to stay. I climb inside my car, and he's there a moment later, holding on to the doorframe. "Let me know if you need anything, Cam. Anything at all."

I nod, because that's all I have in me.

"See you soon, love," he whispers moments before he shuts the door.

I feel more alone now than I did when I first arrived at his house, but I refuse to dwell on it. It's time to take back my independence. It's time to overcome what Cage took from me when he broke into my house. It's time to be me and find my happiness.

As I pull out of the garage and back out of the driveway, I can't help but look at Kellen one last time. His hands are shoved in his pockets as he watches me leave. There's a smile on his lips, but it lacks the usual luster. I glance in the rearview mirror and refuse to look his way again. This is my opportunity to take back my life.

I just wish I didn't feel like I was leaving such a big piece of me behind as I drive away.

Twenty-Seven 27

Kellen

This fucking sucks.

I almost ask her to stay, but I know I can't. I won't.

Watching her pull out of my driveway and head off was the most heart-wrenching thing I've ever experienced, and that's saying something after my parents' divorce and move to Nashville with Kinsley. Then, I chose to stay behind and build my life here. Now, I feel more alone than I ever did after they left.

After several minutes of hoping to see her car return, I finally drag myself back into my house and shut the door. I'm instantly surrounded by silence, and I fucking hate it. Hate. It. Even when she was quiet, I felt her presence. I could smell her familiar shampoo and lotion. Now, even though the scents still linger in the air, there's a void in my space. One I'm not sure I'll ever overcome.

Letting her go was hard, but necessary.

She needs this. She needs to move back home and prove to herself she's strong and capable. That asshole ex of hers took something valuable from her that night, and I know in my heart she's trying to get that back. Having her here helped bridge the gap, but only she can take these final steps to truly heal, and there's not a doubt in my mind she will do it. She'll overcome and persevere, coming out stronger on the other side.

I know it in my heart.

But let's not talk about that particular organ. Not only is my cock pissed off she won't be in my bed anymore, but the heavy thumper in my chest isn't too happy with me right now either. He's hurting. Bad. He didn't want me to let her go. He wanted her to stay. In my bed. In my house. In my life.

Ignoring the pain I feel, I try to keep myself busy, but there's nothing to do. I mowed the lawn and took care of leaves before we left for Philly, and Cameron made sure all the dishes were washed before our little trip. I throw a small load of laundry in the washer, staring at the digital screen as it starts the cycle. The numbers don't move though, no matter how long I stare at them. It stays exactly where it is, which is exactly how I feel. Like I'm in limbo, unmoving.

"Fuck," I grumble, scrubbing my hands over my face. "Get it together. You've had broken relationships before," I chastise myself, even though that's not entirely true.

I've never had a real relationship before, and the kicker is what I had with Cam wasn't one either. It was fake, parameters I set myself from the very beginning. Only I ignored those parameters almost immediately, allowing her to slowly chip away at the hard exterior around my heart. Dammit, I practically handed her the chisel, because I never really tried to keep her out. I liked having her here and that led to this.

Heartache.

Love.

Nothing about any of this feels fake.

It's very much real.

I take a seat at my drum set, ignoring the longing to have her sitting with me. I pound out a hard, heavy melody, trying with everything I have to beat her out of my heart. Does it work? Fuck no. She's permanent, like a tattoo.

Once I'm sweaty, tired, and certain my neighbors are going to call the cops with a noise complaint, I throw the sticks on the floor and get up and make my way to the shower. Hopefully I can burn her memory out of my system.

It's worth a shot, right?

I know instantly the moment she arrives at work. The air changes. It's sexually charged with memories of what happened in our hotel room, but also with recollections of every other night she spent in my arms while we slept.

I pour mugs of beer for three patrons at the bar, while keeping one eye peeled for Cameron. She's wearing a big smile when I finally see her at the servers' station, getting ready for shift change with the lunch crew. Meg is there too, apparently working this evening with her, and says something that makes Cam's laughter carry throughout the bar and land firmly in my balls. It wraps around me like a caress, causing my dick to thicken and memories to replay in my head of hearing that exact laugh in the early morning hours. I never knew sex could be so damn fun. And no, I don't mean it like that. Yes, sex is always fun, but I've never experienced that fun side where you laugh and smile too. It was intimate, but on a whole new level, which is wild because I usually only have one level.

As the night wears on, she makes several trips to the bar for drink orders. Each time, she gives me that knowing grin and is her usual friendly self, but I can see something in her eyes. They're a little puffy, like perhaps she's been crying, and that thought kills me. I've hated every tear she's cried in these last few weeks, and I despise the fact I might have caused a few of them.

Hell, maybe it's not me at all. She reminded me our relationship was fake, so maybe her tears are from being home. Is she scared? Is she worried about someone breaking in again? Will she be able to sleep at night in her own bed without me?

I know with absolute certainty I won't sleep for fuck tonight or any night she's not beside me.

"Hey, stranger," a woman says, pulling me from my own head. I instantly recognize her. She's someone I've spent time with in the past once or twice, and something tells me by the smile on her painted red lips, she's very much interested in another.

"Good evening," I reply with a fake smile. "How have you been?" I ask, even though I don't really care to know the answer.

"Not too bad. Enjoying a few drinks with my friends," she says, glancing over her shoulder to the three other women seated at a round pub table.

"Can I get you ladies a drink?" I ask.

"Four chocolate martinis, please."

I nod, reaching for the glasses. "I'll bring them over to your table. Wanna start a tab?"

"Yes, please," she coos, running her finger across her cleavage before reaching into her purse for her debit card.

I key in the order and swipe the card, placing the whole order on hold for now. Handing back the card, she takes it from my hand, her fingers wrapping around mine in the process. Subtly pulling my hand back, mostly because I hate the feel of her touching me, I give her a smile and say, "I'll deliver those drinks in just a minute." I don't wait for her reply before turning around to get the order started.

Once they're all ready, I grab two glasses and head for where they sit. "Ladies, here ya go," I announce, setting the first half of the order down on the table and quickly retreating to grab the second half. When I return, I find the woman who ordered the drinks—Serena—giving me one of her fuck-me grins as I approach.

Setting down the glasses, she reaches out and places a hand on my forearm. "Can you stay and join us?"

"Sorry, ladies. Not my break time yet," I insist, taking a step back and dislodging her hand.

"Later?" she asks, running her finger around the rim of her glass and then licking the chocolate off the tip.

I smile, even though I don't feel it. "We'll see where the night goes," I reply, even though I already know where it *won't* be going. No way in hell am I going home with her tonight. Or any other night.

She leans forward, her gaze locked firmly on mine. "I know exactly where I'd like to see it go, Kellen."

My heart drops into my stomach at the thought. "You ladies let me know when you're ready for another drink," I reply politely before returning to the bar.

"Her eyes were glued to your ass. I'm surprised you were able to walk with the extra weight," Meg says, waiting patiently for me so I can make her order.

"Not happening," I mutter, grabbing her order slip and jumping into making the drinks.

"No?" she asks, propping her elbows on the bar and watching me work. "I heard you and Cam broke up."

My eyes find hers, and I feel the heaviness of her words like a punch to the chest. It only takes a moment for me to remember everyone here has been under the assumption we've been dating, because that's what we led them all to believe. I hated lying to them, but I hate this feeling of pain even more.

Swallowing over the lump, I reply a quick, "Yeah," before grabbing the bottle of vodka to make the drink.

"Too bad. I really liked you two together," she adds, making me want to shove something in my eardrum. I make a noise, hoping that'll be the end of it, but, of course, Meg keeps going. "She's been different these last few weeks since you two started dating."

"Oh yeah?" I don't look up, refusing to see the truth in her eyes.

"For sure. She's been...happier than I've ever seen her."

"That's probably because she's working the evening shifts with you," I reply, setting the drink on her tray and giving her a wink.

"No, it's you. Everyone sees it."

I exhale slowly, wishing her order wasn't so damn big so she'd leave. Unfortunately, I have five more drinks to make yet, and apparently, she's in a chatty mood. "Well, sometimes things just don't work out," I state, working on the rest of her order as quickly as possible. I'm so hurried I put the wrong liquor in one and have to start over.

This time it's Meg who makes a noncommittal sound, and the whole time, I feel her eyes on me. It's unsettling, really, and causing me to fuck up.

"So, you fell in love with her."

It takes a moment for her words to register, but when they do, they hit me so hard, I drop the glass. "Fuck," I mutter, bending down to pick up the large pieces of broken glass.

"That's all the proof I need," she mutters happily, leaning over the bar and watching me grab a towel to soak up the booze.

Throwing the towel into the dirty bin, I stand up and grab another glass. "What the hell are you blabbering about?"

"You. Falling in love with Cameron. It's so obvious."

It is?

I swallow hard and return my attention to the drinks.

"That woman over there has been eye-fucking you since she walked in. She'll be passing you her number shortly, but I don't think you'll do anything about it. You don't look like a man who's on the prowl after breaking up with a girl he's been seeing and doesn't really care about. You look like a man who lost someone he loves and doesn't know what to do about it."

My heart is beating a thousand beats per second as I take in her words. I'm about to deny, deny, deny, because what else am I going to say, but she saves me from vocalizing the lie.

"It's okay. I'm happy you love her. She needs someone like you, Kel. You made her happy, and she'll see that. Don't give up on her. She knows it in her heart." Meg grabs the tray with six drinks on it, but before she walks away, she adds, "Oh, and don't go home with Miss Genital Warts over there. You'll lose any chance you have at ever getting Cam back if you take home the first barfly on the night after you guys break up."

The smile I give her is real, because there's no way in hell I could think about taking another woman home. My bed only wants Cameron. "Don't worry about that. Not happening."

She nods. "Don't think I didn't notice how you've deflected and refused to answer any of my questions this entire time."

"In my defense, you didn't really ask any questions. You made assumptions."

"I spoke the truth. Now, get that cute ass of yours back to work," she replies with a wink before walking away.

Shaking my head, I look up just in time to see Cameron watching me. She averts her gaze, returning her attention back to whatever task she was doing at the servers' station, but I saw it, nonetheless.

I think about what Meg said the entire night. Even as I turn down the offer for no-strings sex with Serena. Yes, it might put a small Band-Aid over the pain in my chest over losing Cameron, but it would be temporary. If anything, I'd feel worse afterward, and that's something I'm not used to.

The restaurant shuts down at nine, and by nine thirty, the servers have it cleaned up and are ready to go. Meg heads this way, and I can't help but notice Cameron begrudgingly follows. Does she not want to come say goodbye?

"All done, ladies?" I ask, tossing an empty beer bottle into the trash with a bang.

"All done," Meg confirms. "Good tips tonight."

"Yeah?" I ask, but my eyes are on Cameron.

She nods in agreement, giving me the slightest smile and making my heart skip a beat. "Not a bad evening for a Sunday."

"Good deal. You want to stick around for a drink?" I ask, praying they say yes. I have less than an hour to go until I close this side of the business, and the thought of Cam hanging around like she used to when we lived together causes a bubble of hope to erupt in my chest.

"No, I'm ready to head home. I didn't sleep much last night," Cameron announces with a yawn. Her words are instantly followed by a blush, as if she's recalling exactly why she didn't sleep well the night before.

My cock kicks eagerly in my pants, hoping for a repeat of last night's activities, but I have to squash his hopes and dreams, because I can read the look on her face. She's anxious to get home and probably away from me. I might have hoped we'd still be able to consider ourselves friends, but I'm just not sure that's possible. Can two people who have slept together be friends, or will there always be this heavy sexual tension between the two of them? Memories that invade your every waking thought and forbid you to think about anyone but them?

Fuck, this is going to be harder than I thought.

"Well, maybe next time," I reply casually, flashing them both a grin.

"For sure. I'm off to watch *Gilmore Girls* and edit photos from yesterday's shoot," Meg states, sliding her purse over her shoulder. "Come on, Cam. I'll walk you out."

I open my mouth, ready to offer my services, but shut it once I see Jasper standing behind them. I already know he's about to walk them out, probably having just done the same with his kitchen staff.

"Night, Kel!" Meg hollers, throwing a wave over her shoulder as she turns away.

"Night," I reply, my eyes on the woman still standing at the bar.

"Good night," she whispers, a sad smile on her kissable lips.

"Hey," I find myself saying as she turns around to leave. When her eyes meet mine once more, I add, "You know where to find me if you need anything."

She nods and works to swallow. "Yes. Thank you." And then she's gone, spinning around and walking fast to catch up to where Jasper and Meg wait by the back entrance.

I swallow hard, wishing I could say what I really want. Wishing I could take her in my arms and tell her it wasn't always fake. That everything I feel for her now is very real.

But I know in my heart this is what she needs.

Like that old saying if you love someone, set them free. If they come back to you, it's meant to be.

Well, I've let her go to spread her wings and fly and now all I can hope is she comes back someday, because it's been one day and I'm already a miserable sack of crap.

The rest of my life without her is going to be hell.

I slip into my bed, phone in hand. I've typed and deleted the same message a dozen times, wanting to send it but talking myself out of it.

Now, as I lie in bed, the sheets still smelling like her, I know I'm in for a long night. Sleep is not on the horizon for me, despite the fact I'm tired. Twice now I almost got up to go peek in on her next door, only to remember she's not in the guest room. She's across town in her own home, sleeping in her own bed.

I toss and turn for a while longer before pulling up the text message app and typing out the message. I click send before I can stop myself.

I pray it doesn't wake her if she's sleeping, but my need to say the words overwhelms me. I'm in for a long night and hope she's finding peace. Even if we can't be together, I want her to know I support her and am thinking of her.

She's got this.

She's the most resilient woman I know, and even though I hate having her away from me, I understand the why. She's a strong badass, plain and simple.

And I will never stop thinking about her.

Me: I miss you.

Many hours later, sleep comes.

Cameron

I feel like a character on *The Walking Dead*. Not that I've seen the show, but I've watched enough previews.

For a solid week, I've moved through life, barely eating and sleeping, just trying to get through. My hair is a mess, my eyes dark and lifeless, and my skin is more than a little chalky. I thought it would be easier as time went on, but with each passing day, I realize that's a lie. Love doesn't just stop when your heart breaks. It's still growing like a vine in the tiny pieces of your heart, trying to draw them all back together to make yourself whole again. Only problem is my heart isn't complete. A big part of it was left at Kellen's house the day I left.

It's been six whole nights since I spent it with him, wrapped in his arms. Six sleepless nights I forced myself to stay put in my house, even though I don't want to be there. Not because I'm scared. In fact, I feel freer than I ever have in my own space. The problem is he's not there with me, which is probably the biggest problem of all. I've come to need him. To crave his touch and rely on his stability and strength.

That's why I stay here.

Not because I don't want to be with him, but because I *do*. More than anything.

Work has been interesting. We're still on the same shifts every night, thanks to the schedule adjustment when the whole Cage thing was going on. I make a mental note to go see Garreth as soon as possible to get those hours modified a little. There's no need for me to work every single night with him. Not anymore. And seeing him at the bar, smiling at all the customers—especially the women—and acting all fine and dandy is a slow sort of torture I wouldn't wish on anyone.

Not that he's really flirting with anyone. Not like he used to be. He gives them a smile, but it lacks the usual luster and mirth it used to hold. At least not in front of me, and considering I've spent as many free seconds as possible watching him work from the restaurant, I'd have surely seen something by now. A heated look. One of his trademark cocky grins. The flirty banter that mimics foreplay. Yet, I haven't seen any of it in the last week. Not even a cheesy come-on line he knows is going to get him hit upside the head.

My phone chimes with a text message, and I can't stop my heart for speeding up in anticipation. Is it Kellen? I haven't received any from him since that first night we were apart. That simple "I miss you" message pretty much ensured I had a restless, horrible night of sleep. Did he really miss me, or did he just miss me being in his bed? After spending every night for three weeks there, several over the course of that last week getting to first, second, and third base, I'm sure he missed the fooling around. He's a gorgeous guy, after all. One with a healthy sex drive and extensive knowledge in pleasing a woman. I'm sure it won't be long before he finds someone else to fill the spot I vacated.

Well, there's a horrible thought, Cameron. Why not just cut your own heart out with a rusty butter knife and toss it over the Spring Creek bridge?

With a growl, I jump up from my couch and grab my phone. It's a message from Meg, one that brings a smile to my lips.

Meg: This wedding is wild. The groom is wearing a Busch Light cummerbund straight from 1996. His mullet game is on point though. It really ties the whole ensemble together. I think there might be keg stands later. I'll be sure to capture those precious moments.

Me: You have all the fun.

She sends me a pic of the groom and what I assume is his best man shotgunning a beer. In front of the church. Laughing, I fire off a quick reply.

Me: Make sure you behave yourself!

Meg: I don't know, one of the groomsmen looks awfully yummy. I might need to take him for a test drive.

Me: Be safe. Wear your seat belt.

Meg: Always. *insert winky face emoji*

I set my phone down and glance at the clock. It's nearing three, which means it's about time for me to get changed for work. Another shift working with Kellen at the bar. At least it's a Saturday night and that means tips will be good. Maybe it'll be enough I can pay off the balance of my car repair bill at Otto's.

Thirty minutes later, I'm in my Burgers and Brew polo and black jeans and heading to work. It's definitely cooler today. It seems like the moment the calendar flips over to October a couple of weeks ago, the temperatures start to drop and fall settles in. I'll be digging my coat out of the back of my closet soon, which makes me a little sad to think about. I've always loved the warmer weather months.

I pull into the parking lot and park my car, lucky to have one of the closest spots. Instantly, I search out Kellen's truck and confirm he's already here. I'm a few minutes early, so I stay in my car and take a few deep, calming breaths. Working with him is both heaven and hell. It's good to see him but hard at the same time. Relationships and feelings are weird like that, which is exactly why he's steered clear of them his entire adult life.

If only I had done the same...

Deciding to just go in now and hang in the employee break room until my shift starts, I open my door and climb out. Before I can shut the door, however, I hear the back entrance open, and Kellen's laughter fill the air. It makes me pause with its familiarity and beauty and simply soak up the sound like a sponge.

"You're fine. I've got a few minutes before my shift starts," he says into the phone in his hand. "I'm glad you called."

I'm stuck where I stand, watching as he paces from left to right in front of the entrance I need to use. I should climb back into my car, since I'm clearly not going inside right at this moment, but when I hear my name, every muscle in my body freezes.

"Cameron is...well, it's over."

He listens for a few moments, stopping where he stands and exhaling. "Yeah, I fucked up. I should have...I don't know, Kins. I just..."

Again, he's quiet as he listens to whatever his sister is saying. My heart is surely loud enough for him to hear, but he never turns to where I stand just fifteen feet away.

"You know it wasn't real," he says sadly, the words quiet as he slowly starts to pace again. "Yes, I get that, but..."

He growls and stops moving. "Of course I did, but I couldn't say that. That's not what she needed from me."

My eyes burn as guilt hits me. I shouldn't be standing here, listening to his conversation, even if it's clearly about me. Deciding to slide back into my car and wait for him to be done, I pull the door open farther, and it squeaks loudly because my car is a complete POS and gives me away.

I freeze where I stand as his wide blue eyes meet mine. "Cam," he whispers, the softest grin spreading across his mouth as if just saying my name brings a smile to his face.

He seems to snap out of it quickly as he barks into the phone. "No, you can't. We have to work." He pauses for a second before a defeated look fills his eyes. "Fine, but only for a second. We literally start our shift in three minutes."

Holding the phone toward me, he says, "Kins would like to say hello."

There's a tremble in my hand as I shut my car door and take the phone from him, bringing it to my ear. I hope my voice is stronger than I feel as I greet Kellen's sister. "Hi, Kinsley."

"Girl, it's so good to hear your voice. How have you been?" she asks.

I know I need to lie to her to keep her from asking more questions, but I just don't have the strength. "Oh, I'm hanging in there," I concede, making sure to keep my gaze cast downward at the ground.

"You sound as miserable as my brother," she replies. "I hate this for both of you."

"I..." I stop talking because I have no idea what to say.

"Listen, Cam, I know you have to get inside to work, so I will only keep you a minute. Do you remember when I told you he's stupid sometimes and to be forgiving when he messes up?"

I feel the blush creeping up my cheeks as I mutter a quiet, "I remember."

"Well, he's proved it this time. He loves you, even if he's unable to say it. I know my brother, Cam. He's stupid. Don't let his stupidity make you both miserable. Talk to him and forgive him. I like you too much to see him push you away because he's blind. And dumb. And stupid."

I can't help but laugh at the way she talks about her older brother. It makes me yearn for a sibling of my own to tease and torment for the rest of my life. "I hear you."

"Good. Now, put the big dummy back on the phone so I can say goodbye to him before my soundcheck."

"Have a great evening, Kinsley," I say, somehow feeling a little lighter than I did when I first walked up.

"You too, love. And remember, he's stupid, so you're going to have to make the first move."

Shaking my head, I hand the phone over to Kellen, whose gaze is locked on me. "What did you say to her?" He listens for a few seconds before rolling his eyes. "Fine. I love you too. Talk to you later," he adds before hanging up the phone.

We stand there, our eyes locked, as he slips his phone into his back pocket. "Are you okay?"

I nod. "Yeah."

He exhales and runs his hands down his face before looking over at the back entrance. "We need to get inside. Shift has probably already started."

"All right," I whisper, following as he keys in the code for the back entrance and pulls it open.

As we step through, his familiar scent wraps around me, offering me comfort for the briefest of moments. I almost reach out and touch him, my fingers itching for even the tiniest contact of his warm skin. I don't, though. Now isn't the time.

"Thank you," I say lamely, because I don't know what else to say.

He nods. "You better get clocked in."

I turn and head for the break room to put my stuff in my locker and sign in for my shift, wishing I were strong enough to tell him how I really feel.

The evening moves by fast. It's crazy-busy, thanks to a new burger introduction from Jasper. He's been working on the InstaDong hot dog meal ever since Mötley Crüe's drummer, Tommy Lee, decided to post his dick pic on social media, and thanks to our own social media power, we've been packed the entire night with customers wanting to get their mouths on the footlong.

If I never have to hear a giggling woman ask if our menu has a pic of the infamous dick shot or inquire what the creamy white secret sauce is on top of the hot dog, it will be too soon. Plus, I'm pretty sure my blush is permanent at this point in my life. No twenty-three-year-old woman should have to talk about Tommy's dong for this many hours in a row without actually seeing it straight up.

Every chance I get, my eyes are moving to the bar. He's such a natural at work. The customers love him, and not just the ladies. Walker is behind the bar with him, and they have such an easy working relationship together. When they pull out the *Cocktail* drink pouring, made popular by the infamous movie, they're dynamic. The crowds just gather around to watch the show.

Every time I have to place a drink order, Kellen comes right over. There isn't enough time for Walker to help me, and if there is, Kellen pats him on the back and tells him he's got it. I feel his eyes on me everywhere I go, including when I'm just standing there and he's serving drinks.

As he places my latest order on my tray, his finger grazes across my hand as he offers me a wink, but it's not the flirty one I've seen him use over the course of my time working here. It's a knowing gesture with a promise mixed in, and the thought makes my blood heat with desire. Then, he turns to the next customer, offers them a polite, somewhat reserved smile, and makes their drink.

He's different with me.

Meg tried to tell me last Sunday during our shift together, and Kinsley all but told me the same thing earlier on the phone. I think I've known it, probably all along, but seeing it now, having it happen right in front of my face is a little startling.

He loves you, even if he's unable to say it.

Could it be true?

Is it possible everything I've been feeling isn't just one-sided?

But if that's the case, why not talk to me about it? Why remind me of our *friendship* and tell me to call if I needed something?

Feeling just as confused as ever, I return to the restaurant to deliver my drinks. Garreth is near the servers' station, so when I make my way back there, he joins me behind the partition. "How's it going?"

"Really well tonight. I can't believe how busy we are," I reply, filling four glasses of water for my new table being seated.

He laughs. "I told them this new hot dog would be huge. No pun intended," he says with a wink.

I can't help but roll my eyes. "You're terrible."

"What's terrible is designing a new hot dog around Tommy Lee's dick," he mutters with a chuckle. "But the patrons seem to love it, and everyone's talking about the secret sauce."

I groan and shake my head. "Do I even want to know what's in it?"

"You know Jasper. He'll take that secret to his grave."

"Probably," I retort as I carry the fresh waters to my new table and place them in front of the customers.

By the end of the night, I have no idea how many InstaDong footlong hot dogs I've served, but it was a lot. My feet are aching and my neck's in need of a good cracking, and fortunately, it doesn't take too long to close down the restaurant. It helps we get to listen to Jameson play the guitar and sing while we do it, thanks to his playing in the bar.

Of course that only reminds me of the guitar I received from Kinsley that's propped in the corner of my bedroom so I can see it every day. Music in general seems to remind me of Kellen too. I think about those nights we played the drums together; despite the fact I had no clue what I was doing. He led, and I willingly followed. I did it then, and I'd do it now so easily.

When our job is complete and it's time to clock out, I consider going over to the bar and having a drink. Honestly, I'm not a big drinker, but it would give me an opportunity to sit and watch Kellen a little longer like the stalker I've apparently become. Maybe if Meg were here, I'd invite her to stay, but without her, I just don't have the courage to do it.

I head to the break room, clock out, and retrieve my purse from my locker.

"Good night," Jenna says, offering me a wave as she exits the break room.

"Night."

I walk to the back entrance and pause before I push through the door. I can feel his eyes on me, and when I turn around, it's confirmed. Kellen is standing at the end of the bar, a look in his eyes that can only be described as longing stealing my breath. Tears prickle and gather in my lashes as I watch him watch me. My heart is a fast tempo in my chest, beating so loudly I'm certain it can be heard over Jameson's playing.

Slowly, he lifts his hand and waves goodbye, and I feel the pain of that single gesture radiate through my body. Slipping out the back, I hurry to my car, grateful I don't have to go far. As soon as I sit in the seat, the tears fall. Why is love so complicated and hurts so much? Will I ever be able to breathe normally again?

It was never like this with Cage, and definitely not after he left. I was so angry at him, but even if I hadn't been, I didn't love him like this. Not like I was supposed to love him. It took Kellen entering my life for me to really see that, for him to show me what true love is.

I don't care I'm only twenty-three years old, seven years his junior. He's shown me more about myself and about life than anyone ever could or will. I'm not too young to know what's in my heart, and my heart is in love with him.

He loves you, even if he's unable to say it.

I close my eyes and see it. I see it reflecting in his own eyes as he took me to bed that night in Philly. I felt it in the way he touched me, held me. He was unable to say it, but he was showing me. He was communicating without words, and I was too blind to see it.

I angrily wipe my tears away and start my car. Throwing it in reverse, I stomp on the pedal a little too hard as I pull out of my parking spot. When I reach the end of the lot, I don't turn in the direction I should. I let my heart lead me, and it doesn't take me home.

When I pull into his driveway, I park beside where he'd park his truck, when it isn't in the garage. I jump out and head for the back door. I find his key easily and stare down at it. He told me to keep it in case I ever feel scared. Well, I'm scared not to come clean about my feelings for him and possibly spending the rest of my life alone and miserable, so I think that counts, right?

I slide the key in the lock and push open the door. "All right, Kellen. It's time for us both to stop being so stupid," I announce to no one, stepping inside and disabling the alarm.

It's time to set the record straight.

Twenty-Nine 29

Kellen

"Have a good night," Garreth hollers, slipping into his truck and starting the engine.

I climb into my own truck and do the same, really wishing I had somewhere to go other than home. Not that there weren't offers. I had two numbers slipped to me. Invitations for mindless sex after I got off work. Unfortunately for both of those ladies, there was no way that was happening. My dick didn't even get a little excited at the thought of going home with either, which is pretty telling. He's still stuck firmly in Cameronland just like my heart, unwilling to even think about getting naked with anyone but her.

The drive to my house is short, and with every passing intersection, I have to force myself not to turn the wheel and head to her house. Of course, it's late, which means I'd just drive by like the loser stalker I am, and that doesn't sound like much fun either, so I continue in the direction of my house until I'm pulling into my driveway.

I actually stop and blink several times as I stare at the car already there. My mind has played cruel jokes on me several times throughout this last week, thinking I've seen her everywhere, only to find out it's not her, so it wouldn't surprise me if my subconscious dreamed up her car in this exact moment. But when I blink repeatedly for a good ten seconds and the car is still there, I realize my mind isn't making this up.

Cameron's here.

And that's terrifying.

What if something's wrong? Is she scared? Did something happen at her house?

I drive forward, stopping my truck beside her car and almost forgetting to shut it off before jumping out. I click the lock button and take the back steps two at a time until I'm standing in front of the door. My key doesn't go in easily because I'm clammy and frazzled, so it takes a couple of tries to get it in the keyhole and turned.

The alarm starts to beep in warning, and as I stare at the keypad, I completely blank on the code. "Fuck," I mutter, closing my eyes and taking a deep breath. I enter the code correctly the first time, which is a little surprising, and then reset it once the door is locked. Tossing my keys on the table, I head deeper into the house to find Cam and find out what's wrong.

The living room is empty, but I can see that she sat on the couch. The throw blanket is bunched up on the cushion like she usually leaves it after using it. Instead of folding it up and replacing it on the arm, I move toward the guest room. I've stopped and stared into this empty room every night and every morning since she returned to her home, but now the prospect of actually seeing her lying there in bed has my heart trying to erupt from my chest.

Except, when I peek into the room, the bed is empty. The bedding isn't even on the mattress. I took it all off after she left last Sunday to wash and never put it back on.

That could only mean one thing, and I'm trying not to just rush into my room to see if she's there or not. Instead, I take a few calming breaths before turning to face my door. It's wide open, my eyes automatically going to the figure lying in my bed. My cock recognizes her immediately, getting hard as I watch her sleep on my pillow, her delicate arm holding the blanket against her chest.

I take a step toward her, then another until my knees are pressed against the mattress and I could reach out and touch her if I wanted. Oh, don't get me wrong. I want to. Badly. But I won't scare her without knowing the reason she's here.

I don't know how long I stand here and watch her, but it's a while. Her breathing is even, her mouth slightly agape, as if she's comfortable enough to finally fall into a deep slumber.

Suddenly, I find myself taking a seat on the mattress beside her. My hand automatically moves, gently pushing a strand of hair from her forehead. Her skin is warm and so fucking soft, I could touch her forever and never get tired of it.

"I'm sorry, Cam," I whisper, caressing her hair. "Letting you go home was the hardest thing I've ever done, but I knew I had to do it. You needed to prove to yourself you were independent and brave after what happened, and as much as it pained me not to beg you to stay with me, I couldn't do it. So I let you leave, even though it was the last thing I wanted."

I swear I feel her move into my touch, even though I don't physically see her move. "I know you said our relationship was fake, but you have to know, it was never fake for me, Cam. Not once. From the very beginning, it felt more real than anything in my life ever has." I take a deep breath and finally speak my truth out loud, finally vocalizing what's been running through my head and printed on my heart. "I love you. Somewhere between the late night snuggles and the shared breakfasts, I fell completely in love with everything about you."

I sit beside her, wishing I was strong enough to tell her the truth. I'm not afraid of rejection. I'm not afraid of love, even though I've spent a lot of time avoiding it. I'm terrified I'm not who she needs to flourish in this world.

I scrub my hands over my face again and go to stand up. I need a shower to wash the beer and sweat off my body before I climb into bed with this woman. If I have the opportunity to hold her again, I'm not wasting any more seconds.

Turning, I'm stopped in my tracks when a hand grabs my arm. I look down and find Cameron's eyes wide open, her hand gripping me to keep me from moving away.

She swallows hard, her eyes glistening as she whispers, "I love you too."

Okay, wow. First up, I thought she was sleeping. I wouldn't have said anything had I realized she'd woken up at some point during my feelings purge, but now that I have, I can't take any of it back. Not that I want to, considering I think I heard her tell me she loves me too.

"Uhh, can you repeat that, please? I haven't slept well this last week and my mind could be playing tricks on me."

Cameron smiles softly, her hand sliding down my arm and linking our fingers together. "I love you too."

I drop to my knees beside the bed and bring her hand to my lips, kissing her knuckles. "For a big part of my thirty years, I'd always prayed I'd never hear those words from a woman. They always represented something dark, and I never wanted that old familiar pain to affect my life ever again. My parents..." I shake my head and close my eyes for a moment before meeting her gaze once more. "They loved Kins and me, but they weren't good to each other. Over the years, there was so much resentment and hatred between them, it affected me and my sister daily. I swore I would never fall in love, and especially not when I was young. Young love wasn't real, at least in my eyes."

Taking a deep breath, I continue. "But then I met you, and everything I thought I knew about love and relationships turned out to be a lie. This"—I move my finger between us—"is real, Cam. I might have suggested a fake relationship, but my love for you is very real."

She smiles and sits up, slipping her free hand into my hair and drawing her mouth close to mine. "You don't want to just be friends?"

"Fuck, love. What I feel for you and want to do to your body twenty-four seven is anything but friendly," I tell her, kissing her knuckles.

Fire dances in the depths of those green eyes. "Tell me. What do you want to do to me?"

I release her hand and scoop her into my arms, standing and carrying her toward the bathroom. She squeals, wrapping her arms around my neck as she giggles. "How about I just show you?" Moving into the en suite bathroom, I kick the door closed and turn on the light without putting her down. "Wait, are you all right?"

Her eyebrows pull together in confusion. "What do you mean?"

"You're here. I was afraid something happened," I tell her, finally setting her down on the floor in front of me.

She reaches up and cups my jaw. "Yeah, I'm fine. I just realized I didn't want to be at my house anymore. I wanted to be wherever you were, and even if you decided you just wanted to be friends and not together, I knew I needed to tell you how I felt."

"But I beat you to it," I state, big wolfish grin spreading across my face.

"Only because I fell asleep waiting on you to get home."

"You weren't faking the whole time?" I ask, wondering at what point during my confession she woke up.

Shaking her head, she reaches down and pulls the T-shirt she found in my drawer up and over her head, revealing nothing but naked skin beneath it. My mouth goes dry as I drink my fill of this gorgeous woman standing before me. "I woke up after you brushed hair off my forehead. I was going to move, but then you started talking, and I wanted to hear what you had to say," she confesses, a light blush creeping up her cheeks.

"So you were being a big faker," I state, lifting my work T-shirt over my head and tossing it on the floor before bending down and unlacing my boots.

Once I stand back up, she reaches for the button of my jeans, releasing the closure and dragging the zipper down. My cock is achy, hard, and seeping from the head in anticipation and excitement. She glances up and bats her eyelashes at me. "I might have been doing a little faking."

I grasp her hand loosely and pull her nakedness against my body. "From this point on, no more faking."

"No more faking," she confirms, gripping the waist of my jeans with her free hand and trying to pull them down.

It doesn't work one-handed, so I step back and release her hand, giving her free range to do as she pleases. Cameron doesn't disappoint either. She rips my jeans down to my knees and quickly does the same to my boxer briefs. Before I can remove the material, she grabs my cock and gives it a gentle squeeze. I groan in pure bliss and pleasure races through my body. "Fuck, I've missed you. I've missed this."

"Me too," she mumbles, keeping one hand on my cock and wrapping the other around my neck as she presses her tits to my chest.

"I want to come home to you every night. I know you need your own space, but this…"

Cameron shakes her head. "I don't care about my own space. This last week was pure shit."

I can't help but chuckle. "It was. I hated it."

"Me too," she confirms again. "I don't want to be at my house because it doesn't feel right anymore, and not because of what happened there. Because you're not there with me."

It's hard to swallow, but I manage as I reach around her and lift. She drops my cock and wraps her arms around my neck to hold on, her legs threading around my waist. I move to the shower and turn it on, still needing to wash my work shift off me, but also needing to show her what she means to me.

She presses her lips to mine and my heart finally feels whole again. I step inside, the hot water coating our skin as I press her back against the tiled wall. My cock is nestled between us, so damn close to where he wants to slip inside. All it takes is a little shift in our position, and it's there, pressing against her pussy, begging to slide home.

"Shit, I don't have a condom," I mutter, wishing I had thought a little ahead as I was bringing her into the bathroom.

"It's okay. I'm on birth control, and I trust you." Her eyes sparkle with need and faith, and all I can do is claim her sweet lips with my own.

"Fuck, love. I trust you too. I'm clean, I promise. There hasn't been anyone in months. There's no one else but you," I confess, lowering her down slightly and allowing the head of my cock to slip inside. "No one again but you," I add, but it's mostly to myself. I know in this moment there'll never be another woman I love like this. Never another I take to bed and make love to.

She wiggles, taking my cock a little deeper, and I know exactly what we both need. Claiming her mouth, I rock my hips and bring her down to rest on my pelvis, my cock fully seated inside her hot, wet pussy. Our moans mix as I give her a moment to adjust to my invasion.

"This. This is the best feeling in the world," I mumble, carefully lifting her up and bringing her back down on me.

"Yes," she whispers between gasps. "This." Her hands move to my hair as her nails dig into my scalp.

We move in unison, and as much as I try to drag it out, I know it's no use. Not tonight. Not this first time after being without her for a week. "Are you close, love?" I ask, grinding her down on me between pumps.

"So close."

"You want to come on my cock?"

She groans loudly, squeezing her eyes shut. "God, yes."

Ignoring the burning in my arms and legs, I let my desire take over as I drop her down and lift her up, each thrust a little harder than the previous. I feel the squeeze of her pussy, which causes my balls to tighten and draw up. I know I'm about to blow, but I need to make sure she comes with me. "I can feel your pussy, Cam. It's so tight on my cock. Do you feel it, baby?" I ask through gritted teeth, knowing a little dirty talk will help send her over the edge. My Cam loves it when I talk dirty to her, and as suspected, my words do the trick.

She cries out as her pussy clenches hard. Her legs go rigid, and her head falls back against the wall. Too bad I can't bend down and suck one greedy little nipple into my mouth, but right now, my own orgasm is triggered, and it's all I can do to stay upright. My hips move as I release everything I have into her body. I shift forward, pinning her between my sated body and the wall, taking her mouth with mine as our releases slowly subside.

"Mmm," she moans, releasing her hold on my hair and sliding her hands down my neck.

"That was one hell of a welcome home," I mutter against her lips.

"And just think. I could be waiting in your bed every night when you get home from work."

My cock twitches at the thought. "Yes, let's make that happen," I tell her, knowing I need to set her down, but not ready to let her go quite yet.

"All right," she whispers sleepily, shifting her head to rest on my shoulder.

"You're gonna move in with me?" I ask, my question so full of hope.

She looks up. "Do you think it's too soon?"

"Hell no. I can't sleep without you, Cam. I want you beside me every night."

"Then, that's where I'll be," she replies so simply it takes my breath away.

"Perfect." I slowly set her down, making sure her legs will hold her before I release my hold. "Now, let's get washed up so we can go to bed."

"And do that all over again?" she asks, mischief dancing in her eyes.

"Hell yes, love. I plan to show you how much I love you every chance I get," I tell her, reaching for my bodywash.

She reaches down and grabs my half-hard cock. "Good to know. Ready to go again?"

I make a noise, a mixture of a growl and groan, as my cock gets hard all over again. "Be careful what you wish for, Cam. Now I've taken the edge off; this next time is bound to last all night."

A wide smile spreads across her lips. "I just so happen to have nowhere else to be this evening."

I grab the removable showerhead and quickly rinse any lingering soap from our bodies before turning off the water and reaching for her. Gently, I toss her over my shoulder and swat her bare, wet ass. I carefully step out of the shower, the sounds of her laughter filling the room, and wipe my feet on the mat. When I know I won't slip and fall, I head out of the bathroom, the cool air hitting my overly heated skin, and carry her to my bed.

Our bed.

There won't be a night moving forward I won't be in it without her.

Laying her down on the bed, I cover her shivering body with my own. "I love you, Cam."

She grins up at me, wrapping both her arms and legs around me. "I love you too."

Then I proceed to show her exactly how much she means to me until we're both spent. And when I wake again in the morning, I do it all over again, determined to prove to her she's my everything.

The woman I love more than anything.

The one who proved to me I was very much capable of falling in love and no one is immune to it. As long as she's by my side, I can do anything.

She's my entire heart.

My world.

Forever.

Cameron

I give my appearance one final once-over in the mirror and smile at my hilarious Christmas sweater. I don't know which owners' wife came up with the ugly sweater themed staff Christmas party idea, but I love it. My red sweater reads, "I'm so good, Santa came twice," and I can't help but giggle every time I see it.

There's a knock on the bathroom door and it opens right away. "Hello, gorgeous," Kellen says, entering the bathroom. His eyes are zeroing in on my sweater. Well, specifically, on my chest.

"Hey," I reply with a smile.

He stops in front of me and kisses my nose. When he pulls back, he holds out his hand, and there's a small, white box sitting in his palm.

"What's that?" I ask.

"A gift."

"But we just had Christmas two days ago," I counter, recalling how amazing our first Christmas together was. We spent the entire day together, including dinner with Garreth, Reagan, and his family. My parents are planning a visit first of the year, and Kinsley and possibly Kellen's mom will be visiting right after that, once the extension for her tour ends. I'm super excited to see

Kellen's sister again, but a little nervous to officially meet his mom, even though we've talked several times on the phone. His dad and girlfriend aren't planning a trip here, which I think is okay. Dealing with his dad always stresses Kellen out, and neither of them seem to be upset not to spend time together over the holidays.

"This isn't a Christmas present."

I look up at the man I love and shake my head. He's too good to me, and this is just another example. Mere days after the biggest gift giving holiday of the year, and he's already buying me something else.

Sighing, I take the small white box and pull off the top. A gasp slips from my lips as I stare down at the gorgeous ruby and diamond earrings. "Kellen," I whisper, my voice hoarse and dry.

"They were my nana's," he says, taking the box from my shaky hand and removing the studs inside. "When she passed away, Kins and I each got to choose something from her jewelry box. You may remember, Kins selected her cross necklace. She wore it faithfully every day until she passed away. I chose these. She used to wear them every Thursday night when she and my papa would go to the weekly fish fry dinner at the VFW. For years, I remember her putting them in, always sharing the story about how they were the first piece of jewelry Papa gave her when he returned from the military overseas."

I blink multiple times, partially to clear away the wetness and keep my makeup intact, but also because of what these stunning earrings represent. "Kellen, I can't take these," I insist as he holds them out for me.

"Yes, you can," he insists, removing the backs of both earrings.

"These are family heirlooms."

"And they're staying in my family, love, because *you* are my family." He presses his lips to mine. "I love you and want you to have them."

Shaking my head, I forget all about the makeup and let a few tears fall down my cheeks.

"Let me help," he says when my fingers don't seem to work right to put them in. Once both backs are secure, he smiles down at me and turns me around. "See? They're exquisite, just like you."

The red matches my sweater and the diamonds sparkle brightly under the white lighting. "They're beautiful. Thank you."

"You're welcome," he replies, placing a kiss on my neck as he holds me in his arms. "Now, are you ready to go show off these amazing sweaters? I hear Lyndee's forcing Jasper to wear something ugly and festive too, and he's not very happy about it."

I can't help but laugh, wondering if all the owners will be wearing bright, ugly Christmas attire. Spinning around, I wrap my arms around his neck, go up on my tiptoes, and kiss his lips. "I love you."

"I love you," he replies, deepening the kiss until I'm breathless and wondering if we have a few extra minutes before we're due to arrive at Burgers and Brew for the holiday employee gathering. "No, we don't have time," he replies, stepping back and smacking my ass. "But later, you're mine."

My mouth curls upward in a wide grin. "I'm always yours, Kellen McGregor."

"Damn right you are, Cameron Wright." He takes my hand and leads me from the bathroom. "Let's go. I can't wait to show off my awesome sweater," he adds, referring to the green creation I found online for him to wear to tonight's party. It's a cocky Santa with his arms crossed, and beneath it, it says, "'Bout to deliver my big package." I don't even care I spent more on this one sweater than I did my entire outfit for this evening, including my cute new ankle boots. I knew Kellen needed it, and he's not disappointing me either.

He's wearing it proudly.

"Oh, in case anyone asks you about the size of my package, I'm going to need you to really sell it, love. I mean, really push the big," he says before we reach the back door, demonstrating a solid foot length between his two hands.

Playfully, I roll my eyes. "Come on, now. At least let me make it believable," I counter, reaching up and shortening the distance between his hands to about four inches.

A growl erupts from his throat as he lunges for me. "That wasn't nice. My cock is offended by such a preposterous lie."

"I'll make it up to him later. I know how to sweet-talk the big guy," I reply, tapping his cock with my palm before walking right out of the house.

"Damn right you do!" he hollers, setting the alarm and locking the door behind him. "He rather enjoys seeing you on your knees in front of him. In fact, that's one of his favorite positions."

I stop and turn around, going up on my tiptoes and whispering, "I know, Kellen. Be a good boy and I'll swallow him and every drop of cum he gives me when we get home."

I spin back around and get inside the truck, leaving him standing on the sidewalk trying to adjust the erection in his pants. It's the little things that make me smile, and one-upping Kellen every now and again is definitely one of them.

Kellen

"What do you say, old man? She ready to leave you yet?" my friend Tucker says as he takes the barstool beside me.

"What the hell?" I ask with a laugh.

He shrugs, taking a drink of his beer before setting it down on the bar in front of us. "I just figured since you're like, what, ten years older than her, she'd figure out soon you've already peaked and can't keep up with her stamina."

My laugh turns into a full belly roll now, and it takes me several seconds to catch my breath. "There is nothing wrong with my stamina, my friend, and there's only seven years between us. We're approaching thirty-one," I state, referring to the fact we're both the same age. "That's not old."

Tucker snorts. "Sometimes I feel old, man. Chasing a four-year-old around all the time just proves I'm not a spring chicken anymore. Grayson has more energy than a toddler who chugged pixie sticks, a Monster energy drink, and missed his afternoon nap."

I chuckle at the picture he draws in my head, my eyes automatically moving to find Cameron in the crowd of employees. Wonder what she'd look like big and pregnant with my baby? I'm sure she'd look fucking amazing. Edible, even. I should probably convince her to marry me before I put a bun in that oven.

"Why are you looking at her like you want to eat her alive?"

My eyes move to my old friend as I give him a wolfish smile. "Oh, the accuracy," I reply.

He barks out a laugh, taking another drink of his beer as he shakes his head.

"How's Grayson doing?" I ask, referring to his young son.

"Good," he says with a soft smile. "Spent the day with my parents so I could get away for a while tonight."

"Well, I'm glad you're here."

"Because no one else likes you?" he teases.

"Fuck off," I mutter, goodheartedly. "I know we're both busy, but we should catch up again soon. It's been months since we were able to grab a beer together."

"Agreed," Tucker says, taking another pull from his bottle. "Grayson's doing well and loves spending the night with my parents. It's a little easier for me to get out every now and again than it used to be."

"All right. Send me a text if you get a free night soon."

"How about you text me? I'm not the one who works evenings and has a new live-in girlfriend to deal with," he says.

"Good point," I reply, glancing over my shoulder and searching for the woman I love. I find her chatting with a small group of women, including Reagan, Mallory, and Angie.

After a moment, he asks, "You're gonna invite me to the wedding, right?"

A smile spreads across my lips. "Well, there isn't one in the works, yet, but soon. I'm definitely marrying her, man."

Tucker nods and slaps me on the shoulder. "Good deal. It's good to see you so happy, Kel."

Again, I seek her out, much like I do every night we work together. My eyes just seem to move in her direction completely on their own. It's amazing I can get any work done, honestly.

"What the fuck?" I turn my attention to Tucker, who's sitting up straight on his stool. He looks over at Walker, who's behind the bar, and asks, "Can you turn that up?"

My eyes go to the television, and my heart drops into my stomach as I see the words written across the bottom of the screen.

"Country singer Kinsley McGregor's bass player, and husband, was caught backstage before tonight's concert in a very compromising position," the entertainment show host announces before playing the rest of the video.

"Is your friend taping us?" I hear my douchebag brother-in-law ask the tramp he's balls deep in, barely missing a stroke. Even though the act is blurred out, there's no denying what's happening.

"I wanted to have something to remember you by after you leave," the woman coos at Zander.

"And I'm next!" the one who's holding the phone declares with a giggle.

"Hell yes, you are, darlin'," he grunts out, making my blood run cold with rage as the video stops and the show hosts return to the screen.

"Reportedly, that's Zander Houston, husband of Kinsley McGregor, who is set to perform her final show in her very first headlining tour this evening in Charleston, South Carolina. This video was sent in exclusively to our studios just moments ago, and something tells me we haven't seen the last of this unfolding drama. We'll be back with more entertainment news after this."

THE END

Want more Burgers and Brew Crüe? Book 8 will feature Tucker and Kinsley and will release September 2023! Preorder Without You today!

Don't miss a single reveal, release, or sale! Sign up for my newsletter.
http://www.laceyblackbooks.com/newsletter

Books by Lacey Black

Rivers Edge series
Trust Me, Rivers Edge book 1 (Maddox and Avery) – FREE at all retailers
Fight Me, Rivers Edge book 2 (Jake and Erin)
Expect Me, Rivers Edge book 3 (Travis and Josselyn)
Promise Me: A Novella, Rivers Edge book 3.5 (Jase and Holly)
Protect Me, Rivers Edge book 4 (Nate and Lia)
Boss Me, Rivers Edge book 5 (Will and Carmen)
Trust Us: A Rivers Edge Christmas Novella (Maddox and Avery)
    ~ This novella was originally part of the Christmas
    Miracles Anthology
BOX SET – contains all 5 novels, 2 novellas, and a BONUS short story
With Me, A Rivers Edge Christmas Novella (Brooklyn and Becker)

Bound Together series
Submerged, Bound Together book 1 (Blake and Carly)
Profited, Bound Together book 2 (Reid and Dani)
Entwined, Bound Together book 3 (Luke and Sidney)

Summer Sisters series
My Kinda Kisses, Summer Sisters book 1 (Jaime and Ryan)

My Kinda Night, Summer Sisters book 2 (Payton and Dean)
My Kinda Song, Summer Sisters book 3 (Abby and Levi)
My Kinda Mess, Summer Sisters book 4 (Lexi and Linkin)
My Kinda Player, Summer Sisters book 5 (AJ and Sawyer)
My Kinda Player, Summer Sisters book 6 (Meghan and Nick)
My Kinda Wedding, A Summer Sisters Novella book 7 (Meghan and Nick)

Rockland Falls series
Love and Pancakes, Rockland Falls book 1
Love and Lingerie, Rockland Falls book 2
Love and Landscape, Rockland Falls book 3
Love and Neckties, Rockland Falls book 4

Standalone
Music Notes, a sexy contemporary romance standalone
A Place To Call Home, a Memorial Day novella
Exes and Ho Ho Ho's, a sexy contemporary romance standalone novella
Pants on Fire, a sexy contemporary romance standalone
Double Dog Dare You, a new standalone
Grip, A Driven World Novel
Bachelor Swap, A Bachelor Tower Series Novel
Perfect Kiss, Mason Creek Series book 9
Waiting For Love, The Love Vixen Series book 11
Quarterback Keeper, a surprise baby novella

Burgers and Brew Crüe Series
Kickstart My Heart
Don't Go Away Mad
Same Ol' Situation
Wild Side
What's It Gonna Take
Home Sweet Home

Too Young to Fall in Love

Pine Village Series
Pretty Remarkable, a free prequel short story
Pretty Incredible, book 1

Co-Written with *NYT Bestselling* Author, Kaylee Ryan
It's Not Over, Fair Lakes book 1
Just Getting Started, Fair Lakes book 2
Can't Get Enough, Fair Lakes book 3
Fair Lakes Box Set
Boy Trouble
Home To You, a second chance novella
Beneath the Fallen Stars
Tell Me A Story
Royal – Writing as Rebel Shaw
Crying Shame – Writing as Rebel Shaw

Thank you for loving the Burgers and Brew Crüe as much as I do! Your comments, reviews, and messages keep pushing me to write more books, write more of the Crüe.

There are so many to thank during the entire process of publishing this book.

My editing team – Kara Hildebrand, Sandra Shipman, Joanne Thompson, and Karen Hrdlicka. I couldn't do this without you!!

The book team - Photographer, Wander Aguiar; Model, Chase Roback; Cover Designer, Melissa Gill; Graphics Designer, Gel with Tempting Illustrations; Formatting, Brenda with Formatting Done Wright; and Promotions by Give Me Books. Thank you for everything! I work with the best!!

Kaylee Ryan, Lacey's Ladies, Chasidy Renee, and my ARC team, thank you for constant support and pushing me to be the best I can be!

To my husband and kids, thank you for helping me live my dream.

To all the bloggers and readers, thank you, thank you, thank you. I hope you enjoy this story as much as I loved writing it.

About the Author

USA Today Bestselling Author Lacey Black is a Midwestern girl with a passion for reading, writing, and shopping. She carries her e-reader with her everywhere she goes so she never misses an opportunity to read a few pages. Always looking for a happily ever after, Lacey is passionate about contemporary romance novels and enjoys it further when you mix in a little suspense. She resides in a small town in Illinois with her husband, two children, adorable black lab puppy, crazy cat, and three rowdy chickens.

Website: www.laceyblackbooks.com
Email: laceyblackwrites@gmail.com
Facebook: https://www.facebook.com/authorlaceyblack
Instagram: https://www.instagram.com/laceyblackwrites/
Bookbub: https://www.bookbub.com/authors/lacey-black
Amazon: https://www.amazon.com/Lacey-Black/e/B00MW2UGZI
Twitter: https://twitter.com/AuthLaceyBlack
Goodreads:
https://www.goodreads.com/author/show/8414783.Lacey_Black

Sign up for my newsletter so you don't miss a single sale, reveal, or release!
http://www.laceyblackbooks.com/newsletter

www.ingramcontent.com/pod-product-compliance
Lightning Source LLC
Chambersburg PA
CBHW070633260626
47161CB00007B/2681